W9-AFK-885

THE WORLDS WE MAKE

ALSO BY MEGAN CREWE

THE FALLEN WORLD

THE FALLEN WORLD
BOOK 3

THE WORLDS WE MAKE

MEGAN CREWE

HYPERION
NEW YORK

First Edition
10 9 8 7 6 5 4 3 2 1
G475-5664-5-13335

Printed in the United States of America

Library of Congress Cataloging-in-Publication Data

Crewe, Megan.
The worlds we make / Megan Crewe.—First edition.
pages cm.—(The fallen world ; book 3)
Summary: "In the conclusion to The Fallen World trilogy, Kaelyn and her friends must protect the cure they have found from deadly enemies while searching for a true safe haven"—Provided by publisher.
ISBN 978-1-4231-4618-6 (hardback)—ISBN 1-4231-4618-2 (hardback)
[1. Survival—Fiction. 2. Virus diseases—Fiction. 3. Science fiction.]
I. Title.
PZ7.C86818Wor 2014
[Fic]—dc23 2013030343

Reinforced binding

Visit www.un-requiredreading.com

THIS LABEL APPLIES TO TEXT STOCK

To those who follow
paths of their own making

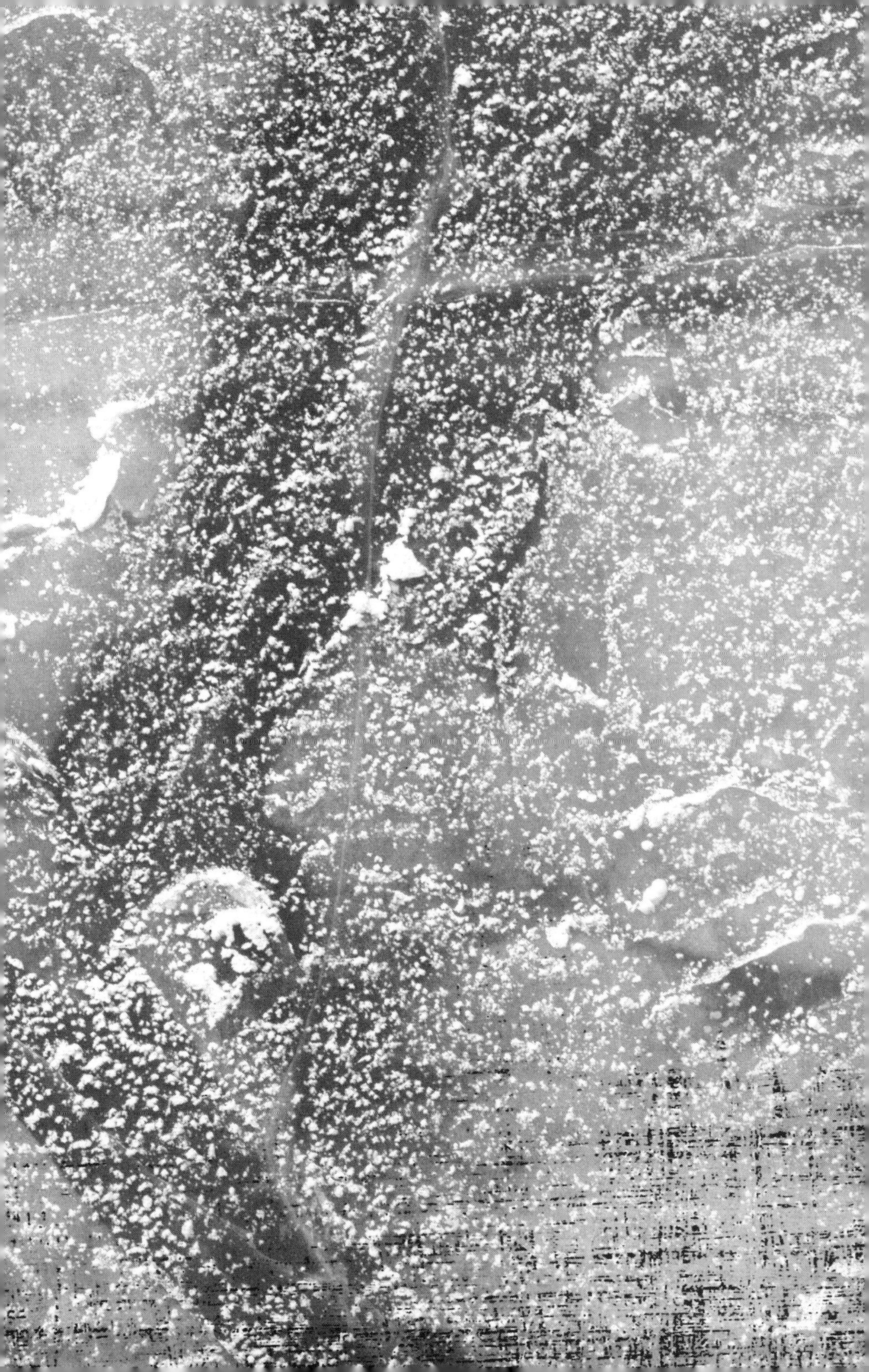

ONE

We'd been on the road for three hours when the stolen SUV lurched over a piece of debris buried in the snow. Anika gave a squeak of surprise, but she held the steering wheel steady. Gav's jaw bumped my shoulder where he was slumped unconscious against me. I tried to adjust my position, but I was jammed tight on both sides. With four of us in the back, Gav and I squished in beside Justin and Tobias, there wasn't much room to maneuver.

Leo glanced around from his spot beside Anika. "Everything okay back there?" he said as if to all of us, but he looked at me.

"Yeah," I said. "We're fine."

As my gaze slid past him to the windshield, where the falling snow was shrouding the landscape, I realized I actually believed what I'd said. How crazy was that? We were on the run from a gang hungry for our blood, and the college girl at the wheel had tried to sell us out to that same gang just a couple days ago. My boyfriend was drugged up on sedatives to stop his virus-riddled brain from making him do anything dangerous. Tobias's skills as a former soldier had helped get us this far, but it looked like he was infected now too. And while Justin was healthy, we'd already seen how much trouble a trigger-happy almost-fifteen-year-old could get us into.

But we were all still here. Leo, the best friend I'd thought I'd lost, was sitting a few feet away from me, alive and well. The vaccine samples that might pull the world out of its downward spiral were safely locked in the trunk. The snow made for rough driving, but it was covering our tracks. We had a tentative destination, and at least a little reason to hope we'd find scientists capable of replicating my dad's vaccine when we got there.

So in those passing minutes, as I stroked Gav's tawny hair and the SUV's tires hissed down the freeway, life didn't seem so bad. It wasn't anywhere near *good*, but it was all right. Acceptable.

Then an indicator on the dashboard started to beep.

"I don't know what that symbol is for," Anika said, waving at it. Her soft voice sounded even more high-pitched than usual. Frazzled.

We should have her switch off with someone else, I thought. She'd been driving since she picked us up at the apartment we'd been squatting in, through the mad dash out of Toronto while the Wardens shot at us, and on into this nearly blinding weather.

Tobias leaned forward between the seats. "Tire pressure," he said, his voice muffled by the scarves he was wearing double wrapped across his face in case he started coughing. His frown showed in his pale blue eyes. "One of them's losing air."

"Why?" Justin demanded. "What's wrong with it?"

"There was that bump a little ways back," Leo said, rubbing the side of his face. Exhaustion grayed his olive-gold skin. "Whatever we ran over, it must have been sharp."

Gav muttered and stirred. My arm tightened around him. The sedatives I'd given him had been veterinary ones, so we didn't know exactly how well they'd work for a person—or how quickly they'd wear off.

"We'd better deal with the tire before it goes completely flat," I said. "Turn off at the next exit, okay?"

If we didn't make it to an exit, if we ended up stranded on the freeway, we'd be sitting ducks for the Wardens. Michael, their leader, had ordered them to keep after us until they'd taken the vaccine. In one of our last encounters, Justin and Tobias had left three of them dead. Given the way they'd fired at us as we fled the city, they were obviously hoping to repay us in kind.

The windshield wipers rasped back and forth as Anika peered through the storm. The indicator kept beeping. Finally, Justin gave a shout, pointing to a sign emerging from the haze.

Anika slowed the SUV to take the curve of the ramp, but the car's frame jolted. One wheel started to thump against the snowy asphalt, tugging the car to the left.

"Crap!" Anika said. Haltingly, we eased down the ramp and came to a stop outside a vacant service station. A few scattered houses stood farther down the road. The snow blotted out the rest of whatever tiny town we'd ended up in.

"Let's see how bad it is," I said with a sinking feeling in my stomach.

As Tobias opened the door, Gav groaned. He was definitely waking up. I shifted into the middle seat to give him more room as the others got out, feeling my coat pocket for the bottle of sedative orange-drink mix I'd made for him. Hopefully I'd be able to talk him into swallowing a little more.

Leo paused by the door. "You need anything?" he asked.

"Not right now," I said. "But I think I'd better stay with him while—"

Without warning, Gav pitched across my lap, clawing his scarves away from his mouth. A shudder rippled through his body, and with a sputtering gasp, he threw up. Orange-tinged liquid splattered the seat.

Leo had jumped back. Up front, Anika made a disgusted noise. Gav sagged against me, and I wrapped my arm around him, fighting the urge to gag at the sickly sour smell already filling the SUV.

He'd refused to eat anything the last two days. Maybe the dissolved pills had been too potent on an empty stomach. Maybe I'd given him too much.

Or maybe, between the virus and the lack of food and our inability to give him even the most basic treatment, his body was giving up altogether.

I blinked hard and shoved that thought away. "Gav?" I said. "Here, let's get some fresh air."

I reached past him to open the other door. The breeze sprinkled snow over us, but it carried away the worst of the smell. Gav mumbled something I couldn't make out.

"You want some water?" I asked him. He didn't answer.

When I raised my head, the others were hovering in a semicircle by the back of the SUV. "The tire's done for," Tobias said. "And there's no spare."

"Okay," I said, forcing myself to focus. "Can you check the garages around here for a car we can take a tire off? I'll look after Gav. Just don't go so far you can't see the SUV anymore. We don't want to lose anyone in the snow."

As they hurried off, another wave of frigid air washed over us. Gav twisted toward it. He pushed himself partway out of the car, and then listed over the ditch, retching. Orange dribbles dotted the snow.

I rubbed his back, wishing there was more I could do. But we weren't going to find any more doctors or medicine out here in the middle of nowhere than we had in the city.

His head swayed with the motion of my hand. Then he started to cough. I grabbed my bottle of regular water, and paused. It might help his cough, but I wasn't sure his stomach could handle anything right now.

He reached back his hand, and I let him take the bottle. He sipped just a little before setting it down on the car floor.

"How're you doing?" I asked.

"Gross. I feel so gross, Kae. And cold," he muttered, in the rambling manner he'd taken on when he passed into the infection's second stage, which caused people to blurt out every thought in their heads unedited. He shivered. "I want to go someplace warm. Back to the apartment. Let's go back there, Kae. We can sit by the fire, just sit and be warm."

"It'll be warm when we get the car going again," I said, trying to sound reassuring around the ache spreading through my chest. The Gav I'd known, the one who'd defended our town's food supply, who'd protected the vaccine he didn't even believe in and made me promise not to give up on this mission, he'd have cringed to hear himself like this. This wasn't him. It was the virus talking.

If I closed the doors and turned on the heat, I'd be wearing down the battery and using up what little fuel we had. And the seat would really start to stink. I needed to clean it.

I straightened up, and Gav jerked around. "Where are you going?" he said, his hazel eyes wild. "Don't go!"

"Hey," I said, "I'm here. I'm just going to look in the trunk."

He watched me as I leaned over the back of the seat. Then his strength waned and he slumped toward the open door. I pawed through the supplies in the hatch area: blankets, camping gear, food we'd scavenged in Toronto. Ripped pieces of sheet. I grabbed one, leaned past Gav to scoop up some snow, and started swiping at the mess beside me. Gav sneezed faintly. Even his symptoms were weakening.

I edged over to reach the farthest splatters, and caught sight of the others trudging back toward the car. "You'd better pull your scarves up," I said to Gav, as lightly as I could manage. Those layers of fabric were all we had to prevent the virus from traveling on his coughs and sneezes and finding a new victim. He grumbled, but he did it.

Our four companions came empty-handed. "Nothing?" I said.

"Not nearby," Tobias said. "Past those houses it looks like just farmland."

"I checked the map," Leo said. "There should be a real town about a mile farther down the freeway."

A mile over uncertain ground, through a storm that could turn into an all-out blizzard at any moment. "I don't think we should risk walking it in this weather," I said.

"So what do we do, then?" Justin demanded, pushing his dark brown ponytail back when the wind whipped it over his shoulder. "We can't drive there with a flat tire."

Anika hugged herself, and it occurred to me that her wool coat was a lot thinner than the down-filled ones the rest of us wore. We'd have to find her a new one. After we found a tire.

"Let's go inside," Gav broke in. "Can't we go inside somewhere? I hate being squashed in this godawful car."

"I checked the houses from the windows," Leo said. "It doesn't look like anyone's still around here. If we wanted to, we could warm up a bit and see if the snow'll die down before we figure out what to do."

Every part of me balked at the idea. We had to keep moving. The Wardens were behind us, tracking us down. The Centers for Disease Control, our goal, was still far off in Atlanta. But we couldn't walk—even if I'd been willing to risk it, Gav wouldn't make it more than a few steps—and we couldn't drive, and I didn't have a single other idea.

Gav staggered to his feet, and suddenly my decision was made for me. "Hey!" I said, scrambling after him. He wobbled around the SUV, supporting himself against it, until I caught his elbow.

"I just want a fire," he said, swaying. "I just want to be warm. Why won't you let me have that, Kae?"

My eyes teared up. "Okay," I said. "We can do that."

As I slid his arm over my shoulders, his legs buckled. Leo hurried over to support him on the other side. Together, we helped Gav walk to the nearest house. Tobias strode past us, tested the door, and slammed his foot against a spot beside the knob. After a few kicks, it burst open. He stalked inside, scanning the rooms.

Gav's feet stumbled and dragged, and as we reached the front step, he lurched forward and threw up the little water he'd drunk, into his scarves.

"Sorry," he mumbled. "I'm sorry."

"It's okay," I said.

He collapsed inside the hall, and I sank down next to him, cradling his head against my chest. The skin above his scarf radiated a feverish heat.

As I peeled the damp scarves away from his mouth, Gav launched into a volley of tiny sneezes, slouching closer to the floor. Justin and Anika, who'd just come in carrying the bags with our blankets, froze on the threshold. One sneeze could mean they'd be just as sick as he was in a couple weeks. Only Leo and I were safe, me because I'd been sick before and recovered, and Leo because I'd given him one of the vaccine samples before we'd realized just how hard it was going to be to keep the few we had safe and viable.

I grasped Gav's arm again. "We need to walk just a little farther," I said.

He wasn't going to be able to sit by a fire the way he'd imagined. But there was a door in the living room near the fireplace, leading into a small home office layered with dust. After we'd staggered in, Gav embraced the patchwork rug as if it were a feather bed. I hurried out to grab a couple blankets and a flashlight. Justin had started smashing apart a chair for firewood, and Tobias was sprinkling the splintered pieces with kerosene from his camping stove. At least we'd have a little warmth.

"Kaelyn!" Gav called out, and I dashed back.

When I closed the door, the windowless room was thrown into darkness. I flicked on the flashlight, set it on the desk, and knelt beside Gav.

"It'll warm up soon," I said. He kept shuddering as I wrapped the blankets around him, despite the fever blazing under his skin.

"I don't want to feel this way," he said. "I hate it, Kae. I hate it so much."

"I know," I said, with a hitch in my voice I couldn't suppress.

There was only one other thing I could give him. I turned off the flashlight to save the batteries and lay down beside him, lending him the heat of my body. We huddled together in the cold, dark room, waiting for the fire's warmth to seep beneath the door.

Time passed with the uneven rhythm of Gav's ragged breath by my ear. After a while, the room felt warmer, but maybe I'd just gotten used to the chill. Gav had curled against me like my little cousin Meredith used to, his head tucked under my chin, his arm looped around my waist. I hugged him tight. He was still shivering, off and on.

The last time I'd held Meredith like this, we'd been hiding from the Wardens in the artists' colony where we'd met Justin and his mother. Where I'd left Meredith, with our friend Tessa, to make sure she stayed safe.

At least I'd saved one person. If she really had stayed safe there.

My heart leapt at a knock on the door. I'd wondered what the others were doing, but I hadn't wanted to disrupt the calm Gav had settled into.

"Everything okay?" Leo asked, nudging open the door.

It wasn't okay, not anymore, but there was nothing Leo could do about that. "We're all right," I said hoarsely, lifting my head from Gav's. "How's the weather looking?"

"The snow's let up a bit, but it's getting dark," he said. "We figured it'd be better to crash here for the night and check out that town in the morning. If that makes sense to you?"

Another night lost. But I couldn't expect them to hike for hours through the dark. And if the Wardens drove past and saw the flashlights . . .

"The smoke from the fire," I said. "Is it still snowing enough to cover it?"

"I think so. And it'll be so dark soon it won't matter. We managed to get the SUV into the garage here so no one can spot it from the freeway."

I should have thought of that. I shook my head, trying to clear it, but my mind spun. I hadn't eaten since our hurried breakfast that morning.

One panicked thought broke through the rest. "The cold-storage box! You brought it inside?"

"Got it right here," Leo said. "I put in some fresh snow. You want it in the room with you?"

Gav stirred. His fingers dug into my coat. I squeezed his shoulder, thinking about Anika out there with the others, still studying us to determine the best advantage. "Yeah," I said. "Thanks." She *had* tried to steal the samples once. Yes, she'd sided with us over the Wardens because of how harshly they'd treated her afterward, but that didn't mean she was any less desperate to protect herself from the virus. Driving the getaway car was one thing. Withstanding the temptation of the vaccine sitting in clear view? That would be hard for anyone.

Leo opened the door to slide the cold box inside, and Gav flinched at the sound.

"Who's there?" he said, and then doubled over, coughing.

Leo shot me a worried glance. At my strained smile, he ducked back out. I brushed my fingers over Gav's hair.

"It was just Leo checking in on us," I said.

He coughed a few more times, and wiped at his mouth. *"Leo,"* he sneered, and something twisted inside me even though I knew his jealousy was unfounded. There had been a time when my feelings for my best friend had gone beyond friendship, and maybe his for me too. Leo had kissed me after an awkward sort-of confession when he'd thought I was leaving on this mission without him and might not make it back. But Gav didn't know about that.

He didn't need to. I was with Gav, and Leo knew I was with Gav, and both of us would have risked our lives to save him from the virus. If only we knew how.

I lowered my head as Gav pulled me closer. "Do we have to keep driving?" he murmured. "All the way to Atlanta. Centers for Disease Control. They really weren't very good at their job, were they? Didn't control this disease at all."

"No one did," I pointed out. As far as we knew, from what we'd seen and heard, the so-called friendly flu had spread across the whole world.

"Why not?" Gav said, his voice rising. "With all those scientists, one of them must have been smart enough, but no one could be bothered to—"

His voice broke with another coughing fit. And I thought, *My dad bothered*. My dad had kept working on his vaccine prototype until the day he died. Gav just hadn't trusted him or it enough to take it when I'd asked him to.

And I just hadn't insisted.

I bit my lip. "Hey," I said, "don't worry about that. You need to rest."

"I've been resting," Gav said. "That's all I've been doing. We should go."

He grabbed the edge of the desk to yank himself upright, his arms trembling. "Gav!" I said. The bottle of sedative-laced water in my coat pocket bumped against my ribs as I scooted over to him. I tugged it out.

“You should drink something,” I said. “This made you feel better before.”

“That orange crap?” he said. “I drank that in the car, and then I puked. No. I’m not taking any more.”

His muscles gave out, and he slumped back down onto the rug. I set the bottle aside.

“Okay,” I said. “Then just stay here with me.”

I’d need to come up with a better plan when we were back in the car tomorrow. Assuming we found a replacement tire. Assuming the Wardens didn’t swarm us in the middle of the night.

But for now, all that mattered was keeping Gav here and keeping him calm. That was going to be hard enough.

TWO

The virus was stealthy and vicious and nearly unstoppable, but it was also predictable. I'd known Gav was sick the moment I'd seen him scratching his wrist when we stood outside Toronto's city hall. I'd known that after five or so days of itching and coughing and sneezing, the virus multiplying through his body would break down the part of his brain that filtered the thoughts and impulses he knew better than to let out, while making him crave constant company. And I knew that, before much longer, his mind would short-circuit completely, into a series of violent hallucinations and delusions.

But knowing it did me no good. For what felt like a few hours, he and I lay on the rug, and Gav slept and woke, slept and woke. Each time he stirred into consciousness, I offered him the sedative drink, until he pushed the bottle away so forcefully it popped from my fingers and half of the remaining liquid splashed onto the floor.

After that, I didn't ask again.

Could we manage to keep him calm in the car undrugged? Was there some way I could trick him into taking one of the pills instead?

It stopped mattering the moment Gav started twitching.

"No," he muttered against his coat sleeve. "No."

I touched the side of his face. His skin was even hotter than before. "Hey, it's okay," I said. "You're okay."

He jerked away from me, and his eyes popped open, fixing on something beyond my shoulder. "No!" he shouted. "Leave me alone!"

He scrambled backward, his arm jarring against the corner of the desk. The blanket tangled around his legs. He thrashed at it while he groped for the bookcase behind him.

I eased upright, my heart thumping. "Gav..." I said, but I didn't know how to continue.

Gav snatched a book off the shelves and hurled it at the opposite wall. I edged to the side, holding out my hands. "There's nothing here, Gav," I said in the most soothing voice I could call up. Only a faint, quivering light was seeping under the door from the living room. I fumbled for the flashlight and switched it on. "It's me. Kaelyn. You're safe."

I'm not sure if he heard me. He slammed himself back against the bookcase, fixated on whatever horror his virus-addled brain had conjured up. I wavered on my feet.

When Meredith had gotten this bad, back on the island, I'd taken her to the hospital and helped the doctor inject her with sedatives and tie restraints around her. All I could do for Gav was watch.

I stepped toward him, and his gaze darted to me, his pupils so dilated they consumed almost all the color in his eyes. He hefted another book.

"Stay back!" he said. "Get away from me!"

The floor creaked on the other side of the door. "What's going on?" Justin said.

Gav's head snapped toward the door. He flung himself at it, falling to his knees as the blanket tripped him.

"I want out of here!" he yelled, pawing at the doorknob. "Let me out!"

I reached for him, and he slapped my hand away. With a heave, he rammed the door open while propelling himself to his feet. Leo, Tobias, and Justin had gathered outside the doorway, Anika poised behind them. They stared at Gav, and he at them. Then he lunged.

I threw myself after him, grabbing his elbow. He spun with a sound I could only describe as a snarl, and slammed me into the door frame. I gasped as pain radiated up my back and though my skull. His elbow slipped from my hand.

"Whoa!" Tobias said firmly, catching Gav by the shoulder. Leo grasped his other wrist.

"He's just sick," I said through the throbbing of my head. "He's just . . ."

"Let go of me, let me go, let me go!" Gav cried, struggling, but he must have burned through whatever strength he'd had left in his starved body. As he sagged toward the floor, Leo and Tobias hauled him back into the office. Justin shifted, eyeing me.

"You all right?"

"Yeah," I said, but I staggered when I tried to straighten up. A fresh jab of pain shot up the back of my head. My eyes watered, and my gut clenched.

Gav had done that. Gav had wanted to hurt me.

Not him, I reminded myself. The virus. Only the virus.

"No!" Gav was shouting. "No, no, no, no!" Tobias and Leo stumbled out of the room, Leo clutching the cold box. Tobias shoved the door shut, and an instant later fists pounded against it. The knob rattled.

"Don't let him out," Anika said, backing away. Her face had gone sallow in the firelight. Leo braced himself against the door.

"Put something in front of it," Justin said, and Tobias pointed to the dining room armoire. They dashed over and pushed it along the wall to the office door. The knob thumped against it. Gav's frantic voice carried through the wood.

"You can't! Don't leave me here! It's going to—Please, let me go!"

I covered my ears, tears welling behind my closed eyelids. Someone touched my shoulder—lightly, but I flinched.

"Kae?" Leo said. "How badly did he hurt you?"

"It wasn't him!" I snapped. It wasn't him we'd trapped in that room, alone with the images that were tormenting him. It wasn't.

Because in every way that mattered, the Gav I knew was already completely gone.

Through the night, I sat in the corner while Gav raved and raged on the other side of the wall. Despite the warmth wafting from the fireplace, the others retreated to the second floor. I didn't blame them. How could anyone sleep there in the living room, hearing him?

I rested my head against the wall, listening to his fists grow weaker and his voice more ragged. Tears streaked down my cheeks. He was fighting so hard, battling the enemies his muddled mind had conjured up, just as he'd always fought. He'd put everything he had into helping our town and then getting me across the country. And this was where he'd ended up. I'd set out to save the world, and I couldn't even save the person who'd supported me the most.

The sun rose. Light splashed through the living room window.

The others crept downstairs, moving through the kitchen and the dining room. I closed my eyes. Gav was crying in the office, in heaving gulps. My fingers curled into my palms, nails digging into the skin.

After a while, Leo came into the living room. He stopped a few feet from where I was crouched. I looked at his boots, the scuffs and scratches in the brown leather like a map of how far we'd already come. Gav kept sobbing.

"Kae," Leo said. "Is there anything I can get for you?"

I shook my head. My throat was too tight for me to speak.

"We're going to check out that town, look for a replacement tire," he went on. "Me and Justin and Anika. Tobias thinks it's safer if he stays on his own upstairs. But if you need him, just shout; he'll come right down. And we'll try not to be gone too long."

I nodded. He paused, and then set something down with a clunk on the coffee table. When I glanced over, I saw he'd left me a plate of crackers spread with peanut butter. I hadn't eaten in twenty-four hours, but seeing the food just made my stomach knot.

They were going to town to find a tire. When they came back, it'd be time to go. Time to leave Gav for good.

A few days ago, Gav had made me promise to keep trying to find someone who could make more of the vaccine, to hold on to that hope. The day after that, I'd looked into his fevered eyes and kissed him and promised I'd stay with him, always. But there was no way we could take him with us, not like this.

A ripping sound pierced the wall. Over and over, as if Gav was tearing up all the pages of all the books in the room. He was murmuring instead of yelling now, but that was almost worse.

I couldn't make out what he was saying, only the low panicked tones of his voice.

Metal screeched against metal. Fingernails scrabbled at the door frame. I squeezed my eyes shut again. And something other than despair lanced through my chest, sharp as a gulp of alcohol.

I raised my arm, wanting to hit something, hard. But that would just scare Gav, and maybe bring Tobias hurrying down. So I held my clenched fist to my mouth instead. I pressed my knuckles against my teeth and bit down until the stinging ache dug just as deep as the fury inside me.

I hated them. Not the virus—I hated it too, but I'd felt that way since the beginning. I hated the people who had forced us into this position. I hated Michael, the man I knew only from Anika's and my brother Drew's stories, the man who'd marched across the country gathering like-minded people to guard the food, generators, fuel, and medicine he hoarded, refusing to help anyone who couldn't pay his price. I hated the doctors who'd gone along with the Wardens instead of standing up to them. The government officials who'd fled. That stupid sick man who'd rushed at us and exposed Gav to the virus.

Epidemic or not, maybe we would have been okay if it hadn't been for all those people who'd thought only of themselves. And right then, I wished all of them dead.

I didn't remember falling asleep, but at some point, exhaustion took over. I woke up in a dark room. The day had passed, and night crept back in on us. I was still alone, but the fire was crackling behind me, which I guessed meant the others had come back.

My neck throbbed when I lifted my head from my knees. And I realized the space on the other side of the wall was finally quiet.

My body went rigid. I stood up, swaying, rested my hand against the chipped plaster, and listened. There was only silence.

I tugged the armoire away from the door. Just far enough so I could slip inside.

Gav was curled up on the rug, as he had been before the hallucinations took over. His blanket lay in a corner, torn down the middle, and shredded papers scattered the floor around him like a deranged nest. His coat hung open, the stitching torn. The desk and chair had been tipped on their sides against the wall.

I knelt down beside him. He lay so still, his shaggy hair drifting over his forehead. The flush of his fever had faded. He could almost have been sleeping.

His skin was cool when I touched his cheek. My hand slid down to hover by his mouth and nose. His lips were parted, but the air was still above them. The tips of his fingers, limp by his face, were raw and bloody. His knuckles too. A smear of blood marked his chin. The wall around the door was dented and scored and dappled scarlet. A wave of nausea rolled over me.

I sank down, setting my head against his chest. No rise and fall of breath. Not the faintest heartbeat. I drew my knees up, huddling against him. My own breath started to sputter out in halting gasps. My eyes burned, but I must have cried all the tears I had already. Nothing came but pain.

"I'm sorry," I said into the fabric of his shirt. In our island hospital, the patients had lived longer. They'd had doctors making them eat and drink, medication to calm them down, bindings to stop them from wearing themselves ragged.

It was better for it to have happened sooner, if we couldn't have saved him anyway, wasn't it? Less horror, less suffering.

I swallowed thickly, tears finally pooling in my eyes. It wasn't right. It wasn't *right*. I kicked out at the mess of papers. Even in the dim light, my eyes caught on bloody smudges. I stumbled to my feet, sweeping at the pages with flailing arms, shoving them all away against the wall, fumbling for the scraps I'd missed, wheezing and crying and swiping at my face with my sleeve, but not stopping until the rug was clear.

The surge of energy left me. I dropped to the floor across from Gav, tucking my hand around his wrist.

"I'm here," I said, my voice watery. "I was here the whole time. I didn't leave."

I lay there for the rest of the night, inches from Gav's motionless body. I couldn't say I slept, but I couldn't say I was all there either. I didn't notice movement beyond the office door, or anything except the stabbing pain inside me, until a crackle of static cut through my stupor.

"Attempting to contact the CDC," Leo said in the living room. His voice echoed in the radio transceiver's microphone. "If anyone's listening, please respond. Over."

It had been Drew, working as a sort of double agent alongside the Wardens in Toronto, who'd suggested we go to the CDC. But we'd had to leave him at his post in the city. Leo was the only one in our group who was familiar with the center, because he'd been in the US at his New York dance school when the epidemic broke out. He'd said that the CDC had still been operating the last he'd heard.

Now, he waited. Then there was a click as he twisted the dial to a new frequency. I opened my eyes. Gav's hand felt stiff and cold beneath my fingers. Bile rose in my throat. I pushed myself onto my knees.

"Attempting to contact the CDC," Leo repeated. I hesitated, afraid to go out, to make what I saw in here that much more real by putting it into words. As Leo worked through the bandwidths, my arms started to tremble.

"Please respond," Leo said, for what felt like the twentieth time. "Over." And a guttural voice snaked through the static.

"Vaccine thieves," it growled. "We've been listening for you."

I flinched, and on the other side of the door, Leo went silent. The voice laughed. "Not interested in talking? We'll be face-to-face soon enough, kids. You better believe we're going to track you down, and when we find you we're going to take what's coming to us and rip you open from—"

Leo slammed his hand down on the radio, and the transmission cut out.

"Hell," Justin said from across the room. "They can't tell where we are, can they?"

"I don't see how," Leo said shakily. "I didn't say anything about our location. But I think we'd better leave the fire out until tonight. Maybe they have some idea how close to us they are now."

Before I knew I'd made a decision, I was on my feet. I wobbled and gripped the edge of the bookcase. Nausea swept through me again, too fast for me to contain it. I hunched over, snatching at the wastebasket.

I had nothing in my stomach. Acid seared my throat as my stomach heaved, and I spat into the basket. A fit of harsh coughing filtered through the ceiling from the floor above as I wiped my mouth.

Tobias. Leo had mentioned he'd isolated himself up there. He was getting worse.

In a few days he'd start to go the same way Gav had, if we didn't get to someone who could help. If we didn't get past the Wardens.

The anger I'd felt last night flared inside me. How dare they call us thieves, when they were trying to steal from us? I'd tried to be *kind* to them, I'd chastised Justin for shooting at the three who'd tracked us down on the journey to Toronto, and I'd asked Tobias to only hurt, not kill, the ones who'd chased us out of the city. And if it wasn't for them . . .

I touched Gav's cheek. The coolness of his skin made me wince.

I wasn't going to let this happen to Tobias, or anyone else.

Dragging in a breath, I straightened up and walked to the doorway. Justin was poking at the ashes in the fireplace. Leo was sitting on the couch, sliding the radio back into its case. He ran a hand over his smooth black hair, which was starting to look almost as unkempt as when he'd first made it back to the island from New York.

Both their heads jerked up when I stepped around the armoire, their faces apprehensive. They knew. Of course they knew.

"We're not staying until tonight," I announced in a voice that wasn't much more than a rasp. "We're getting out of here as soon as we can." Even if we had to walk it.

And I'd kill every single Warden Michael had appointed before I let them get in our way again.

THREE

I wanted to bury Gav, but that was impossible. From the front porch I could see only yard upon yard of snow, the ground frozen solid beneath it.

He deserved something. Something better than being left sprawled in the midst of that wrecked office room.

Leo stepped out beside me, his breath clouding in the frigid air. He touched my back, tentatively, and I shifted toward him. For a moment we just stood there, his arm tight around me, holding me together. Like when we were kids, when that tourist looked at my skin and hair and called me a mutt, when I'd cut my head open falling from that tree. My best friend. How much more broken would I have been right now if I hadn't at least had him?

"What can I do?" he asked.

"I don't know," I said. "I guess . . . we could bring him to one of the bedrooms?"

So we did. We carried Gav's stiff body upstairs, to the room beside the one where Tobias was snuffling. A light blue sheet was still tucked around the double bed's mattress. I reached to drape it over Gav, and my hand shook. My fingers clenched.

Leo gripped my shoulder. "It wasn't your fault," he said quietly. "You know that, right?"

The concern in his warm brown eyes jarred loose too many of

the feelings I wanted to smother, one after the other, in a jagged chain. The memory of the one kiss we'd shared. The boy lying in front of us who I would never kiss again. All the ways it *was* my fault: for deciding to come out here, for letting Gav come with me, for not pushing him enough to take the vaccine.

I groped inside for the anger that had steadied me earlier. *Think of the Wardens. Think of Michael on his imaginary throne.* If it was my fault, it was even more theirs.

I crossed my arms over my chest. "Give me a minute?" I said.

Leo inclined his head. "We found a tire yesterday," he said. "The SUV's ready, whenever you are."

After he left, I stood there, staring down at Gav's body. It looked so vacant, as if there had never been a glint in those eyes, a smile on those lips. My gaze caught on a small lump in the pocket of his jeans. I balked, and then, skin creeping, slipped my fingers inside. Maybe it was a pack of matches or water purification tablets he'd been carrying.

I pulled out a strip of folded cardboard: a flap torn off of a box of cookies. A scrawl of blue ink on the other side caught my eye.

Kae,
I love you.
I love you.
I love you.
Keep going.

I blinked hard, sucking in a breath that was almost a sob.

He must have found the box and a pen in one of the rooms he'd stayed isolated in back in Toronto, before his mind started to go. Left it in his pocket hoping I'd find it after the virus's awfulness was over. So he could give me this one last message from the real him.

Keep going.

"I will," I said. Carefully, I slid the note into the pocket of my own jeans, and folded the sheet over Gav's body.

I covered his face last. My hands fell to my sides, and for a second I couldn't move. At least, when he was found, whoever found him would know someone had cared about him. He hadn't died alone.

Tobias sneezed in the next room. On heavy feet, I walked into the hall and stopped in front of his door.

"Tobias," I said. "We're going to head out."

He gave a startled cough. "Now?"

He didn't know, I realized. I hadn't seen him downstairs since the night when he'd helped move the armoire. The thought of explaining overwhelmed me. He'd figure it out fast enough.

"Yeah," I said. "You good to go?"

"I've got my scarves." He paused. "Maybe I should take some of those sleeping pills. I guess I'd be a lot less contagious if I'm knocked out."

"We can do that," I said. Anika had brought us several bottles of the veterinary sedatives as her peace offering, so there were plenty left.

Tobias opened the door, and I found myself glancing away from his wan face. No matter how nonchalant he tried to sound, I knew he was terrified. He'd been terrified since he'd first told me about the itch he couldn't scratch away. And while I'd been holding vigil over Gav, Tobias had been inching closer and closer to the same horrible fate.

"Fully equipped and ready to march," he said with a salute, but I could hear the strain in his voice. We didn't know if we'd find scientists who could treat him, if we made it to the CDC. Or whether the treatment would save him even if we did.

But it was all the hope we had.

"We're going to make it to Atlanta," I said, forcing myself to meet his eyes. "As fast as we can."

The house's pipes were frozen, nothing but a groan coming out when I tried the faucet, so I brought some melted snow into the bathroom for a hasty scrubbing before changing into some of the fresh clothes the others had scavenged from a store in town when they'd been looking for the tire. Then I checked the cold-storage box. All three samples were secure, the ice packs still frozen. I stuck the bag holding my dad's notebooks in on top, so it'd be easier for me to grab everything if we had to make another run for it.

"We found a US road atlas in the gas station shop," Leo said as we headed out to the car. "It should be enough to get us to Atlanta."

Tobias gulped down a couple pills and got into the back of the SUV, coughing faintly into his scarves. Justin tugged his own scarf up and followed. He sat with a careful gap between him and Tobias. Anika watched beneath the immense hood of her newly acquired parka, her usual mask of eye shadow and lipstick washed away, fear naked on her delicate features. She hesitated by the door, and Tobias's shoulders tensed.

"Wait," I said. "I can navigate from the back. Justin, let me sit in the middle." Where I'd be a barrier between Tobias and the people he could infect.

Justin shuffled out to make room, and Anika scrambled into the front. I took one last look at the house before I slid in beside Tobias. I couldn't see the window of the room where we'd left Gav. But what lay in there was nothing more than a shell. Justin shut the door, and I turned my gaze forward.

The border was less than fifty miles away. In a couple hours, I'd be leaving the only country I'd ever lived in. The last scraps of my old life.

The engine revved, and Leo aimed the car toward Atlanta.

I charted a course with our old Ontario maps, keeping us off the major roads as much as possible. The Wardens might not have realized we'd stopped, so they were probably well ahead of us now, but I suspected they'd be patrolling every major highway between here and Atlanta until they caught us. They'd heard Leo's broadcast; they knew where we were heading.

Leo flipped through the radio stations a few times. He used to drive his dad crazy when we were little, switching stations every few songs because he wanted to hear what all of them were playing. Today there was only the dull fizzle of static.

He stiffened when we approached the border, and I remembered his story of his weeks in the containment camp when he was trying to get home. But the booths and the lanes between them were empty. Several of the barriers were broken. And then we rumbled past the darkened windows and left Canada behind us.

Through the next day and into the night, we pulled over every few hours—to switch off the driving, to grab food from the back, to quickly siphon gas when we passed a cluster of houses that all had cars parked in their driveways. We never stopped moving for very long, but our progress was slow. The snow tugged at the tires, and twice we had to backtrack around a road where it was heaped too high. I tried to nap in the back during one of my breaks, but every hitch of the suspension startled me awake. Whenever I closed my eyes, I imagined Gav lying there in that room, the cold freezing him down to his bones. By the time the sun peeked over the horizon the next morning, I was chilled through.

As I peered out the window, a new worry broke through my exhaustion. The forestland we'd been traveling through for most of the night was giving way to open fields. Fields across which the Wardens might be watching from the larger roads we'd been avoiding. We hadn't seen another soul so far, but that didn't mean anything. The Wardens would be keeping a particular eye out for this SUV, the one we'd stolen from them.

"Anika," I said, and she blinked to attention at the wheel, where she'd been staring through the windshield as if hypnotized. "You know the Wardens better than we do. You said Michael had headed down this way a little while back—how many people do you think he could have looking for us?"

She seemed to swallow a yawn. "I'm not sure," she said. "I mean, I was never in with them—I've never even seen Michael. But from what I picked up, listening in on the talk on the street, he's really good at winning people over. And he brought a bunch with him when he headed south. He's had, like, a month now to get organized—he could have set up groups in a few different cities by now. If he wants the vaccine this much, he'll have a lot of people keeping an eye out."

"Maybe we should get another car, then," I said. "One they wouldn't recognize."

Beside me, Leo rubbed his bleary eyes. "That might be safer."

"They're going to come after any vehicle they see, aren't they?" Justin put in, setting the road atlas on his lap. "It's not like there's any traffic for us to blend in with. If we stop to find a new car, we're just giving them a chance to catch us."

Anika frowned. "This one *would* be really easy to spot, though. I mean, the black against the snow."

"So we'd need a *white* car," Leo said. "That could take a while. We've had trouble just finding any car at all that's drivable."

He was right. Since none of us had any skill at hot-wiring, we needed to stumble on not just a white car capable of handling the snow, but its keys too. What were the chances?

Tobias's breath rattled through his scarves from where he slumped against the opposite window. We had to get him to the CDC as soon as possible.

But we wouldn't make it anywhere near Atlanta if we got caught because we were driving this dark SUV amid a sparkling snowy landscape. Or because we stopped to look for a different car. Or because one of us fell asleep at the wheel and got us into an accident.

I brought my hand to my forehead. How were we supposed to pick the safest option when every one was so risky?

The shadow of a telephone pole slid over the SUV's hood, and a compromise occurred to me.

"The black would blend in at night, if we put something over the headlights to dim them," I said. "We could stop off for the day, find a place to hide, and we can all get some sleep. And then when it starts getting dark, we can keep going."

"Sounds good to me," Justin said.

Leo nodded. "I'd feel better about driving more if I could get a little real rest first."

We drove several miles farther, until we reached a campground with a cluster of abandoned rental cabins in a clump of forest. By then, Tobias was waking from his pill-induced sleep. He peered around groggily as we parked behind one of the cabins.

"Shouldn't stay in this one," he murmured. "Tire tracks would lead 'em right to us. We walk"—he pointed—"through the trees so no one sees where the trail ends, and go to one farther down."

The evasive skills he'd learned in his military training hadn't failed us yet. So we followed his instructions, looping through the forest to the cabin closest to the road, where we'd hear if anyone else drove into the campground. We crashed on the cabin's living room floor, bundling in our blankets and sleeping bags inside the army-issue tent, to keep in the warmth in the absence of a fireplace. Tobias, since he'd slept plenty already, sat by the window to keep watch.

When I crawled out of the tent hours later, Leo was already up, fiddling with the radio transceiver in the day's fading light. "Anything?" I asked.

"Nope. No CDC, but no Wardens either, thankfully." He studied my face. "Did you sleep all right?"

"Kind of hard not to when you're that tired," I said, with an attempt at a laugh that came out strained. "You don't have to worry about me."

"If you need to talk, about Gav, or—" He stopped when I shook my head sharply. "You're pushing yourself really hard," he added.

"I have to," I said. My eyes flickered toward Tobias at his post by the window, and I lowered my voice. "We don't have a lot of time."

"I know," Leo said. "But you're not alone here. We're all in this as much as you are."

Well, he was, and Justin and Tobias. I wasn't sure about Anika yet. But the coiled tension inside me loosened a little at his words.

"I know that," I said. "Thank you."

He cracked a smile. "Couldn't get rid of me if you tried."

As Justin and Anika roused, we disassembled the tent and gathered our things. Anika swore at the sleeping bag ties that kept slipping through her fingers when she tried to knot them, and Justin reached over to help.

"I guess I'm officially pathetic now," she said.

"Just a little," Justin said, and to my surprise he flashed a grin at her. Apparently sometime in the last few days, he'd finally forgiven her for trying to screw us over. When she'd come back asking for a second chance, he'd been the loudest opposition.

Tobias was watching them. He turned his head when I noticed him, snapping open the cap of the pill bottle. I remembered how he'd turned pink in Anika's presence when she'd first joined us, his gaze following her wherever she went. *It's nothing*, I wanted to tell him. *She's four years older than Justin. The two of them—it's never going to happen.* But she hadn't shown the slightest interest in Tobias either. So I kept my mouth shut as I tramped with the others back to the SUV.

I took the wheel first. Beneath the swathes of fabric we'd fixed over them, the running lights provided just enough illumination for me to follow the road as it wound along a stretch of farmland. I didn't think their pale glow would stand out across much of a distance.

After an hour, the road ended at a T intersection. Beside me, Justin squinted at the road atlas. "Looks like we should take a left, and then turn onto the first road to the east," he said.

"How close is this taking us to the highways?" I asked when we reached the second turn.

"Not too close," Justin said. He measured with his fingers. "I think there's still at least a mile between us and the nearest one."

"We don't know for sure the Wardens are sticking to the highways," Anika said. She paused, fidgeting with her gloves, and then added, "If Michael was smart enough to do everything else he's done, he's probably smart enough to figure out we'd try to slip by on the side roads."

"Well, if we meet any Wardens, we'll just blast through them like last time," Justin said, as if he'd been the one doing the shooting when we'd fled Toronto, not Tobias.

"I'll be happier if we don't run into them at all," Leo said. "Any 'blasting' is going to make other people want to see what's going on. The Wardens aren't the only dangerous ones around."

True. There'd been plenty of dangerous people back on the island, where no one had heard of Michael.

"I'm surprised he trusts anyone that much," I said. "I mean, the people who catch us, what's to stop them from just using the samples themselves?"

"Michael would probably have them killed," Anika replied,

matter-of-factly. "Anyway, I think he's given some people the idea that, if he got the vaccine, he'd somehow let everyone who's loyal to him get a piece of it."

Did he think he could split up the samples and just a fraction would be enough to protect people? Or—Drew had said Michael had recruited doctors. Maybe he figured one of them would have the know-how to duplicate the vaccine in small batches with whatever equipment they'd scrounged up, so he could dole it out to whoever paid the highest price.

I realized I was gripping the steering wheel much more tightly than I needed to. Screw Michael. Justin was right. We'd beaten the Wardens before, and we'd do it again if we had to.

As I flexed my fingers in an effort to relax, a muted *boom* echoed across the field to our right. My head snapped around, my foot hitting the brake. We slowed to a halt.

In the distance, to the west and ahead of us, a streak of light flickered. It flared brighter as another booming sound rang out, and a second light leapt up beside it. They wavered, dipping and swaying, like lines of flame.

"Wow," Justin said. "Something big just blew."

Leo leaned between our seats. "I wonder what?"

I strained my eyes, but all I could make out through the darkness was the quaking of the distant fire. "It could be anything. Maybe just an accident. There must be factories around here, with all kinds of chemicals stored in them that no one's looking after anymore."

More than just factories. How many nuclear power plants were operational in North America? Would the workers have taken the time to make sure they were safely shut down, in the midst of the epidemic panic? A shiver ran through me. Just one more in a long list of possible horrors the future might hold.

"Are we going to keep driving this way?" Anika asked, bringing my thoughts back to the car. I hadn't even turned off the engine—we were wasting gas.

I lifted my foot and the car eased forward. "I think whatever's going on, it's far enough away that we don't have to worry," I said, hoping that was true. "We might as well get past it before it gets much worse."

My hands were clenching the wheel again, and this time I knew there was no point in trying to relax. The lights edged closer to the snow-blanketed road. Whatever the fire had caught on, it was obviously spreading. Within ten minutes, it had crept across a space twice as large as before. A dim glow hazed the clouds above it.

We were almost directly across from it when another light glinted off the snow, about fifty feet ahead of us. The circular gleam of a flashlight.

"Hey!" Justin said. A moment later, I made out a cluster of figures huddled around the person holding the flashlight, a couple of them child-sized. They waved to us, obviously having seen the SUV before we saw them. I slowed.

"Where did they come from?" Justin said, craning his neck. There were no buildings in sight.

"They could be getting away from wherever the fire is," Leo said. "Or they could have started it. Be careful, Kae."

They were calling to us now. I could hear them faintly over the sound of the engine: "Please stop! Help us!"

"What do they expect us to do?" Anika murmured. "The car's full."

"I guess we could give them some food?" Justin said doubtfully.

We had hardly enough for ourselves. But wherever these people had come from, they looked as if they had even less. As if they had nothing but one another now, stranded in the snow.

A pang shot through me. But as I wavered and we rolled toward them, I thought of Gav. Gav, who would have been saying right now, "We should at least talk to them," who felt it was somehow his responsibility to help every person he saw who needed it. Who *had* felt. My resolve hardened.

Nine times out of ten, when we'd tried to help anyone, they'd stabbed us in the back the first chance they got. I wasn't letting that happen again. I could only look out for our group now.

"They could be armed. It could be a trick. We don't know them; we can't trust them," I said. A woman holding a bundle that looked like a baby stepped to the side of the road, and in that moment guilt tugged at my gut. But only for a second. I jerked the wheel to the side to swerve around her and pressed down on the gas. The engine roared, drowning out the shouts they hollered after us. The SUV jolted forward. I fixed my eyes on the road ahead, nothing left inside me but relief.

The next time I let myself look in the rearview mirror, the drifters and their flashlight had faded out of view.

FOUR

"Anyone who comes within miles of that place is going to notice the fire," Leo commented a little while later.

I glanced over my shoulder. The flickering light was finally hidden by the small town we'd passed through, but it had been visible for a long time and it could still be getting larger.

"So what?" Justin said. "If some Warden sees it, why would they think it's got anything to do with us?"

"If someone patrols by here, they'll probably take a closer look," Leo said. "And that group's probably still out there, walking the roads and flagging people down. The group that saw us."

"Who could tell the Wardens a black SUV went by less than an hour ago," I finished for him, my heart sinking.

"Yeah."

"Oh, hell," Anika said under her breath.

I bit back an echoed curse. Maybe the fire would die out long before any of Michael's people happened by here. Maybe that group had already found shelter somewhere. But with a little bad luck and a couple radio calls, Michael could know exactly where we were. For all we knew, he already had every Warden he could spare speeding straight toward us.

"Let's get off this road," Leo suggested. "It'd be the first place they'd search."

"Right," I said.

Justin jerked open the atlas. "There are lots of little roads all over the place around here," he said. "We just have to watch out for dead ends. And if we go much farther west we'll hit a big freeway."

"So we go east, then," I said. "And let's turn every chance we get. I don't want to give them an easy path to follow." Until it snowed again, our tire tracks would reveal our route, but at least a winding path would make it harder for anyone to set up an ambush. "You tell me when the intersections are coming, and which way to go to keep us east and south. Okay?"

"Got it," Justin said. "About a mile from here, you can take a left."

I pressed my foot against the gas pedal, pushing the car faster than we'd risked before. Twenty miles an hour . . . twenty-five miles an hour. I eased off only when I felt the tires start to skid on the snow. It was even and fairly shallow here, but it still offered much less traction than the plowed roads I used to take for granted.

We reached the turn and turned again fifteen minutes later. And then the good luck we'd had so far started to run out. The farmland gave way to forest, and the wind sweeping over the trees had left the snow sloped across the road. It was still shallow enough for us to drive through, but the slant threw off the tires. I had to creep along, hugging the ditch, braced against the slightest drift to the side. The dark tree trunks slipped past the faint glow of the headlights like looming phantoms. A bead of sweat trickled down my back, but I didn't dare stop to unzip my heavy coat.

It was almost an hour before we came to another viable turnoff. A sprinkling of snowflakes fluttered down—not enough to cover our tracks, just speckling my view through the windshield. My ankle was starting to ache from holding my foot steady on the pedals. But we'd hardly covered any distance at all.

Unfortunately, the SUV couldn't run on determination alone. The fuel indicator had dipped below the ¼ mark.

"We're going to need more gas soon," I said. "Is there any extra in the trunk?"

Leo shook his head. "I poured everything we had in before we left the cabins."

The road ahead of us looked particularly lonely, but so far we'd been more successful siphoning from vehicles left at isolated houses than in towns, maybe because other scavengers had already made the rounds in more populated areas.

"Shout if you see a mailbox," I told the others.

The first two houses we came across, down lanes between the trees, were car-free. Then the forest receded by a row of country houses only about an acre apart. I eased up and down the driveways, munching on potato chips from the bag Justin had opened as a hurried lunch.

We peered at each house before getting out of the car, but all of them looked abandoned. The weather hadn't been kind. A huge crack bisected a living room window. The roof over one of the porches had collapsed. We found a little gas: an old truck gave us a couple gallons, which we sucked down our length of plastic tubing into the jugs we carried. Then, after a few empty garages, a van offered a few more gallons. But it wasn't enough.

As we edged onward, Tobias snuffled and shifted in the back, his most recent batch of sedatives wearing off.

"What's going on?" he asked.

"Looking for gas," I said.

Through the rearview mirror, I watched him fumble with the pill bottle. His face was even pastier than usual. If the pills were upsetting his stomach like they had Gav's, he wasn't complaining, but it couldn't be enjoyable staying constantly knocked out in that artificial sleep.

"Hold on," I said. "Why don't you help search these places? It'll go faster with more people."

So at the next property, Tobias got out, quickly veering away from us as he coughed into his scarves. Leo and I checked the garage, Justin and Anika headed for the house to peer through the windows, and I sent Tobias to take a look around back.

We repeated the pattern at the next few properties. As we pulled up yet another driveway, the lights caught a line of shadows in the snow. I jammed my foot on the brake.

"Interesting," Justin said.

"What?" Anika poked her head around his seat.

A trail of footprints crossed the snow between the house and the garage. Human footprints. I turned off the engine, studying the windows as silence settled over us. No light in the house. No smoke above the chimney. Just a looter passing by, then?

Even if it had been a looter, they could have crashed here for the night. The muted glow of the SUV's lights didn't reach far enough to tell me if the footprints led away from the house on the other side.

"What do you want to do?" Leo asked.

"Go carefully and keep our eyes open," I said. "And let's leave the house alone. We'll take a look at the garage and then we'll move on."

I touched my coat, running my fingers over the shape of Tobias's flare gun in my pocket. Leo and Tobias both carried real pistols. If someone confronted us, we could probably convince them to leave us alone.

Dragging in a lungful of frigid air, I stepped out. We converged on the garage. A keypad was mounted beside the sliding door, requiring a code we couldn't provide, and the knob on the side door didn't budge when I tried to turn it.

Locked up tight. Which meant maybe there was something valuable in there. Something the looter hadn't gotten to.

Or there was no looter, only an owner protecting his supplies.

A figure materialized at the edge of my flashlight's beam, and my pulse skipped a beat before I recognized Tobias. He'd ducked around behind the house as usual. He jerked his head toward the backyard. "You should take a look at this."

We tramped through the calf-deep snow to a log shed almost as large as the garage. The door hung ajar. Tobias held up the padlock he must have busted off it. He hung back, scratching his elbow, while the rest of us stepped inside.

"Holy crap," Justin said, and Anika laughed.

Our flashlights revealed a snowmobile parked in one corner of the shed, beside a stack of gas cans. At the other end of the building stood a thick wooden table, with several animal skins hanging on a line above it. Mostly rabbit, two that had once belonged to squirrels, and what looked like a raccoon's bushy coat. A salty, musky smell reached my nose through my scarf, thicker than the piney scent of the logs.

Some of the skins were fresh. The footprints hadn't been a looter's. Someone lived here.

I backed up instinctively. Tobias was still standing guard by the door. He sneezed a couple times, and cleared his throat.

"I don't think anyone's home right now," he said. "There's a spot where another snowmobile must have been sitting around back, and a trail heading off toward the trees that looks recent. I'll keep watch."

Leo nudged one of the gas cans with the toe of his boot. "We could get pretty far on this," he said, but he just stood there, looking at them.

Justin didn't seem concerned about politeness. He marched over to the wall beside the table and poked through the tools hanging there. "I bet this could come in handy," he said, grabbing a wrench. "And these." He snatched up a pair of wire cutters.

My flashlight grazed Anika's back—she was stuffing something into her pocket. I smothered the urge to protest. Leo had raised his eyes toward me.

Everything here belonged to someone else. Someone still alive, who'd done nothing to harm us. But we needed it too. We needed it *more*. Whoever owned all this didn't have a murderous gang tracking him down. He didn't need to protect a vaccine that might save everyone in the world who was still living.

"We'll take all the gas," I heard myself say. "And anything else that could be useful. But let's get the gas first—that's what's most important."

"And we don't know when the homeowner might show up," Tobias put in.

"If he doesn't appreciate the cause, I guess we'll just have to convince him," Justin said, waggling the wrench.

"You and your violent solutions," Anika said as they hefted a couple of the gas cans.

"Hey, I know when to back off," Justin protested. "I haven't gotten us into any trouble since we left the city. But sometimes you've got no choice, right?"

"I suppose sometimes it's good to have a man of action around," Anika said drily, but she aimed a crooked little smile at him that looked almost sincere. When he glanced back at her, his cheeks faintly flushed in the hazy light, the smile vanished so quickly I wondered if I'd imagined it, and then she was hurrying out to the SUV.

Leo picked up a couple cans too. Tobias backed away from the door as we passed. His gaze followed Anika for a moment before he turned back toward the yard.

We emptied cans into the SUV's tank until it was full. Then we stacked the extra cans in the trunk. When we were almost done, Justin went to have a look at the garage—to see if he could "crack the code," he said—and Leo and I made one last trip to the shed.

Only three cans remained by the wall. The space looked horribly empty. Without meaning to, I imagined the owner coming back from his hunting trip and finding his stash gone. The anger and panic he'd feel. I tensed.

"Hey," Leo said, lowering his flashlight. "We can always leave the last few."

I didn't mean to say what I was thinking, but the words slipped out. "Gav would have."

"Yeah," Leo said. "I bet he would."

"They'll get us that much closer to Atlanta," I said. And wherever we might have to go after, if it turned out the CDC was a dead end. "Maybe this guy's got an even bigger stash in the garage. He'd probably take everything we have if our positions were reversed."

"That doesn't mean we have to," Leo said. "It's your decision, Kaelyn. We're with you either way."

I knew he meant it. But at the same time, there was a rawness in his voice that took me back to the time a couple weeks ago when he'd confessed how he'd stolen from and abandoned friends, people who'd tried to help him, to make it back to the island alive. When he'd admitted he no longer believed he was a good person, and how much that horrified him.

Back then, I'd told him I still thought most people would do the right thing, if they were given a real chance. I'd wanted him to believe that, to believe in me. Remembering that made a sickly heat rise in my chest. Maybe before, I'd have left a few cans for a person I didn't know.

Maybe if I'd been a little more callous before, a little less naive, Gav would still be alive.

Good and bad didn't apply here. It was about surviving or ending up dead.

"We take all of it," I said firmly. In that instant, Leo's gaze flickered, in a way that sent an anxious twinge through my chest. But he nodded and reached for the remaining cans.

He understood, I told myself as I grabbed the last one. He had to.

On our newly filled tank, we wove through the back roads until the brownish haze of the dawn lit the horizon. Time to hole up for the day. I picked the house: a three-story Victorian positioned like a fort on a small hill. The thought of the view from the windows, overlooking the road and the fields and forestland beyond its long backyard, made me feel a little more secure.

As before, we didn't park at our chosen hideout, but a few homes down. We crossed the backyard there, tramped to the house on the hill through the forest where our path would be hard to spot, and then set up camp in the Victorian's living room. After our hurried dinner, I stepped out to repack the cold box with snow. My scooping mittens uncovered tufts of yellow grass.

The snow was starting to thin. I didn't want to think about what that meant. One small hike in temperature as we continued south, and it would all be melting away. Leaving us with nothing to cool the vaccine.

I guessed, when that happened, we'd just have to make one long run for the CDC. And hope they had the facilities to keep the samples cool there. And if no one was there at all . . .

I shoved that thought aside and headed back in. But as I watched Justin spread the blankets inside the tent, a restlessness worked its way through my bones. I wasn't ready to sleep yet.

"I'm going to watch the road, just for a bit," I said. Tobias had taken the second floor bedroom at the front of the house to keep watch, but it couldn't hurt to have two sets of eyes on the lookout. Maybe the third floor would be a loft room, with windows at both ends so I could see all around us.

My gaze passed over Anika, and I nudged Leo. "Keep the cold box with you?"

"Sure," he said.

Upstairs, a yank on the thin chain in the hallway brought down the steps to the next level. The gust of freezing air that came with it carried just a hint of sourness. I hesitated, and then climbed up.

The room above stretched the entire length of the house, as I'd anticipated. It was set up as a bedroom, with a canopy bed and short bookshelves lining the walls beneath the vaulted ceiling. Everything was a delicate shade of lilac, even the bedspread. Which made the body in the mint-green dress that lay on it stand out despite the gauzy canopy curtain.

Something clenched inside me. I sucked in a breath and made myself walk to the front window first. From there I could see as far as the closest highway, more than a mile away. Beyond it, the landscape rippled, rolling hills rising into rounded mountains lifting to distant peaks that grazed the clouds. The branches of the trees in a nearby orchard wavered in the wind. Nothing else stirred.

The world was as still as the corpse on the bed.

I didn't want to have to look at her, to see whose house we were appropriating and what had happened to her, but I couldn't help stopping at the foot of the bed on my way to the back window. Maybe I owed it to her to find out. I turned my head.

If I hadn't seen dead bodies before, this one might have been more disturbing. But there was no blood, no open wound, no evidence of violence. The woman behind the curtain looked so peaceful I might have been able to believe she was simply resting, if not for the icy tinge on her coppery skin and the dribble of vomit seeping from the corner of her parted lips. The winter had kept her perfectly preserved. There was no smell of rot yet, only a faint sour tang from the vomit.

The woman's eyes were closed, but her head was tipped toward the opposite side of the bed, where she'd laid out a collection of photographs. I eased the canopy to the side so I could make out the images. An older couple standing on the deck of a cruise ship. The woman before me in a wedding dress with her red-haired groom. School portraits of two little boys. What appeared to be a New Year's Eve party with a group of friends raising their cocktails.

Beside the photos lay a diamond necklace, a plastic beaded bracelet, a dog-eared novel, a ratty stuffed elephant toy. And an open, empty bottle of painkillers that had rolled against the clock on the bedside table.

I'd braced myself for a wave of nausea, for shock or disgust. All that washed over me was sadness, fading into a dull sort of resignation.

There wasn't any sign she'd even been sick. But maybe this wasn't such a bad way to go, if you were going to go somehow eventually: in a little world of her own making, a shrine to all the things she must have loved. Better than the way Gav had gone—clawing and shrieking and terrified.

Except, since when was I assuming it was better to die than go on? Why wasn't I horrified that the epidemic had brought her to the point that suicide was the best option?

What was wrong with me?

I dropped the canopy and walked away. When I reached the back window, I leaned my forehead against the glass. But the chill didn't wake up any emotions; it just blended into the numbness.

There wasn't much to see out back, only the shadowy forest and another line of hills beyond it. My head was getting heavy, my eyelids drifting down. Maybe I was just tired. Too much stress from across the night, catching up with me now.

I came downstairs to the familiar crackle of the radio's static. "Attempting to contact the CDC," Leo said, so wearily I could tell he'd been at it for a while. I found him in the dining room.

"I couldn't sleep either," he said before I could ask. "Everything look okay?"

"As good as we could hope," I said. The thought of telling him about the woman upstairs just made me feel more exhausted. As he turned the dial, I peeked into the living room. The tent's flap was closed, with Justin and Anika presumably dozing behind it.

"If anyone from the CDC, or with information about the CDC hears this, please respond," Leo said. "Over." He paused, and then sighed, rubbing his face.

"Just leave it," I said. "We're probably not—"

The static buzzed. "Hello?" a voice said, breaking through. "This is Dr. Sheryl Guzman from the Centers for Disease Control. I hear you."

FIVE

The first time I'd heard a voice emerge from Tobias's radio a few weeks ago, I was flooded with excitement. Now, my skin went cold. That first time, we'd thought we'd found help on the road to Toronto, and it'd turned out to be the Wardens manipulating us into giving away our location. And then they'd come to take the vaccine and kill us. I had no doubt they'd try to trick us again if they had the opportunity. But if we'd reached an actual person at the CDC, that could make the difference in whether we got the vaccine safely to people who could make more. We had to take the chance.

I pulled up a chair next to Leo. He offered the mic to me. I blinked, and then accepted it. The vaccine was my dad's; I'd said before that this mission was mine. I supposed that meant I should do the talking. Leo gave my arm a reassuring squeeze, and I bent over the transceiver.

"We hear you, Dr. Guzman," I said. "You're at the CDC now?"

"I am," she replied. The volume dipped and rose, but I could hear wariness in her soft southern drawl. "Where are you? What's this about?"

As long as we only shared information the Wardens already knew, we should be fine. "We have samples of and notes on a new vaccine for the friendly flu," I said. "A vaccine that works. We've been trying to find someone who can make more of it—the CDC seemed like our best shot. We're headed your way now."

There was a pause, and for a second I thought the transmission had dropped off completely. Then the static crackled, and the doctor spoke again, angrily. "People like you are why we let the radio monitoring slide. Making up stories isn't going to get you in here. We're not that much safer here than you are out there. We don't have time for this."

"Wait!" I said. If this was some special tactic by the Wardens to prove their authenticity, it was awfully convincing. "Don't go. I'm not—We really—" I fumbled for something to say that might make her believe me.

Leo squeezed my arm again. "Your dad talked with them?" he murmured.

Of course! If he hadn't, they should at least have heard of him. "You know the name Gordon Weber, don't you?" I said into the mic. "The first vaccine that was released—he was the Canadian microbiologist who worked on it with the World Health Organization. In Nova Scotia, where the outbreak started."

Another pause, and a sigh. "Give me a minute."

I set down the microphone. My heart was thudding. I hadn't thought before about having to prove ourselves to them. I glanced at Leo.

"Do you remember, was my dad's name in the news when they talked about the epidemic?" I asked.

"I don't think so," he said. "I was always listening for people I knew, after I found out about the quarantine. Mostly the reporters quoted people from World Health and the other agencies."

“Then maybe giving his name will be enough to convince her we’re legit,” I said. “If it really is the CDC.”

He tapped the side of the transceiver, his mouth twisted like he wasn’t sure whether or not to smile. “Yeah. We have to test *them* too.”

How? The woman on the other end—this Dr. Guzman—wasn’t acting like someone trying to draw us in. But maybe Michael had realized we’d be too suspicious if they used a direct approach again.

In the living room, the tent rustled. “What’s going on?” Justin asked groggily, zipping open the flap. “You get someone on that thing?”

“We’ve got a woman who says she’s at the CDC,” I said. “She seems to think we’re making things up. We’re not sure yet whether she is.”

“What about the notebooks?” Leo said, tipping his head toward the cold box where it sat beside his chair. “Maybe your dad wrote down something we could use.”

“Right!” I said. Dad had been so involved in working on the vaccine, he must have recorded information only someone on the inside would have known. Leo passed over the bag with his notebooks, and I pulled out the top one, the earliest volume.

“You figure the Wardens are messing with us again?” Justin said.

“Too early to tell, but there’s no point in risking it.” As I turned back to the radio, I flipped to the pages where Dad talked about the development of the first vaccine, the one his team had sent to the States for further testing. The one that had failed.

The static fizzled. “Are you still there?” Dr. Guzman said.

I snatched up the mic. “We’re here.”

“What exactly does this have to do with Dr. Weber?” she asked.

Her tone was more urgent now, her drawl thicker. "Is he there with you? Can I speak to him?"

Justin shrugged off his blanket and crept over to stand by the table. Anika scrambled out of the tent after him, her eyes wide.

"Dr. Weber's—" Even after all this time, after everything I'd seen, that fact stuck in my throat. I swallowed. "Dr. Weber is dead. I'm his daughter, Kaelyn. I guess you'd know about the quarantine that was set up on our island? When we lost contact with the mainland, my dad was working on a new vaccine. He finished it and started testing it. I have samples and his notes."

"All right. Can you confirm something for me, then? What was the working name for the first vaccine?"

So she wasn't finished testing us yet. "Hold on," I said, scanning the notebook's pages. The letters stood out in sharp capitals a couple dozen entries in. "FF1-VAX," I read.

"And which testing facility was it sent to after the initial formulation?"

I searched farther, looking for the dates when I knew the first vaccine had been ready. "Fivomed Solutions," I said. "In New Jersey."

"How come she gets to ask all the questions?" Justin grumbled.

"Okay," Dr. Guzman said. "Okay." She gave a little laugh. "I'll have to talk this over with everyone else, but this is good. Where exactly are you?"

"I'd rather not say right now," I said. "Actually, I'd like you to confirm a few things for us, just so we know for sure who we're dealing with."

From her silence, it appeared she hadn't expected that. My

stomach twisted. If this conversation ended up being just another chance for the Wardens to taunt us, I was going to scream.

"What do you want to know?" she asked.

"Well, it sounds like you have files on the first vaccine," I said. I frowned at the page in front of me. "How many samples were sent to Fivomed?"

"Twenty," she said after a moment.

"And..." Leo tapped a name near the top of the page, and I nodded. "Which Public Health Agency official traveled to New Jersey with the vaccine?"

"Ah, Dr. Henry Zheng, it looks like."

The tension started to drain out of my shoulders. "Yes."

"So will you tell me where you are now?"

Even if we were sure this was the CDC, the Wardens could have stumbled on our conversation and be listening in on their own radios. "I still don't think it's a good idea," I said. "We've had some trouble.... There are other people who want the vaccine, and our transmissions aren't secure."

She'd passed the test, but I still felt wound up inside. Some part of me refused to be relieved. "Look," I added, "we're trying to reach Atlanta as quickly as we can. Now you can at least be ready for us. It's really good to know someone's there. Is there anything you can think of that would help us get to the city?"

"Well, you clearly already know to be careful," she said. "I have to admit I'm not sure there's much we can do for you from here, even if we knew where you are. We haven't had contact with anyone very far afield in quite some time, and the situation here has been... Well, we'll do whatever we can once you make it to the city. Will you keep checking in? We'll have someone monitoring this frequency as often as possible. Any questions you have, we can at least try to advise on."

"We'll do that."

"At the very least, make sure you get in touch before you come into the city," Dr. Guzman said. "We'll work out with you the safest route to the center."

"All right," I said. And then, automatically, "Thank you."

"Thank you!" she said with another laugh. "I have to tell everyone else."

Her voice faded away into the static. I reached to flip off the switch.

"Ha!" Justin said, raising his hands. "We found them. We're *heroes*!"

Leo let out a ragged breath, smiling more openly than I'd seen in a while. I started to grin back at him. "I guess we are," he said. "The CDC came through."

Gav wouldn't have believed it. He'd wanted to, for me, but he'd been so sure everyone in power had abandoned us. My grin faltered. If only he'd had a chance to see this moment.

If only we'd been able to come straight down to Atlanta, instead of having to hide from the Wardens and sneak around them. Maybe Dr. Guzman and her colleagues could have saved him.

"There's really going to be a vaccine," Anika said. She grasped the edge of the doorway as if knocked off balance. "I mean, for everyone. We're all going to get it. We're going to be okay. I kind of thought—*Michael* thought he was going to get to be king over everything. He's going to be so pissed!"

She crowed the last words, but at the same time she looked almost as if she was going to cry.

"Good thing you hooked up with us, eh?" Justin said, and she swiped at her eyes.

"Oh my god, yes."

I wanted to feel that exhilaration too. I wanted to feel more than this tangled knot of hurt and frustration. This was even worse than my absence of guilt over leaving those people behind in the snow, my absence of horror at the woman's body upstairs. Why wasn't I happy? The scientists we'd come all this way to find—now we knew they really existed.

But somehow they still seemed so far away.

Coughing echoed through the ceiling, and my focus snapped back to the present. Now we knew where to go to make sure no one else had to die.

"I'm going to tell Tobias," I said.

I walked upstairs alone. The floor creaked after I knocked on the closed bedroom door.

"Are we heading out already?" Tobias asked hoarsely. "We just got here."

I hadn't considered leaving, but all at once I wanted to say yes. We were going to get in the SUV and keep driving until we were face-to-face with Dr. Guzman at the CDC. But the Wardens were still out there looking for us.

"No," I said. "But there's good news. We managed to reach someone at the CDC on the radio."

I'm not sure how I expected him to respond, but I expected something. All I got was silence.

"Tobias?" I said. "There are scientists still working there. I'm sure they'll have the equipment to do a blood transfusion—they can do the same procedure for you that cured Meredith, with my antibodies."

"If we can get to Atlanta," he said slowly.

"We've managed to get this far."

"But it's going to get harder," he said. "I've been keeping track, Kaelyn. It was four days ago I first got the itch. That means my mind could start to go as soon as tomorrow, doesn't it? We're not making it there that fast."

"They could still cure you," I said. Maybe. My dad had tried a similar treatment on other patients and hadn't succeeded, but if Meredith had been lucky, Tobias might be too. "Meredith was already hallucinating when—"

"That's not what I meant," he rasped, cutting me off. "I saw what Gav was like. What if you can't convince me to keep taking the sedatives? How're you going to keep a low profile if I'm shooting my mouth off and running around like a lunatic?"

"We'll manage," I said.

I was going to say we'd managed with Gav. But we hadn't. My throat tightened. I closed my eyes, willing back the grief. I had to think about the people who were still alive. About Tobias. Because he was right. If the virus broke down the part of his brain that controlled his inhibitions before we made it to the CDC, the rest of the trip was going to be hard. Really hard.

If I'd offered to let him take one of the vaccine samples when we were leaving the island, like I had with Leo, we wouldn't even have to worry about this. I couldn't have known we'd need to make it this far, or that the soldier who'd been a stranger then would end up helping us so much. Tobias himself had said that he didn't think it was right to risk using up another of our few samples, when we'd first arrived in Toronto and Gav had gotten sick. But right then I wished I'd made that offer, and that he had taken it, so this awful conversation would never have had to happen.

To mention that regret seemed even more awful. "We'll manage," I said again.

Tobias shifted on the other side of the door. "I'm glad," he said, and for the first time since I'd given him the news, he sounded like it. "Your dad's vaccine will get made; people will be protected. I was a part of making that happen. Pretty amazing when you think about it, for a guy who spent his whole life with everyone thinking he wouldn't amount to much. Anika—and Justin—they won't have to be so scared anymore." He paused to cough weakly. "I've been doing everything I can to make sure they're safe. I don't want anyone getting sick because of me."

"We know that," I said. "We've all been so careful. I'm sure they're okay, Tobias. They'll stay okay."

"It's a strange feeling, seeing people be afraid of you," he said, the lightness in his voice fading. He went quiet, as if he was talking more to himself than to me. "I never asked for anything. If Anika would rather talk to that kid than me—"

A sneezing fit interrupted him. "We could be there as soon as a couple days," I said firmly, before he could continue. "We're going to crush this virus right out of existence. Hold on to that, okay?"

"You're right," he said after a moment. "I will. I'm just rambling. You should all sleep while you can. I'll keep on watching."

"Thanks," I said. "I—we all—really appreciate it."

"I know," Tobias said. "Thank *you*, Kaelyn."

I lingered outside the door a few seconds longer, half-expecting him to add something. When he didn't, I headed downstairs.

Justin and Anika were back in the tent, the fabric muffling their murmuring voices. Leo was standing in the hall as if he'd been waiting for me.

"You're happy, aren't you?" he said quietly as we grabbed our blankets. "You knew we'd find someone, and—there they are."

"I'm not sure I'll be really happy until we're right there in the CDC," I said. Tobias's worries buzzed inside me. "It still feels like a long way to go."

As soon as I'd said it, I wished I hadn't. Leo's face fell, just fractionally, before he caught it and pushed his mouth back into a smile.

"Well, we haven't let 'a long way to go' stop us yet," he said. "It's getting to be our specialty."

"No kidding," I said, managing a small smile in return.

Justin and Anika fell silent as we ducked into the tent. I slid under the spread sleeping bags, setting the cold box between me and the thick canvas wall. As soon as I was lying down in the darkness within, exhaustion crashed over me. I let it drag me down into sleep, like a swimmer too tired to fight the undertow.

I drifted and dreamed, the images slipping by in blurs and fragments. I was being suffocated by the sense that I needed to reach out, that someone—*Gav?*—waited in the fog just inches from my fingers, when a shrill dinging pealed into my ears and through the haze. I jerked upright, my pulse hiccupping.

The others were scrambling up too. I kicked away the sleeping bag and fumbled with the tent's flap. The room outside was dark with the passing evening. My head snapped around, following the dinging noise. The kitchen. I stumbled out and hurried down the hall.

In the fading light, I didn't immediately recognize the objects in the shadows on the counter. But as the others came up behind me, my vision adjusted. I groped for the off switch on the back of the old-fashioned alarm clock that I didn't remember being here in the morning. Its hands marked the time as seven o'clock.

"What the hell?" Justin said, pushing his rumpled hair away from his face. "Did you set that, Kaelyn?"

"No," I said, and Leo broke in.

"Is that . . ." His voice trailed off, and we all stared at the counter.

Just beyond the alarm clock lay a large black pistol. A pistol that, I was pretty sure, belonged to Tobias. Beside it sat a flashlight, a pack of batteries, a compass, and a granola bar. Things he'd been carrying in his coat.

My heart plummeted. I turned and ran to the stairs. "Tobias?" I called as I pounded up them. "Tobias!"

The door to the bedroom was open. I jerked to a halt on the threshold, one glance confirming what deep down I'd already known.

He was gone.

SIX

Leo and Justin had followed me upstairs. Justin pushed past me into the room, swiveling to survey the furniture as if Tobias might be hiding somewhere.

"What the hell!" he said. "He acts like he's so *mature* and responsible, and then he just takes off on us?"

"I don't think it's like that," I said. The words Tobias and I had exchanged earlier swam up through my memory with an uncomfortable chill. "He was worried he'd get us caught before we made it to the CDC, once he got sicker. He did this to help us."

"Oh." The flush of Justin's anger drained from his face.

"He probably hasn't gone far yet," Leo pointed out. "Knowing him, he wouldn't have left us without someone on watch for very long."

Which was why he'd set the alarm clock—so we wouldn't be sleeping for hours unguarded.

"Come on," I said, hurrying back to the stairs. "We have to find him. Before—"

Before he did something even more stupid. Oh no. I considered the items we'd found on the counter. He'd left behind everything he'd had on him, except his bottle of sedatives. Maybe he didn't think it was enough just to walk away from us. Maybe he was planning on eliminating the "problem" completely, like the woman in the attic.

I raced to the back door. Several sets of footprints marked a path through the shallow snow across the backyard, down the hill, and into the forest at its foot. The tracks we'd made when we walked here from the other house where we'd parked the SUV. I couldn't tell if a fresh set had been laid over them. Tobias would be using his military evasive skills against us now.

"Someone check if he went out the front!" I called over my shoulder.

"Doesn't look like it," Leo answered. He came through the kitchen, scooping up the flashlight Tobias had left. Anika had hesitated by the counter. Near the pistol. The memory of the violent ringing of shots, the thud of falling bodies, reverberated through me. But someone needed to take it. And if our lives were on the line, I still had the feeling Anika would save herself at the expense of the rest of us, given the chance.

I stepped inside, grabbed the gun, and stuffed it into my coat pocket. Anika turned toward me, her expression hidden behind her scarf. We all headed out into the backyard.

Leo cast the flashlight's beam over the snow. "Tobi—" Justin started to shout, and I threw out my hand.

"Quiet!" I said, keeping my voice low. "He doesn't *want* us to find him. If he knows we're looking for him, he'll take off even faster."

I strode toward the trees. Of course, he had to realize we'd go after him when we saw he was missing.

Or would he? Could he really believe we'd be glad to get rid of him? The way he'd talked before, about the danger he was putting us in, about Justin, and Anika—I should have made sure he understood how much it mattered to me to get him to Atlanta, to help him beat the virus. If he'd known there was no way we were giving up on him, maybe he wouldn't have done this.

We stepped into the thicker darkness beneath the branches of the oaks and pine trees. The trail of footprints veered to the left, and no new ones split off from them. I walked faster, my breath coming in puffs of mist. The night air stung my cheeks. I hadn't thought to grab my scarf.

Leo swept the flashlight across the forest around us, and I tracked its light. The surface of the snow between the trees remained smooth and unbroken, other than a faint scattering of rabbit prints and a dimple here and there where a twig must have fallen. We followed the downward slope of the ground to the base of the hill.

My hands balled in my pockets. There had to be a way to track Tobias down. I wasn't letting him sacrifice himself when we had a chance to save him.

I was trying to think of what our next best move would be, when there was a sharp inhalation behind me. Anika had frozen. She pointed through the trees.

A low mechanical hum reached my ears. An engine. Leo flicked the flashlight off without a word.

My mouth went dry. I took a few steps forward, toward the edge of the forest. There, I could see across the lawns to the road beyond.

Two pale lights glimmered into sight. A Jeep with its running lights on, cruising slowly over the snow.

"Wardens?" Justin said.

"I don't know," I murmured. It was possible some other group of survivors was traveling down the same road we'd taken, wasn't it? But as I watched, the Jeep crept past the house we stood behind, past the two after, and eased to a stop by the fourth. After a pause, it turned down the driveway, toward the spot where the SUV was parked.

Whoever was in the Jeep, they were following our tracks. It could be the Wardens, or other raiders just interested in a new car and supplies to steal. Either way, it was bad.

My mind leapt to the cold box in the corner of the tent, back at the house we'd left undefended, and panic jolted through me. I couldn't see the Jeep now, but I heard the thud of the doors closing. As soon as our pursuers realized the house we'd parked by was empty, they might start checking the others.

"Go back!" I whispered. "Fast but quiet!"

We rushed along the trail the way we'd come. Without the flashlight, it was harder to avoid the sticks that crackled underfoot and the shrubs that rasped against our clothes. Every noise seemed to echo. By the time we reached the edge of the Victorian's backyard, my skin was damp with perspiration.

The gleam of a quarter moon showed the way across the yard. I peered behind us to where the Jeep had stopped. Our pursuers hadn't made any noticeable sound since they'd gotten out. I didn't know where they were now. They might be able to spot us leaving the forest, even at that distance, if they were watching.

"Run for it," I said to the others. "Around the far side of the hill and then up. So we'll stay mostly out of view."

I waited only long enough to catch their nods, and then I darted onto the open ground. My heart thumped as I dashed across the brief stretch between the forest and the steepening slope of the hill. Then I was around the far side, hidden from anyone south of us. At the top, I ran for the back door. Inside, the cold box was in the tent where I'd left it. Letting out a breath, I grabbed the handle and scrambled up to the second floor. In the smaller bedroom that faced south, I stared out the window.

The people from the Jeep were in the house we'd both parked by. Flickers of what must have been flashlight beams glinted through its darkened windows.

The others gathered around me. "Do you think they saw us?" Justin asked.

"I don't think they'd be looking in that house if they had," I said.

"It's got to be the Wardens," Anika said, shifting on her feet. "Who else would be driving around in the dark on random back roads, chasing tire tracks? We're screwed."

"We're not," I said. "We just have to . . . figure out what to do."

"They're going to find our footprints," Leo said. "When they see we're not in that house, they'll go back to the SUV to check where else we walked, and follow our trail back here. But that was part of the plan, wasn't it?"

"It was." I closed my eyes, pushing through the anxious jumble of my thoughts. Tobias had talked us through the whole strategy. If our pursuers followed the path we'd made through the forest, we could head down the road in front of the house without being seen. Get back to the car. Get away from them.

"So we wait until they head into the forest," I said. "As soon as they do, we go along the road, jump in the SUV, and take off. I'll keep watching. The rest of you, pack up all our things downstairs, okay?"

They slipped out without argument. I studied the path of the distant flashlights, biting my lip.

It was far from a foolproof plan. What if our pursuers left someone behind to guard their Jeep? And even if they didn't, as soon as they heard our engine, they'd come running back after us.

The last time the Wardens had been at our heels, we'd only been able to escape thanks to Tobias's sharpshooting. We didn't have him now. We didn't even know where he was.

Unless he came back on his own, and soon, to get out of here safely we'd have to leave him behind.

I swore under my breath, feeling sick. He'd suggested this strategy, and now we were going to use it to abandon him. If only I'd noticed something was off in his attitude earlier—if only I'd said the right thing to stop him from leaving. Now there was no time.

Our pursuers' lights were wavering past the back of the house. They glinted off the glossy paint of the Jeep and the SUV. I tensed. The window clouded when I exhaled. As I rubbed the condensation away, the lights wove back and forth, and then bobbed farther from the driveway, toward the forest. Following our tracks, like we'd hoped.

"Come back, Tobias," I murmured. "We need you *here*."

The flashlight beams made slow progress, sweeping over the yard in all directions. The hall floor creaked behind me. "Ready to go," Justin announced, his voice quivering with what sounded like nervousness as well as excitement. Good. We could count on him as long as he didn't get cocky.

"It's not quite time yet," I said. The glow of the flashlights had just reached the trees. Justin came up beside me and handed me a bundle of scratchy fabric. The scarf I'd forgotten in our frantic rush.

"I figured you'd want this," he said.

"Thanks." I felt surprised by his thoughtfulness, and then guilty for being surprised. He might be younger than the rest of us, but he had started pulling his weight all right.

As I wrapped the scarf around my face, Justin lowered his head. "So Tobias took off because he didn't want to infect the rest of us?"

"I think so," I said. "That, and he knew he wasn't going to be able to control his own actions soon, and he was worried he'd make it hard for us to get to Atlanta. You remember how tough it was to avoid drawing attention after Gav... got bad. And we weren't on the move for most of that time."

"We still could have handled it. I know I complained a lot, but it really wasn't *that* bad with Gav, with all the precautions we took." He scuffed his boot against the rug. "Do you figure... I wasn't exactly being friendly with Tobias the last few days. I didn't want to get sick! But I don't have anything against the guy. Do you think that's maybe why—"

"I don't know," I said. A lump filled my throat. "Maybe it was how all of us acted. Or maybe there wasn't really anything we could have done to stop him." He was just trying to protect us, like always. A bunch of teens he hadn't even known until a month ago.

"And now he's out there on his own."

"Yeah," I said. I didn't mention the sedatives Tobias had taken with him. For all we knew, he was sitting there in the forest less than a mile away, with the entire contents of that bottle in his stomach. I crossed my arms over my chest, hugging myself. *Go away*, I thought at the distant flashlights. *Go back to wherever you came from. Don't make us leave him.*

They ignored my silent plea. Finishing their sweep of the open ground, the lights dipped between the trees, winking in and out of view. As Justin and I stood there, the glimpses became briefer and less frequent, and then stopped altogether. I counted the seconds in my head. Ten . . . twenty . . . thirty . . . They'd vanished. Which meant they wouldn't be able to see us either. This was our opportunity.

I turned, squashing down my emotions. I had one person out there and three here, counting on me to get them out of this alive. My hand dipped to brush the pocket that held Gav's last message. *Keep going.*

I didn't have a choice, not really.

"Let's get moving," I said.

Leo and Anika were waiting by the front door. They handed bags off to Justin and me wordlessly, Leo stopping for just a moment to press his hand against my shoulder, his mouth slanted unevenly, his expression pained. Then we hurried out into the frigid wind.

"We'll walk faster in the tire tracks, where the snow's packed down," Leo whispered when we reached the road.

Our boots rasped over the gritty treads. I watched the road, and the dark shapes of the trees beyond the houses, as we marched down the hill. Our pursuers were still so deep in the forest that I couldn't make out their lights. Would they continue to go cautiously, or would they be hurrying too, now that they were sure they'd picked up our trail?

My fingers started to ache from clutching the handle of the

cold box. We passed the house at the bottom of the hill, and its neighbor. As the fourth house came into view in the dim moonlight, I sped up, as close as I dared to a jog. The others hustled on behind me.

When I reached the driveway, I pulled off my mitten and fumbled in my coat pocket for the car keys. My hand bumped the cool edge of Tobias's pistol. I paused, and then held out my arm to slow the others.

If someone was guarding the Jeep, we needed to be ready.

I drew out the gun and fit my forefinger around the trigger. It felt too large and heavy in my hand. Beside me, Leo took out his own gun, one we'd confiscated from the first Wardens we'd tangled with—the people Justin and Tobias had shot with the pistol I held now.

As we crept up the driveway, my heart pounded against my ribs. I'd never fired a gun before. But if it was them or us, I was pretty sure I could.

We hesitated by the side of the house and peeked around back. No figures waited by the back door, or the vehicles. I lowered the gun.

We tossed our belongings into the SUV—I scrambled into the driver's seat, and Leo climbed in beside me with the road atlas. As Justin got in the back, Anika cocked her head at the Jeep. She walked over to try the doors. They didn't budge.

"Come on!" Justin said.

"They're going to come running as soon as they hear us start the car, aren't they?" Anika murmured.

"Yeah," I said. "It's not over yet."

Her hand dipped into her coat, and she grinned. "Then let's buy ourselves a little more time."

She pulled out a long, sheathed hunting knife. That must have been what she'd taken from the shed the other night. She jammed the blade into the side of a tire. As the air hissed out, she repeated the gesture with the others. I felt a grin tug at my own lips. Suddenly our escape didn't seem half as impossible.

"I'd like to see them catch up with us now," Anika said.

"Great thinking," I said. "Now let's get out of here."

"Sweet!" Justin whispered to Anika as she hopped in beside him.

"Call it payback," she said.

I shoved the key into the ignition. "Same rule as before?" Leo asked. "Turn at every intersection?"

"You know what?" I said. "Let's find a stretch of straight road first, and get as far as we can as fast as we can. We can worry about muddying the trail after we've got some distance on them."

I couldn't help one last glance toward the forest, as if I might see Tobias running across the yard toward us. It was as still and empty as ever. I set my teeth and turned the key.

The sound of the engine reverberated out into the night. I jerked the wheel, backed up the car, turned, then sped down the driveway. In the distance, I heard something that might have been a shout. And then we were racing along the road, leaving both our enemies and Tobias behind.

SEVEN

We'd been roaring down the road for about fifteen minutes before the panicked thumping of my heart eased off enough for me to think clearly, and it occurred to me that we could use the Wardens' strategies against them.

"Justin," I said, "the transceiver's back there?"

"Yeah," he said. "Why? It didn't sound like that woman at the CDC is going to be able to bail us out up here."

"I know," I said. "I don't want to talk to anyone. I want to listen. If those were Wardens back at the house, they'll be radioing the others, right? Since they're close, maybe we can pick up some of their transmissions, get an idea of how much they know, how many of them we have to watch out for."

"Ha!" Anika said, sounding as amused as after her revenge on our pursuers' Jeep.

Leo's eyebrows lifted. "It'd be nice to get the jump on them for once."

"I'm on it!" Justin said. He pulled the transceiver onto his lap. As I drove on, the flick of the switch and the hum of static carried from the backscat.

"Go through the frequencies quickly," I said. "We don't want to use up too much of the battery."

"Right." The dial clicked as he scanned the airwaves. The static popped and fizzed. Leo leaned his head against the side of his seat, his ear cocked toward the back.

"Wait!" he said. "There. Tweak that dial a little." He pointed, and Justin complied. And a wavering voice emerged from the crackle in fits and starts.

". . . headed south . . . the same SUV they reported . . . half an hour from . . . Michael's looking into the choppers, and . . . you take Highway Sev—"

After the last incomplete word, the voice disappeared into the static. Justin fiddled with the dials some more, but nothing else came out.

"We lost them," he said.

"Or they finished talking." Leo straightened up. "I guess that confirms it. *Someone* saw the SUV, anyway. But—choppers?"

That word had stood out in my mind too. "I guess there must be helicopters around that they could use, if they found someone who knew how to fly them." My gaze flickered from the road to the star-speckled sky. "Do you think they could fly around at night, when there aren't any lights on the ground to navigate by?"

"I don't know. We'll just have to be extra careful about hiding the SUV when we stop in the morning."

"It figures," Anika said, her good humor gone.

"Well, we might as well stick to the original plan for now. No highways. Get away from here fast and then lose the trail," I said, trying to ignore the knot of tension in my chest. We hadn't heard enough to know how to avoid the Wardens, only to know they were on to us, and that they had even more resources than we'd realized.

But we had something too. We had the certainty of the CDC waiting for us. We just had to make it there.

We drove on in a straight line for two more hours, and then Leo directed me down a winding series of back roads, skirting the mountains that loomed closer as we continued south through Ohio. The Wardens didn't cross our path, but they were out there, somewhere, searching. The tension inside me tightened into a sharp ache. It pinched every time I breathed.

Late in the night, we ended up down a lane swimming with snowdrifts. It took an eternity of pushing and tire spinning to back out and find another route. But as we neared the West Virginia border, the coating on the ground thinned. When we stepped out to rotate positions and fill up the gas tank with the rest of the fuel we'd taken from the hunting shed, I packed the cold box with as much snow as it could safely hold before climbing into the passenger seat.

As we rotated again at about five in the morning, a light drizzle began to fall. Within half an hour, it had dissolved what remained of the snow on the road, leaving a slick sheen of ice on the asphalt. Anika, now at the wheel, pumped a spray of antifreeze over the windshield. She'd eased on the gas, her face whitening every time the tires started to slide. I clamped down the urge to tell her to speed up again. At least now we weren't leaving a trail for the Wardens to follow.

Staring out the rain-streaked window, my thoughts drifted back to Tobias. Was the weather the same back by the house on the hill? Was he sitting in it right now, wet and cold and just waiting for it all to be over, not even knowing we'd tried to look for him? The image made my gut twist.

It was far too late, and too dangerous, to go back for him. Too dangerous to do anything but keep driving. But that didn't stop me from hating the fact that I hadn't found some way to help him.

My frustration must have shown in my expression, because a second later Anika said, "We had to go. The Wardens were right there."

"I know," I said.

"I can hardly believe we made it," she went on, with a brief breathless laugh.

The naked relief in her voice pricked at me. Before I could catch the words, I was saying, "And I guess it's nice for you not to have to worry about the sick guy in the car."

Anika's mouth opened and closed and pressed into a thin line. A rush of shame washed over me. I could hardly blame her for being happy to be alive.

"I'm sorry," I said. "That was mean. I'm just so angry we had to leave him."

"I don't know," Anika said finally, quietly. "Maybe you're kind of right. I *was* nervous, having him with us. I don't want to end up like that. But I'm not *happy* he took off."

I couldn't blame her for being scared of the virus either. It'd seemed like the only right thing to do, bringing Tobias with us. But by trying to help him, I'd put Justin and Anika at far more risk than they'd have faced otherwise, hadn't I?

I just wanted to keep everyone okay. It shouldn't have been so hard.

My head was starting to ache now—from my fractured sleep, from the stress of our escape, from the endless patter of the rain. I pressed my hand against my temple.

"We did everything we could," I said, as much for her as for me.

"You end up leaving people behind, one way or another, right?" Anika said, with a forced lightness. "That's just how it goes. I don't even know what happened to half of my friends. When everyone was getting sick, I just started fading out of people's lives so I didn't have to worry. . . . It's so weird; I used to be hanging out with them, partying, whatever, just about every night—I hated being on my own. And then being alone was the only thing that seemed safe." She laughed again, more stiffly this time.

I imagined her in another time, perched on a bar stool with a group of friends, grinning as she spun through the whirling lights on a dance floor. Free from all this fear.

"What were you studying?" I asked. "At college?"

She paused. "Special-events planning," she said. "I thought I was going to be arranging charity galas and movie-release parties. Well, so much for that."

"But you liked it."

"Yeah. I—" She cut herself off, her eyes darting over to me and back to the road. Then she shrugged. "Whatever."

"You never know," Justin said, behind her.

"Whatever," she repeated, her voice going flat.

Leo's coat rustled as he shifted in the backseat. "We still have a future," he said. "I mean, we're all going to end up somewhere. Obviously there's a bunch of things we can't do anymore, but from what I've seen . . . you've got to figure out what's important to you, what you *can* do, and do it, or *you're* getting left behind."

I wondered if he was thinking of Tessa. Who had left who, there? Leo was the one who'd continued on while she'd stayed put at the artists' colony. But she was the one who'd really broken things off with him. She'd seen a place where she could accomplish what felt most important to her—more important than boyfriends or friends or even the possibility of a vaccine.

I still missed her sometimes, her calm practical way of looking at things that I'd gotten so used to while we were working together on the island, but remembering how she'd lit up in the colony's greenhouse, I couldn't wish she'd chosen differently.

"Anyway, I don't think what's important to you always has to make sense," Leo went on, more breezily. "I'm going to keep wanting to dance even if every studio in the world is closed. It's in my bones. Might as well let it out."

"At least you guys had plans and stuff," Justin said. "I was just goofing off with my friends and making sure I passed my classes so my parents wouldn't be pissed."

"You're fourteen," I said.

"Fifteen in a month!" he protested.

"Same thing. My brother Drew used to talk about how so many of the guys he knew who were applying for university, *they* didn't really know what they wanted to do with themselves; they were just going through the motions. So you're normal."

"Being normal's not much good to anyone now," Justin said. "The *world* isn't normal. I didn't take off with you and get myself chased by guys with guns to be normal."

No. He'd wanted to come with us so he could do more than just waiting and hiding, like he'd been when his dad was shot after the looting had started.

I was trying to find the right compassionate words to say when Anika's mouth twisted as if she was trying to suppress a grin. "If it helps," she said, "I think you're pretty weird."

"That's not what I meant," Justin grumbled, and I couldn't help giggling, and just for a moment, the tension in the car split with tired laughter.

Then my gaze slipped to the fuel indicator. Any lingering traces of amusement vanished.

"The gas is getting low," I said. I'd been so distracted by the fading snow and the rain and my guilt about Tobias that I hadn't been paying attention to it since I stopped driving. In the last few hours, it had dipped to almost empty. We'd burned through the stash we'd stolen yesterday. "We'll have to do some more scavenging."

"We've covered a lot of distance since the Wardens caught up with us," Leo said, but he sounded as apprehensive as I felt.

We drove into a tiny town that appeared to have been completely abandoned. All the driveways and garages were empty, the yards and streets strewn with soggy litter, as if no one had lived there for years. Had everyone fled after a few of their neighbors got sick? The sight of it made my skin crawl.

"Come on," I said. "We shouldn't stay in any place too long."

After the town, we passed two farmhouses, one with a truck with a dry tank, and another offering no vehicles at all. The droppings on the front hall floor suggested the house had become home to several nonhuman squatters. The drizzle was lightening, though moisture still tapped my cheeks when I hesitated before getting back into the SUV. Sunlight was creeping through the clouds along the horizon. In less than an hour, the field and forest below us, and the mountains to our left, would be lit with daylight.

"Maybe we should stop for the—" I began, and a sharp sound rang out across the field. All four of us jerked around.

Nothing moved on the stretch of snow-dappled field, but as I eyed the dark clump of trees about half a mile distant, the sound came again. The distant staccato of a barking dog. A couple dogs, actually.

Anika stepped toward the car door. "They could be ones that've gone wild," she said. "Hunting."

I shook my head, thinking of the coyotes I used to watch on the island, the puppies I'd helped look after at the vet clinic where I'd volunteered. Had that really been less than a year ago?

"A dog wouldn't bark like that if it's hunting," I said. "It would scare away the prey. They sound playful." But grown dogs didn't usually bark much when playing with one another. Were there people over there? People who were doing well enough that they could provide for pets?

"We should take a look," I said. The last place we'd found where someone was living, wc'd also found gas.

"Are you sure we want them to know we're here?" Leo asked.

"No. But if we're quiet and don't get too close, we can at least scope them out."

"I'm in," Justin said.

Anika shook her head. "I don't like dogs."

"Well, someone should guard the SUV anyway," I said. "Why don't you and Leo stay here, and Justin and I will see who we're dealing with?" I might understand her a little better now, but it still didn't seem wise to leave her with free access to our only vehicle and the vaccine.

"Works for me," she said.

"Here." I handed the flare gun I'd been carrying to Justin, since I had a real gun now.

"You don't need to tell me," he said. "I won't shoot anyone unless there's nothing else I can do."

"Good," I said, "because I don't even know how well that thing will stop someone."

I took out Tobias's pistol. The memory of seeing it on the counter, realizing why he'd left it there, flashed through my mind, and my throat tightened.

"Can you show me how to use this, quickly?" I said to Leo. "Just in case we run into trouble?" I might not be looking to attack anyone, but if these strangers spotted us, who knew whether they'd be friendly?

Leo accepted the gun, handling it carefully but with practiced efficiency. "The safety has to be off for you to shoot, but leave it on the rest of the time," he said, demonstrating with a snap. "You look along here to aim. You should steady it with both hands or the bullet will probably go wild."

I practiced, pointing the pistol at the garage, trying to copy the wide stance I'd seen Tobias take. Leo stepped closer, looking over my shoulder. He nudged my hands up slightly. "Be careful, okay?" he said by my ear, his voice low. "I don't want anyone shooting at *you*."

His breath warmed the side of my face, and for an instant my body snapped into vivid awareness of how little space there was between us, how his arms had almost encircled me to adjust mine. An unexpected heat tingled over my skin, and the gun dipped in my grasp, bringing my mind back to the task at hand. I moved to the side, stuffing the pistol into my pocket where it would hopefully stay.

"I know," I said without looking up. We needed to find gas—that was what I had to be thinking about. "We will. Thanks. We won't take long."

Justin shifted restlessly at the edge of the driveway. "Okay, let's go," I said, and he raised his head. We headed out across the field.

The snow that dusted the grass had dissolved into little more than slush, which hissed against the soles of our boots. One of the dogs barked again. It sounded far away, though the trees must have muffled some of the sound. The breeze was pushing against our faces, cool and cedary, so our scent wouldn't be carrying to them. That would let us get closer.

"Can we talk?" Justin murmured.

"For now," I said quietly. "What is it?"

"I've just been thinking, since we heard from the doctor at the CDC. You don't think they had anything to do with the virus, do you?"

"What do you mean?"

"Well," he said, "like, in the movies, when there's some killer flu on the loose, it's usually because government scientists were experimenting and accidentally let it out or something."

"Oh," I said. "I don't think the CDC does that kind of work. Biological weapons would be more a military-lab thing." I paused, considering the early response on the island. "The Public Health and WHO people that helped my dad, they didn't know anything about the virus beforehand—it was a big deal when they isolated it. If someone had made it, they would already have had samples, records. And in my dad's notes he talks about the friendly flu being a natural mutation of the virus I caught before, the one that gave me partial immunity." It was by using part of that earlier version in combination with bits of the new one that he'd finally been able to create an effective vaccine.

"It just seems strange," Justin said, "the way it came out of nowhere."

"I don't know," I said. "No one knows where Ebola came from. And it took a long time for doctors to figure out AIDS. Viruses just appear—they can be lurking somewhere isolated until people stumble along, or a sudden mutation makes them more deadly or lets them leap from some other animal to us. We're probably lucky that nothing this bad ever hit us before."

Justin nodded, but his face had fallen. It would have been easier to blame an actual person for the virus than having to think nature was just screwing with us the way nature tended to do.

I glanced back toward the house when we reached the edge of the forest. Leo held up his hand. I waved in return, and stepped between the trees.

The cedars were interspersed with elders and maples, and to my relief the leaves they'd dropped during the autumn had turned into a wet mush that dampened our footsteps. Still, I walked cautiously, easing around bushes and low branches. A few paces in, I stopped, and Justin stepped beside me. A faint canine whine reached my ears. Not close yet. We walked on.

We'd been sneaking along for maybe five minutes longer when the daylight ahead of us started to brighten. The trees were thinning. I crept from trunk to trunk, peering between them. After several steps, I made out a clearing maybe ten feet ahead. Within it, a boxy-looking metallic structure that glinted in the morning sun stood behind a tall chain-link fence.

Justin raised his eyebrows at me. I tapped a finger to my lips and eased forward. A couple steps from the clearing, I came to a halt.

The fence appeared to stretch around the entire clearing,

surrounding a whole row of the boxy metal structures. A grid of bars and railings, like some futuristic jungle gym, loomed over them, and farther in I could see a squat concrete building with a high voltage warning sign mounted on the door. No wires crossed over the fence, but the place reminded me of the electrical substation on the island. Wires could run underground.

And it *was* running. A faint hum of electricity hung in the air. The substation was connected to a plant somewhere—a plant that was still operating.

A movement caught my eye. As I turned my head, a girl who looked no more than ten years old ran into view on the other side of the fence. A golden retriever panted as it raced after her. She waggled a rawhide bone. Behind her, beyond the substation's buildings, I spotted a cluster of dark green tents set up along the fence. Two shacks that looked as if they'd been constructed out of crates and broken furniture stood nearby. A woman slipped between the tents, moving toward a spot beyond my view. The breeze carried a wisp of smoke to my nose, the tang of burning wood.

It was a smart place to set up camp. They had the fence for protection, and access to electricity as long as the plant was in operation. Maybe they were the families of the plant workers who were keeping it that way. But the substation made a smaller, less obvious target. I couldn't imagine Michael's group would fail to go after a functioning power plant if they realized one existed.

Of course, maybe they already had. Maybe these people were indebted to the Wardens. It seemed like half the survivors we'd run into since leaving the island were.

I gestured for Justin to follow me, and stalked along the border of the clearing, away from the tents. Around the curve of the fence, the camp had an odd kitchen setup: three fridges, a basin with a tap, but no oven. I guessed they were cooking over the fire. Farther on, a rectangle of soil had been broken up and tilled in rows, as if they were hoping to start a garden when the weather got a little warmer. Then I caught sight of a small delivery truck and a gray sedan, parked on the grass between the concrete building and the fence.

If they had vehicles, they'd have gas.

A few steps more, and I made out a line of huge plastic drums on the other side of the truck. Several smaller gas cans were stacked on the grass around them.

Justin pointed, and I nodded. "Think they'd be up for a little trading?" he asked under his breath.

I made a gesture of uncertainty. What did we have that they didn't? Other than the vaccine samples, which I couldn't offer. From the number of tents, it looked as if there were several more of them than there were of us. Had they survived this long through kindness and generosity? For all we knew, the second we presented ourselves, they'd attack us and grab everything we had.

"I don't trust anyone anymore," I said.

Justin shrugged. "Then we take it."

As he said it, I realized I'd already made the same decision, somewhere in the back of my mind. We'd cleaned out that one hunting shed—stealing a little from people who had so much was no worse. I saw our options with a cold certainty that brought back the ache in my chest. It was either them, or us. There was no middle ground left anymore.

The only question was how we were going to get what we needed.

I studied the clearing. The fence stood seven or eight feet beyond the last of the trees. The gas cans lay only a few steps farther on the other side. But the fence itself was at least twice my height, topped with loops of barbed wire.

"Hey!" Justin whispered. "The wire cutters. They're back at the SUV. We can hack right through."

Perfect. "Go get them, quickly," I said. "We don't have a lot of time." Any minute the breeze could shift and the dogs catch our scent. And they might not react kindly to strangers.

EIGHT

Justin slunk away through the trees. I crouched down behind the trunk of a maple, listening, watching. Smelling. A salty greasy scent that made me think of frying bacon was drifting through the compound. Maybe it *was* bacon. My mouth started to water.

Footsteps brushed across the damp grass somewhere to the left. A fridge door sighed open. Glass clinked, and the door closed with a thud. I tipped my head against the bark. If we could have trusted these people, we could have asked them to hold on to the vaccine samples for us, where they'd stay cold. We wouldn't have had to worry about losing the snow.

A second later the thought seemed so absurd I grimaced. Who wouldn't turn on us while we were carrying something that valuable?

Beyond my view, childish laughter rose, and the dogs barked again. If breakfast time for people meant breakfast for the animals too, that would help distract them.

At home on the island, my ferrets, Fossey and Mowat, were probably wondering where everyone had gone. I hoped when they finished the bags of food Leo had opened for them, they'd find their way out of the house to forage.

A new sound carried through the fence. I stiffened. On the other side of the compound, someone had broken into a coughing fit. The coughs sputtered out and started again, and hinges creaked.

"Why does Corrie get to play with Rufus all the time?" a thin voice called. "I want to see him too! There's nothing to do in here."

There was a murmur of conversation I couldn't make out, and then a man's voice said, "Here, Devon, you can have a turn now." He whistled and, I guessed, ushered the dogs into whatever building the boy was quarantined in. A wooden door thumped shut.

The cool wind cut through my scarf. So the virus was here too. How careful were they being? How many of them were infected? One more in the long list of reasons to avoid talking to them face-to-face.

Another set of footsteps approached, this time from behind me. Justin was walking over, the wire cutters he'd taken from the hunting shed clutched in his gloved hand. They looked tough enough to handle the chain link.

"Leo didn't seem really happy about the idea when I told him," he murmured as he reached me.

Because he was worried we'd get caught? Or . . . Or he didn't totally approve of us stealing from strangers in the first place. An uncomfortable twinge ran through me, and I closed my eyes. He wouldn't really think less of me for doing everything I could to keep us on the road and alive, would he? He knew what it took to survive, in this new world. I couldn't think of a single alternative I could call "good."

My previous certainty settled back over me. "This is our best chance," I said. And I was going to make the most of it. I held out my hand for the clippers.

Justin shook his head. "I'm doing it."

"I'm smaller than you," I said. "I won't need as large a hole." He was only a couple inches taller than me, his body still gangly with adolescence, but his shoulders were broader, his coat bulkier.

"No way," he said quietly. "You're our leader. The general doesn't take the dangerous solo missions. What'll we do if something happens to you? I'm going. Throw something at me if you see someone coming."

I didn't have a good enough argument in the moment, and time was slipping away. So I watched him go. Smoothing my hand over the ground, I found a small rock to pelt him with if I needed to alert him.

Justin hunched down and stalked across the clearing as if imitating a military commando in a video game. Maybe he'd picked up a few useful skills from all that goofing off with his friends after all. When he reached the fence, he tested the metal links with his fingers. Then he raised the clippers.

The blades made only a faint clicking sound as he cut through the wires. He moved from one to the next, carving an oval in the fence. Nothing was moving in the compound within my line of sight. I kept my ears perked as Justin clipped the last few segments and gave his makeshift door a nudge. The wires squeaked faintly as they bent, and a pot clanged in the distance. He flinched, but no one came.

I held my breath as he pushed through the gap, the metal edges snapping threads on his coat. And then he was inside. My fingers squeezed around my rock. Justin glanced both ways, and then hurried to the gas cans.

He was just bending down to grab a couple when a low baying

broke the quiet. With a thunder of heavy paws, a Great Dane charged around the concrete building.

I jerked to my feet. Justin snatched up the nearest can, spun, and scrambled toward the fence. "Hey!" someone yelled. Pounding footsteps raced after the dog, and a woman burst into view, carrying a rifle. "Stop!"

I ran across the clearing, grasping the flap in the fence and yanking it up. Justin stumbled over a dip in the dirt, and the can's handle jolted out of his fingers. The can thumped to the ground. The Great Dane snarled, scattering slush as it crossed the short distance between them.

"Leave the can!" I said. With a grimace, Justin lunged forward. In the space of a heartbeat, he ducked through the flap and we shoved it back down.

The dog skidded to a halt, teeth snapping at the spot where Justin's arm had been an instant before.

"I said stop!" the woman hollered, lifting the gun. I grabbed Justin's elbow and we dashed for the trees. The pistol in my pocket bumped against my ribs, but I didn't trust my aim to save us. In a minute we'd be outnumbered anyway.

We'd just reached the forest when the shot crackled through the air. A yelp broke from Justin's mouth. We threw ourselves forward into the shelter of the trees. My ears rang with the echo of the gunshot and the dog's frantic barking.

For a second, I thought we'd made it, that we'd both dodged out of range in time. Then Justin sagged against a trunk. Blood bloomed around a tear in his jeans, just below his knee.

The woman with the rifle was striding closer, and the Great

Dane was biting at the flap in the fence. I hauled Justin's arm over my shoulder and tugged him deeper into the forest.

He limped alongside me, his breath turning into a gasp every time he moved his injured leg. "'M okay," he said, with a pained grunt that told me exactly the opposite. I swallowed hard.

"You're not," I said. "But we're going to get out of here, and then we'll make sure you *are* okay."

My pulse pounded at the base of my throat. We had no time at all now. That gunshot would have been audible for miles around. If the Wardens were anywhere nearby, they'd be heading straight here.

As we staggered out on the other side of the forest, Anika was waiting halfway across the field. She rushed over to us. Leo watched, gun at the ready, from beside the SUV.

"What happened?" Anika asked, reaching for Justin's other arm.

"Stupid dogs," Justin muttered. "I almost had it—I should have at least gotten one can."

"They caught him inside the fence," I said. "He's been shot in the leg."

Anika winced in sympathy. Justin pushed her hand away, but he didn't say anything else. A sheen of sweat had broken out on his forehead despite the chilly air.

"Start the car," I told Anika. "We need to get out of here fast."

She nodded and ran ahead to the house, her highlight-streaked hair streaming behind her as her hood slipped from her head. When she spoke to Leo, he handed her the keys. He edged over to the passenger door without shifting his gaze from the forest behind us. The unhappy curve of his mouth made my stomach clench.

I was the one who'd agreed to Justin's suggestion of breaking into the compound. I'd let him go in. I knew how sensitive dogs could be to one unusual sound or scent—maybe I should have realized the risk was too high. If that woman had aimed differently, he could have been dead now. For a couple cans of gas.

Justin gave a little sigh of relief when we reached the house. I helped him into the back of the SUV and jumped in beside him. Leo hopped in the front, jerking his door closed, and Anika jammed her foot on the gas. I glanced up and down the road as she roared toward it, but there was no sign of pursuit. Yet.

"Backtrack," I said quickly. "The people from the substation might come down to the road over there to ambush us. You have the atlas, Leo?"

"Right here," he said.

As we veered onto the road, he started giving Anika directions. I leaned over the back of the seat to grab the first-aid kit from the trunk.

"Let me see your leg," I said to Justin.

He leaned back against the door and lifted his injured leg onto the middle seat between us, inhaling sharply at a lurch of the tires. "I guess we have to get the bullet out?" he said, his voice strained.

"No way," Leo said before I could answer. "It's better to leave it in. My dad went over what to do in an accident every time he dragged me out on a hunting trip. You start digging in there, you'll just get bacteria inside. The most important thing is to stop the bleeding."

I pawed through the kit for the scissors, and then cut open the fabric of Justin's pants so it sagged away from the wound. Blood seeped down Justin's pale, hair-speckled skin. But the wound was a gash, not a hole—a thick ragged line slicing along his calf. And while it looked painful, it didn't appear to be very deep.

"I don't think the bullet's in there," I said, my voice shaky. "It looks like it just caught the side of your leg."

"Well, I guess that's good news," Justin said, and sucked air through his teeth as I dabbed at the wound with an antiseptic wipe. Our last one, since I'd used the others when Meredith had cut her hand.

"Sorry," I said. He grimaced in answer, his lips pressed tight. Holding the wipe against the gash, I fumbled with the roll of gauze, almost losing it as the car swayed around a turn. There was only enough left to wrap it around his leg four times.

"Pass the scissors," Justin said. When I handed them over, he cut a swath of fabric from the other leg of his jeans and tied that around his calf over the bandage. "You figure that'll do it?"

"It'll have to," I said. Sifting through the contents of the kit, I found another roll of gauze, but I thought we'd better save that so we could clean the wound and rebandage it later on. If we *could* clean it properly, without an antiseptic. I didn't think the bullet had done any permanent damage to his leg, but even a shallow cut could get infected. We had a couple bars of soap. That was better than nothing.

And we only had to look after it until we got to the CDC. The doctors there would know what to do for a bullet wound. They'd have antibiotics.

If we could actually make it there.

A sudden longing swelled inside me, so intense my eyes went watery. I didn't know what Gav would have thought of my plan, or its outcome, but I didn't care. I just knew that if he'd been here right now, he would have pulled me close and told me I was amazing to have gotten us even this far, and maybe I'd have believed him.

Then my mind flickered back to those last few days, to his complaints about how far I'd dragged him and the way he'd begged to go home. My throat closed up. Some part of *him* hadn't believed this journey was worth it.

But I had to anyway, if I was going to get through this.

"Have you seen anyone else on the road?" I asked as Anika took another turn.

"So far, all clear!" she replied.

Justin shifted back in his seat. "Take it easy, okay?" I told him.

He rolled his eyes. "I should have been faster."

"I shouldn't have let you take the chance with the dogs there," I said. "It wasn't your fault."

He made a face and turned toward the window. Fields, forests, houses, and barns whipped by. Leo directed Anika along a winding route that avoided all but the smallest towns. While I'd been bandaging Justin's leg, we'd managed to swing around to head south again. The roads were clear, the night's ice melting into puddles on the asphalt. Without snow slowing us down, we might be able to make it all the way to Atlanta by tonight.

But not without fuel. As we crested a small hill, about an hour after we'd raced away from the substation, the engine sputtered. My hopes plummeted.

"Shit," Anika said faintly. The engine's noise stilled to a purr, sputtered again, and then choked off completely.

* * *

Using the momentum of the slope, we managed to steer the SUV down a lane behind a rusty silo. I climbed out into mid-morning air that felt faintly warm against my skin. We were stranded, exposed, in the midst of a tract of farmland that sprawled out beyond the foot of the shadowy mountains. Only thin rows of trees divided the open fields. The nearest house, a broad brick structure on the other side of the road, looked to be at least a fifteen-minute walk away. And just a few small splotches of snowy white glinted amid the fallow soil. In an hour or two, I suspected they'd have melted away completely.

"What the hell are we going to do?" Anika said, pacing beside the SUV.

Justin leaned out past the open door. "We can't just sit here."

"No," I said. We had to keep moving—that I knew for sure. "We'll have to leave the SUV. Obviously. Either we find another car that works and we go on in that, or we find gas and we come back here."

"If we might not come back, let's see how much we can carry," Leo said.

He popped the hatch, and we stared at the heap of supplies inside in silence. We'd brought a few of the sleds we'd used on the road before, but they'd just slow us down without snow to coast on. Tobias had contributed a couple army packs along with his other equipment. I pulled the one that held the tent and the camping stove over my shoulders, trying not to think about where Tobias might be now, how far we'd left him behind.

Leo stuffed the other pack with bottles of water and cans of food, what remained from our scavenging in Toronto. We each shoved a flashlight into a coat pocket. Anika gathered up the bags holding our blankets. Justin had brought the first-aid kit out from the backseat, and squeezed it into the rolled sleeping bag he swung onto his back. I hefted the cold box and two of the jugs we used to siphon gas, and Leo picked up the radio transceiver in its plastic case. It sat awkwardly in his arms. But we needed it if we were going to contact the CDC for further instructions.

Justin slid out the hunting rifle we'd lifted from the first Wardens we'd confronted, gripping the muzzle and bracing the butt against the ground like a walking stick. The flaps of his cut-up jeans wavered around his calves. We had extra sweaters and hats, even two extra coats, but no good pants to give him.

"We'll check the houses for something better for you to wear," I said, and he looked down at his legs as if he hadn't even thought about it.

"It's not too cold," he said. But as we set off across the field, he walked with a noticeable limp, his hand tight on the rifle. After several hurried steps, his forehead was gleaming with perspiration.

"Hey," I said, grasping his shoulder. "We can go a little slower. If you push yourself too hard, we'll end up having to carry you."

"I can take the sleeping bag," Leo offered.

Justin shook his head vehemently, but he eased up his pace, hobbling as the rest of us ambled along the road toward the nearest house. I kept my ears perked for the faintest hint of an approaching vehicle. We were like wounded ducks fluttering around in a pond here, hoping the hound would miss our scent. And it didn't usually turn out well for the ducks.

I stopped once, while the others continued ahead, to scoop what remained of a mound of snow into the cold box. This might be the last time I filled it, I realized as I snapped the lid shut. We were so close, just a couple states from Georgia, half a day's drive now that the snow was gone. And it could all be ruined without gas.

As we came up on the house, I saw a tree from the yard had collapsed against the back, presumably during a winter storm. Its branches had shattered the second-floor windows and caved in the roof.

The garage held only a workbench and the smell of mildew. I assumed from the state of the house that no one could possibly be living there, but as we approached the door, a weak sneeze carried through it. All of us froze. Then we hustled on without a backward glance.

My back began to throb under the weight of the pack. Leo shifted the radio in his arms, tucking it under one for a short while, and then the other. Anika rolled her shoulders, her face looking pinched. And Justin limped on, his jaw set and his gaze determined.

The breeze carried a slightly rancid scent to us as we skirted a field of crumpled cornstalks. My nose wrinkled reflexively. Maybe something—or someone—had died in the midst of the crop. I focused on the hemlock trees that lined the border of the next field over, where hopefully we would leave the smell behind.

We were only a few steps away, catching a glimpse of another house just a short distance beyond them, when an oddly familiar whirring sound split the air.

Leo spun around. "Helicopter," he said, at the same moment I recognized it. A dark speck hung in the sky to the north. In the second I stood staring at the shape, it doubled in size. It was heading our way.

Michael's looking into the choppers, the voice had said on the radio.

"The Wardens," I said, turning back toward the trees. "Come on! We have to get out of sight."

NINE

We ran for the hemlocks. Leo held out his hand to Justin, and this time Justin didn't refuse help. The trees offered only a couple feet of open space beneath their lowest branches. I crouched down and crawled under, pulling the cold box and the backpack after me. Anika scrambled in beside me. Beyond her, the guys were clambering under the neighboring tree.

I squirmed around on the damp soil and elbowed my way back toward the open ground. Peering through the branches, I made out the glint of the sun on the helicopter's windows and a sheen of blue and white on its body. It looked as though it might pass us by to the west rather than go directly over us, but it was hard to tell. And I had no idea how far they might be able to see from that high up.

I tracked the shape of it growing in the sky. "Are they coming after us?" Anika asked. She was hunched by the trunk of the tree, untangling a strand of her hair from a clump of needles.

"I don't think so," I said. "I don't think they saw us. But it's a good thing we were close to the trees." If they'd snuck up on us while we were in the middle of one of those fields, they couldn't have missed us.

"They just aren't going to give up." Her voice quavered. "I knew it."

“It doesn’t matter,” I said. “Once we get to the CDC, there’s nothing they can do.” I hoped.

“If we get there before Michael moves on to tanks and stealth jets,” she muttered.

I eased a few inches forward to keep the helicopter in sight, and my elbow knocked the hard angle of the pistol in my pocket against my ribs. A picture flashed through my mind: pulling out the gun, aiming at the chopper, and seeing it burst into a ball of flame. Just one of our problems blasted away; just one victory over the Wardens. It was a ridiculous image—something from a movie, not any reality I knew—but it gave me a momentary satisfaction.

The helicopter prowled on, appearing to follow the line of the main highway, about a mile from here. My heart stopped for a second when I thought of the SUV, but we’d left it in the shadow of the silo. We hadn’t been walking that long. It should still be hidden.

Finally, the chopper passed us completely. As the drone started to fade away, I rolled onto my side. Anika was staring off toward the sound, still fidgeting with the hair she’d freed.

“You know,” she said, “my parents always used to tell me my life was so easy. I only had to worry about friend problems and boy problems and school. The two of them, and my mom’s parents, they lived through most of the war in Bosnia before they managed to get out and come to Canada.” She paused, and pursed her lips. “But I don’t think that war could have been any worse than this. I guess I wasn’t so lucky after all.”

She laughed without much humor. Hunched there, her back rigid and her eyes shiny with fear, she made me think of the squirrel I’d caught in a makeshift cardboard box trap when I was ten.

I'd felt so awful for frightening it nearly to death that I'd let it go right away.

But I couldn't beat myself up over the horrible situation we'd found ourselves in. I wasn't the one who'd trapped Anika here. I was just as trapped as she was. At least I was doing everything I could to get us someplace better.

"You're alive," I offered.

"Yeah," she said. "There's that."

The helicopter's rumble dissolved into the breeze. I waited another minute, and then crawled out. Leo and Justin were doing the same. Their clothes were streaked with mud, like mine, but our winter coats had protected us from the worst of the damp.

"You both okay?" I asked, and they nodded. But Justin stayed sprawled on the ground, his hand resting on the knee of his injured leg, while Leo stood.

"Helicopters," Justin said, gazing off in the direction the chopper had gone. "That's just crazy."

"We know how much Michael wants the vaccine," I said. My hand tightened on the handle of the cold box. In this world, a working vaccine was worth a million times more than helicopter fuel. "Come on. We'll stick as close to the trees as possible from now on, in case those guys turn around."

So we took the long way to the next house, around the edges of a field of yellowed bean plants. Anika fell back beside Justin, giving him a hand where the ground was uneven, so quickly he didn't have time to argue. She kept her expression impassive, but her eyes periodically darted toward the sky.

The farmhouse's double garage held a dented station wagon, its hood popped and tires stripped, picked over for parts. I checked the tank with the siphon hose just in case, unsurprised to find it empty. But the house's door had already been broken open, and in a quick search, we turned up a pair of khaki pants that were only a little baggy on Justin.

As we passed a field of sagging hay, the wind shifted. The rancid smell rose up again, more pungent now, like greasy fast-food–restaurant refuse left in the sun to spoil.

"What *is* that?" Justin asked, making a gagging sound.

"Something dead," Anika said. She looked faintly green. My own stomach was churning. But turning our search in the opposite direction would mean we'd have to recross all the ground we'd already covered. Well, where it stank this much, at least we weren't likely to encounter other scavengers. I pulled up my scarf.

At the edge of the hay field, we had to clamber over a metal fence. Leo and I helped Justin over. We descended into another field, which stretched wider than the others we'd passed, dotted with a frost-shriveled crop I didn't recognize. Up ahead stood several large aluminum-sided outbuildings, but nothing like a home.

"Looks like a big business operation," Leo said. "I guess we could find something useful."

The stink intensified as we hurried toward the buildings, until it smelled like a hundred restaurants' rotten scraps. I coughed into my scarf, swallowing the bile that had started to rise at the back of my mouth. If the business owners had left anything behind, we'd better find it fast.

When we reached the first building, a long structure with scratched-up red paint, I marched straight to the door and yanked on it.

Whoever had worked here last hadn't bothered to lock it. The door whined open at my tug. The stench hit me like a putrid punch, slamming right through my lungs and into my gut. I doubled over, yanking my scarf aside, and puked what remained of my last meal onto the straw-strewn floor.

Rows of narrow metal stalls stood in the dim light of the barn, and in each slumped the carcasses of what had once been pigs. Flies buzzed over their sightless eyes and picked along their emaciated necks, which were dark with rot and ravaged with sores where they must have tried to force their way free against the bars.

I backed away, wiping at my mouth. Horror welled up over my nausea. The farm's owners, they'd shut the place down, or the workers had just stopped showing up, and they'd abandoned the animals in here without food or water or hope of escape.

How long had the pigs survived, pushing at the bars, gnawing at the straw? I closed my eyes, imagining the sounds they must have made as they slowly gave up and died.

Justin leaned inside and then jerked back with an, "Oh, *gross.*" He pressed his fist against his mouth. Anika hung back, her arms folded tightly over her chest and her lips pressed flat.

"Hey." Leo touched my shoulder, and I leaned toward him. His hand smoothed my hair back from my face. "At least it's over—they aren't in pain anymore," he said raggedly.

I nodded, wanting to sink into him but knowing I couldn't feel comforted with that smell still all around us. "Let's keep moving," I forced out.

We made it about halfway past the barn before Justin's control broke. He ducked around a bush with a heave of breath and the choking sound of vomit, then rejoined us with averted eyes.

"It's so stupid," Anika said. "They should have let the animals out if they weren't coming back."

"I don't know if the owners of a place this big would come by very often," I said. "They could own a bunch of farms and run them from an office somewhere. And the employees might have been worried they'd get into trouble, if the epidemic stopped after all."

"It wouldn't have been that hard," Leo said. "Things were so chaotic, no one would have known who'd opened the stalls."

"Yeah," I said, the sour taste of stomach acid lingering in my mouth. Maybe the pigs wouldn't have survived the winter anyway, but at least they'd have had the chance.

How many other farms around the world had turned into coffins? My stomach rolled again. Sometimes it seemed people had brought almost as much death as the virus had.

And our little group wasn't exempt, were we? The people we'd passed on the road might have frozen. Whoever we'd stolen the gasoline from might die because he didn't have enough left to get to his hunting grounds. Maybe we should have left some.

But if we had, would we have made it this far, or stalled somewhere the Wardens would have caught us? I bit my lip. We *had* to get the vaccine to the CDC—that was the only sure thing I knew.

The smell started to ease off once we'd left the barn behind. Another identical structure stood off to its left, but I was afraid to discover a similar array of cow or goat or sheep carcasses. The immense building with the maroon-shingled roof up ahead looked promising. That huge square door suggested something drivable was kept inside.

We crossed a wide cement lot, the butt of the rifle tapping along with Justin's lurching steps, until we reached the garage-like door. There was no discernable way to open it. So we veered around the side of the building until we found a person-sized entrance. It was locked, but there was a large window in the wall just a few steps away. Leo set down his load and picked up a rock to smash it. When he'd cleared away the shards of glass, I boosted him inside and he unbolted the door.

"I think our day just got better," he said as he opened it for us.

We stepped into a dark cavernous room. I found a light switch on the wall beside the door, but nothing happened when I flicked it up and down. We all pulled out our flashlights.

The beams glanced over steel frames and giant tires. My breath caught. Before us stood an assortment of farming vehicles, most of which I didn't know the names for, which I assumed had been used for plowing and seeding, harvesting and processing the crops.

We circled the room, our cautious footsteps echoing through the shadows. The vehicles decreased in size as we approached the far wall, where several farm tractors only a little larger than the SUV waited in a row. No proper cars though. I guessed, since no one lived on-site, it wasn't likely that any personal vehicles would have been left behind. But I'd started to hope for at least a van or a pickup truck.

As I paused, Justin limped over to a door beyond the last tractor. He lifted the latch and tugged it open.

"Now we're talking!" he said.

We joined him, filling the small storage room with the combined glow of our flashlights. Dozens of keys hung from hooks on the wall beside the door. Repair tools and a couple spare tires sat on a metal shelving unit. And next to it stood five rectangular tanks stamped with a flammable warning sign and the words DIESEL FUEL. Each one of them looked large enough to hold a hundred gallons.

A jolt of excitement raced through me before I came back to reality.

"We can't put diesel in the SUV," I said. "It runs on regular gas. The wrong kind of fuel would mess up the engine, wouldn't it?"

"Probably," Leo said with a sigh in his voice. "But everything around here should work with it, I guess."

"And we've got the keys," Justin said, waving to the hooks.

I studied the farm vehicles in the dim light that seeped through the grimy windows. The plows and harvesters and tractors—how fast did they even go?

How many options did we have?

"We should keep looking around, see if there's any regular gas or a car we can use," I said.

Justin shrugged, but as he shuffled back into the main room, his face spasmed with a wince so intense he couldn't suppress it. He was so good at acting tough, I'd let myself forget it was only a few hours ago he was shot.

"Wait," I said. "We don't all need to go. Justin, you should stay here, give your leg a break."

"I don't think any of us should hang around here alone," Leo said. "There could be other people interested in this place."

"True. You know what, I want to take a closer look at what's in here, in case this is all we've got. Can you two do a quick circuit of the rest of the buildings? I think they're all pretty close."

"Sure," Anika said without much enthusiasm, and Leo dipped his head.

“We’ll keep an eye out; stay out of sight,” he said.

“Of course,” I said.

His fingers brushed my forearm, giving me a brief squeeze. I found myself searching his expression for some sign of how he felt. Some reassurance that he wasn’t disappointed in me after the debacle at the compound. But he just looked tense. Well, we were all tense, weren’t we?

Even though I knew that, a little pain pierced my chest as he turned toward the door. My hand dropped to my hip pocket, to the fold of cardboard there.

Keep going.

How? Would Gav have climbed into a tractor and declared it the solution, or been as overwhelmed as I felt? I tried to picture him here, but the image of his rigid face just before I’d pulled the sheet over him swam up instead. I shoved it away, the pain digging deeper inside me.

Gav had never really been confident, not after we came over to the mainland. He’d tried to pretend, for me, but he’d have been so much happier if he’d stayed on the island. And he’d probably have still been alive.

The door clicked shut behind Leo and Anika, and Justin started toward one of the tractors. I jerked out of my regrets.

“Hey!” I said. “Sit down. Here, there’s a chair in the corner.”

He made a face at me, but to my surprise, he didn’t protest. Maybe his leg was hurting even more than I’d guessed. I had to keep a closer eye on him.

I walked over to the tractor he’d been checking out. There was only one seat in the sealed cab, but there might be enough room for a person to lean against the back window. Definitely not space for four, though, especially with the supplies we needed to carry. The tractor beside it was the same size. I paced around them, frowning.

"We could take two," Justin said from his corner. He was following my movements with his flashlight.

"Then we'd need twice as much gas, and we'd be twice as noisy."

He craned his head. "We could use that trailer over there. A couple people and our bags could ride in it while the tractor pulls it."

The beam of his flashlight had hit what looked like a low-walled metal box on wheels, about the same length and width as the tractor. A hitch protruded from its front end.

"It's totally open," I said. "If it gets cold again . . ."

That wasn't really the problem, though, was it? The problem was the weather getting *warmer* as we headed farther south. If the temperature outside continued rising, I didn't think we could assume the snow in the cold box would stay frozen for more than ten or twelve hours. None of the vehicles in here looked like they could move fast enough to cross six hundred or so miles in that time. And none of what we'd gone through would be worth it if the vaccine samples spoiled.

Frustration bubbled up inside me. We knew where to go. With a real car, with gas, we'd have been so close. Without that, with the Wardens on our tails, Atlanta might as well have been across the ocean. Why did every part of this journey have to be so *hard*?

I kicked at a tire and was rewarded with a stinging pain in my toes. Tears that had nothing to do with my foot welled in my eyes. I stepped away from the light, gripping the edge of the tractor's hood.

"What's our biggest problem?" Justin said after a minute, tentatively. "I mean, we're probably not going to find something perfect, right? So what's most important?"

Focusing on the details steadied me. "We have to keep the vaccine cold," I said. "And we have to make sure the Wardens don't catch us. With that helicopter, they might be able to see us from fifty miles away."

"So we need cover. A road where there are more trees blocking the view. Right? That sounds like what Tobias would say."

It did. I set down the bags I'd been carrying and pawed through them for the road atlas. With it open on the floor, I stared at the spread of the whole country. Green splotches marked the largest forests, the national and state parks, including a huge one that stretched from West Virginia down through Virginia and along the North Carolina–Tennessee border, ending in Georgia just a short distance from Atlanta.

Only a few small towns speckled that area. Because it wasn't just forest, it was mountains, I realized, thinking of the giants that loomed to the east of us. The roads would be winding and difficult. But a higher altitude would mean colder weather. If there was still a little snow down here, there might be a lot on the slopes. There might be snow all the way to Georgia. Then it wouldn't matter if the trip, in one of these slow tractors, took us a few days instead of one.

"Don't let this go to your head," I said, "but you're a genius."

Justin chuckled. It sounded pained. My head jerked up, but to my relief he didn't look sick or suffering. Just sad. He lowered his gaze, the glow of his flashlight bouncing off the floor and tinting his face a sallow yellow.

"I wish he was here," he said. "I wish we hadn't had to leave him."

Tobias. "Yeah," I said quietly. "I wouldn't have, if there'd been any other way."

"I know. But it still bothers me. You know, I don't think I ever really *respected* him. Like, he was amazing with a gun, but I always thought he was kind of wimpy about everything else. The way he'd get so freaked out if we saw anyone sick . . . But he wasn't a wimp. He was obviously really smart about things like getting away from the Wardens. And he gave himself up for us, so he wouldn't hold us back. How freakin' brave was that?"

"Yeah," I said again, my throat tight.

Justin leaned forward, resting his arms on his lap. "I've been thinking about my mom too," he said. "How I ran off on her to come with you guys. I thought *I'd* been a wimp, hanging around the colony, all of us hiding from anyone who looked a little scary, but it was a pretty chicken move not telling her I wanted to leave, wasn't it? She probably doesn't even understand why I did it. The note I left—I didn't really go into a lot of detail."

"Maybe it was chicken," I said. "But you've helped us protect the vaccine, and that's a good thing. You really have done a lot, Justin. I'm glad you've been with us." I hadn't realized quite how true that was until the words came out of my mouth. I closed the atlas and stood up. "When you get back to the colony, you can tell her all that. I think she'll understand then."

"If I manage to make it back," he said. "What if those guys in the Jeep had caught us? What if the woman with the rifle had got me in the head instead of the leg?"

"They didn't, and she didn't," I said, as firmly as I could. "We're doing our best. You'll survive a leg wound."

He raised his head then, to meet my eyes. He looked more serious than I'd ever seen him. "Sure," he said, and his mouth twisted into a half smile. "But just in case I don't, I want to know I really helped, more than I screwed things up. *I'm* going to do my best. Okay? And if—if we don't all make it, you'll tell my mom, right? Why I came? What I did?"

"Of course," I said, staring back at him. He must be terrified, to talk like that. But I couldn't think of another honest thing I could say to take that fear away.

We stayed like that for a minute, silent. Then he tapped the rifle against the floor and gestured with it toward the tractors. "So which one are we taking?" he said with more of his usual bravado.

I considered them. It would still be better to have a car. But I doubted Leo and Anika were going to find one hiding behind a silo, gassed up and ready to go.

This was the best we had, so we should use it. We could drive toward the mountains, watching for a better vehicle along the way. And if we didn't find one, we'd just continue on with the tractor. Whoever was riding in the trailer behind it would have to bundle up, but we could switch off regularly. Those huge tires would be good if we did run into snow on the slopes. Even with a winding route and tractor-level speed, we could probably make it to Atlanta in just a few days.

"I'd say this one," I said, patting the back of the one that appeared to have the biggest cab. "So, do you know how to hitch a trailer?"

Justin smiled with his whole mouth this time. "I bet I can figure it out."

TEN

When Leo and Anika returned with the news that there were no other vehicles on the farm, I'd managed to drag the trailer over to my chosen tractor and Justin had helped me attach the hitch. I explained the plan as we tossed all our supplies—except the cold box, which I wanted to keep within reach—into the trailer. Neither of them argued.

I'd been thinking we'd head for the mountains immediately. But I saw Leo sway and grasp the side of the trailer for support after hefting his backpack over the side, and when I stopped to let myself breathe, I realized how heavy my own head felt. Justin was smothering a yawn. None of us had slept since the alarm clock had gone off last evening. We'd been chased and shot at and faced with a disgusting scene that still stank up the air around us, and on a normal day we'd have set up camp hours ago.

I couldn't remember the last time we'd eaten, either. But I couldn't even swallow water with the smell of rotting livestock lingering in my nose.

"We'll go a little farther and then wait until it's dark," I said.

"Right," Anika said, as if reassuring herself. "Helicopters won't be able to see us at night."

"We'll keep an eye out for spotlights," Leo said, without much humor.

The diesel tanks weighed far too much for us to lift them, so we topped up the tractor's fuel and then filled the empty jugs we'd brought with us, as well as a large plastic barrel I'd spotted near the trailer. It was impossible to know exactly how much we'd need for the rest of the trip, but what we had seemed like a lot. Leo and I tested the controls in the cab, and then I eased the tractor out the wide door we'd been able to open from inside. Anika pressed the button to close it again and scrambled into the trailer to join Justin. And we were off.

The grinding of the tractor's huge wheels over the road felt impossibly slow—the speedometer on the dash only went up to twenty miles an hour—but it was a lot faster than walking. After a few minutes, Leo rolled down the window to let in the breeze.

"Well, we've gotten away from the stink," I said.

"That's progress," he agreed, but he still looked weary.

Of course he did. But I couldn't help going on, even though the words tried to stick in my throat.

"The whole thing, with the compound, trying to take their gas," I said. "We didn't have anything to trade with, we didn't know anything about them, and it was getting light, and the Wardens . . . It seemed like the best option we had."

"I get it," Leo said. "I know you wouldn't have tried if you'd thought they'd shoot Justin."

I needed more than that. I didn't just want him to get it; I wanted him to say it made sense, that he realized I'd done the most right thing I could see at the time. There was still a hint of distance in his voice.

"Justin's probably just happy he's got an excuse to carry around a gun now," Leo added, letting out a huff of amusement, and I relaxed a little. I was so wound up, it was making me paranoid.

Before much longer, we came to a smaller farm with a clapboard house and a garage big enough to squeeze the tractor and trailer in beside a rusty Chevrolet, the tank of which turned out to be empty. I looked back down the road, thinking of the abandoned SUV, wondering how quickly the Wardens would find us if they stumbled on it today.

Not as quickly as if we stayed on the roads in full daylight and that helicopter came by.

"I'm taking first watch," I said, and waved Justin off when he opened his mouth. I didn't want him or Leo being self-sacrificial and letting me sleep through what should be my turn.

For two hours, I sat in the shadows by the living room window, listening to the weathered porch swing creak in the breeze. The sun rose in the now-clear sky, and I unzipped my coat in the midday warmth. For a few minutes, shortly after noon, I thought I heard a distant mechanical whirring. I tensed, holding my breath. But the sound drifted away, leaving me wondering if I'd just imagined it.

When my time was up, I traded off with Leo and dove inside the tent. I couldn't have kept my eyes open if I'd wanted to. My mind tumbled into dreams that flickered in and out of focus and dissolved without warning. I woke from them with a jolt, my pulse racing, unable to remember what I'd thought I'd seen.

The tent felt strangely empty. I heard the rasp of sleeping breath to my right, but the space at my left was vacant. Then a hushed voice carried through the canvas.

"Really? That's not what it looks like."

Justin. Maybe it hadn't been a dream that had woken me.

It was Anika who answered.

"What does it look like, then? I'm not taking anything. All I've got on me is what I found myself—you can check if you want."

"I wasn't saying that. You're planning on taking off. I saw you, looking at the door like you're trying to figure out when it'd be safest to leave."

Oh, hell. My hand leapt to the cold box, but it was still there, secure, by my head. I pushed off my blanket and ducked out of the tent.

Anika's gaze snapped toward me from where she was wavering in the doorway between the living room and the front hall. Hazy late afternoon sunlight streaked the walls. Justin was standing just outside the tent, his weight on his good leg. I straightened up beside him, studying her. She was wearing the coat she'd scavenged back in Canada, no bag over her shoulder or at her side. Even if she was lying, she couldn't have taken much.

"What's going on?" I said.

"She's planning her escape," Justin said, jerking his chin toward Anika. His hands were balled at his sides.

"I'm not!" Anika protested. "So I looked at the door a few times. What's the big deal?"

"I was watching you," Justin said. "I can tell." He paused. "I know what it feels like when you want to get out of a place so bad you could crawl out of your skin. You looked like that."

Anika glanced from him to me and back, her shoulders hunching defensively. "I'm not going to say I'm loving this. I'm scared, okay? I knew the Wardens were going to be after us, but I didn't realize it was going to be this bad. So maybe I've thought about how it might be easier for me to keep out of sight, not get noticed, if I was on my own. Can you blame me?"

"No," I said, before Justin could reproach her. The weight of my responsibilities pressed down on me. Was I supposed to tell her to do what she thought was best for her? Try to convince her to stay? Did I even know which would be more dangerous? At least, staying together, we could help each other. Alone, she'd have no one if the Wardens caught her trail, if she got hurt or ran into someone infected.

And we wouldn't have her.

The tent flap rustled, and Leo poked his head out. He took in the scene silently, his eyebrows rising.

"I don't blame you," I said to Anika. "And I won't force you to stay with us if you think you'd be safer on your own. But I'd rather you stayed. The next few days, I think we'll need all the help we can get."

"You really think I'm such a great person to have around?" she said. "It was pretty much me who drove Tobias away, wasn't it? As if I should have . . . *pretended*, just because he wanted, I don't know—he was sick! And even if he hadn't been sick, he wasn't my type! What was I supposed to do?"

I could have laughed. Apparently we'd *all* been blaming ourselves. If she'd been there when Justin came to me with his guilt—if she'd seen inside my head . . .

"No one thinks he left because of you," Leo said, standing.

"And it wasn't your fault any more than it was the rest of ours," I said. "I talked to him, right before. Tobias wasn't upset with you." Sad that things hadn't been different, maybe, but accepting.

"I don't know why any of you care whether I'm here or not,"

Anika said, as if we hadn't spoken. "I'm not good at this—looking out for other people. I had to just stop caring about anyone else, to stay alive."

I'd suspected as much of her, but I found myself arguing.

"You've still helped," I said. "You brought us those pills that kept Gav calm so we could get out of Toronto—so Tobias wouldn't infect you or Justin in the car. You got us the car. You drove, you've carried supplies, and you found a way to stop the Wardens in the Jeep from chasing us. We don't need more than that."

"You really don't care what happens to the rest of us?" Justin asked, with a tinge of hurt.

Anika hesitated. "I don't *want* to. It makes everything so hard."

I lowered my gaze. Maybe that was why I'd kept my distance from her, held on to my suspicions. Because when you cared and you lost someone, it was awful. I couldn't have saved Gav, but maybe we all could have saved Tobias if we'd made an effort to show how much we wanted him with us.

I hadn't made any effort for Anika, not really, and now she was ready to go too. I'd thought, when we were hiding under that tree, that we were trapped in this situation in exactly the same way, but it wasn't true. I had my immunity from the virus, one less thing to fear; I had a personal connection to this vaccine through my dad and the island, to keep me focused.

Maybe I hadn't trusted her, maybe I still didn't completely, but I knew I didn't want to lose one more person. And I had to prove it.

The answer was suddenly obvious.

"The vaccine," I said. "It hasn't been fair, the two of you being vulnerable while Leo and I are protected. I have to hold on to one backup sample, just in case, but there are three. I could give you each half a dose—it should still give you some defense."

Anika's eyes widened. "Are you serious?"

"If you'll stay with us, and we all work together to get to the CDC," I said. "I think it's only right. I really don't know if we'd have gotten this far without you. Or you," I added, glancing at Justin, who was gaping at me.

"Kaelyn's right," Leo put in. "You two deserve to be protected just as much as I do."

They could take it and still leave. But this wasn't about bribing them. It was about showing how much keeping them meant to me.

Justin broke from his daze first. "No," he said, shaking his head. "What if the CDC will need all the samples we have? I'm not going to be the one who messes this whole thing up." The color had drained from his face, as if he was frightened by the words coming out of his mouth, but his voice was firm.

"Damn," Anika said. She slouched back against the door frame. Her head turned toward the tent, where the cold box still sat. Then she looked at me. "You really would, wouldn't you?"

"I wouldn't say it if I didn't mean it."

"I don't even know what I'm doing. I came this far, didn't I? Where the hell would I go? I just . . ." She trailed off, and then squared her shoulders. "You know what, I'm tired of being scared to death of those guys. Screw the Wardens. They haven't managed to catch us yet. And you can keep the samples. I should be able to handle at least as much as this kid." She jerked her thumb toward Justin, who bristled at the *kid* even as a grin tugged at his mouth.

Relief flooded me. I didn't know how long her change of heart would last, but it felt good. Screw the Wardens. We could do this.

"Who's supposed to be on watch?" I asked.

"This *chick*," Justin said, nodding at Anika. She rolled her eyes, but she was smiling too.

"Then you should get some sleep," I told him. "And get off that leg already!"

"Yeah, yeah." He swiveled toward the tent. His face pinched as he knelt down by the flap. My relief faded.

"It's worse, isn't it?"

"It's fine," he said tightly, but I could see how awkwardly he held it as he crawled inside.

We'd have to take another look at the wound before we left. Try to wash it. But what if it was already infected?

"The CDC people will take care of it when we get to Atlanta, right?" Anika said. Her smile had fallen.

"Yeah," I said. When we finally got there.

"The doctor said to check in if we needed any help," Leo said. "Maybe they'd know something we can do for him on our own."

"Good point," I said. "I'll see if I can get a hold of them. You two go back to what you're supposed to be doing." I fixed Leo with a mock glare when he opened his mouth to protest. "I need you awake enough to drive when it gets dark."

"You make sure you're getting some rest too," he said. "If you can't reach them now, we can call out again in a few hours."

"I won't try for too long," I promised.

I took the transceiver up to the second floor, where the noise wouldn't interrupt anyone's sleep. The duvet in the master bedroom was rumpled, and a musty smell hung in the air. I could immediately picture a figure lying on the mattress, throwing back the covers as their fever rose. There was no body here, but the sense of sickness filled the room. My legs balked. I headed into the second bedroom, which appeared to be an unused guest room, and set the radio on the dresser in the corner.

As I lifted the mic, my mouth went dry. I'd talked on the radio before, but I'd never been the one calling out. For a second I had the absurd impression that it wouldn't work for me.

I shook the feeling off and flicked the power switch. Justin had set the frequency back to the one we'd had it at yesterday morning. I dragged in a breath, and then pressed the call button.

"I'm looking for Dr. Guzman at the CDC. Is anyone at the CDC listening? Over."

The static hummed. My mind started to wander. What were the chances of the Wardens stumbling on this transmission? Well, I wouldn't be giving the doctor any details about our location anyway.

I was about to get up to confirm the frequency against the note I'd made in Dad's journal when a voice crackled out of the speaker.

"I'm here, Kaelyn," Dr. Guzman said in her soft drawl. "Is there any news? Are you all right?"

She sounded a lot more anxious than she had yesterday. I guessed she'd had a chance to talk to the other scientists, for the idea of a working vaccine to sink in.

"We're . . . mostly okay," I said. "I wanted to talk to someone there because—we don't have much in the way of medical supplies. What are the best things we can do to stop an injury from getting infected?"

She paused. "What kind of injury?"

"One of my friends was shot," I said. "In the leg. The bullet just grazed him, so we managed to stop the bleeding, but the wound's pretty open. We've cleaned it as well as we can, which isn't much."

"All right," she said, her demeanor becoming more businesslike. "It's good that you stopped the bleeding. If the wound needs stitching up, we can take care of that when you arrive. In the meantime, you should do your best to keep the area and the bandage clean. I'm not sure what you have access to. If it's not already infected, soap and clean water—I'd boil it first—may do the trick. Or water with a lot of salt added. And make sure anyone who touches the bandages or the wound has washed their hands first as well."

I had no idea how dirty my hands had been when I'd wrapped Justin's wound. At least I'd had the disinfectant wipe.

"And if it gets infected?" I asked. "Is there anything we can do then?"

"A salt solution can help, especially if you soak the affected area. If you don't have enough salt on hand to manage that, you can try bleach, diluted with water. About a one-to-ten ratio is best. It'll hurt, but it should kill the bacteria in the area too. And have your friend put as little strain on the leg as possible."

I bit back a grimace, thinking of the miles Justin had walked that morning. From now on, he was sitting as much as I could make him. And while I wasn't sure if we could find much salt—that might have been grabbed with food by the local scavengers—I doubted anyone had been hoarding bleach.

"Thanks," I said. "That helps a lot."

"As soon as you get him here, we can give him full medical care," Dr. Guzman said briskly. "How many are there in your group exactly?"

"Four," I said.

"And are you close to the city yet?"

"Oh." I could already tell she wasn't going to like this. "Um, we've had to change the way we're traveling, which means it's going to take us a little longer to get down there than I expected before. But I think we should still make it in a few days."

"I see. I'm sorry to hear that." She fell silent for a moment, and I thought I heard her mutter something under her breath that was lost in the static. "I wish we could send someone to pick you up, Kaelyn, I really do. The situation here, it's the most unreasonable—"

"It's okay," I said.

"No, it's not. You need help. And these people, the kind who'd shoot at you—the kind who go around hacking at our walls and staking out our gate—it isn't right. We can't take a vehicle out unnoticed. One of my colleagues drove out three weeks ago to try to see what was happening at the hospital, because the phone lines have been down, and he made it just two blocks. They swarmed the car. They—" Her voice broke.

I didn't want to imagine what might have happened to him. Didn't want to ask whether he'd made it back. "I'm sorry," I said.

"Yes. Well." She cleared her throat. "I suppose they'll regret it when everyone else is getting your vaccine."

"What?" I said.

"Let's just get you here," she said. "You be as careful as you can be, all right?"

An uneasiness settled over me. It sounded like she was suggesting they'd withhold the vaccine from people. Even people who'd just been defending their property like the woman in the substation? I wasn't happy that they'd shot Justin, but I could understand why they had.

She couldn't mean they'd punish people for just protecting themselves. I hadn't explained the whole story.

"We will," I said, but my chest still felt tight.

"Is there any other way I can help?" Dr. Guzman asked.

"No," I made myself reply. "Thank you for what you already told me. I'll try to get in touch again when we're close to Atlanta."

"Please do. I don't want anything else happening to you. Look after yourselves."

I listened to the meaningless buzz of the static for a few seconds before I switched the radio off. Dr. Guzman was our one hope of getting the vaccine to the rest of the world. She might not even have meant that comment; maybe she'd just gotten caught up in her frustration. Why was I worrying about exactly how the CDC planned to distribute it, when we couldn't even say for sure we'd make it there?

ELEVEN

By the time we started climbing the undulating slopes of the mountains the following night, I'd given up hope of finding a faster vehicle. But the tractor was serving us well enough. Its sturdy tires ate up the road slowly but steadily, even as snow returned to the ground in the higher altitudes. I'd convinced Justin to keep lounging in the trailer, where we'd set up the tent and the sleeping bag to fend off the worst of the deepening cold. When I'd checked his wound that evening, it had looked raw and painful, but his skin had no reddish streaks of infection. As long as he took it easy, I thought we could get him through this okay.

With dense forest sheltering us on all sides, we switched to driving during the day, when the sunlight could help us navigate the twisty mountain roads. In places, the snow hardened into a thick crust that cracked under the wheels. I tried not to agonize over the deep tracks left in the tractor's wake. The Wardens would have to follow us up into the mountains on guesswork before they'd stumble on our trail.

Twice on the first day we heard the whir of the helicopter again. We drove the tractor as far onto the shoulder as we dared and stopped to wait. All I could make out beyond the branches overhead was clear sky. I hoped if we couldn't see the chopper, that meant no one in it could see us either. Obviously they weren't giving up anytime soon.

We traded off driving and map duties, someone always sitting in the back with Justin. Leo was at the wheel and Anika leaning against the side of the cab when I spotted a stream of smoke ghosting into the sky from somewhere up ahead. I leaned over the front of the trailer to knock on the back of the cab, and pointed to the smoke. Anika rolled down her window.

"There's a town about five miles down this road," she said. "Maybe someone there's still alive."

I eyed the smoke warily. If Michael had headed into the States only a little more than a month ago, he'd hardly had time to bring every survivor here over to his side, and I doubted isolated mountain towns would have been his priority. Still, even if the local survivors weren't with the Wardens, they weren't necessarily amicable.

"Is there another route we can take?" I asked.

She looked down at the road atlas, frowning. "Sort of. We'd have to go back to that turnoff we passed, like, an hour ago."

"Let's do it," I said. "I'd rather take a little more time than risk being noticed."

"Sounds good to me."

Overnight, we kept the tent in the trailer and bundled up there after a hasty dinner of canned stew. The next day, we wound through North Carolina until I figured we were less than eighty miles from the Georgia border. Soon we'd have to leave the shelter of the mountains. But not long after that, I could be putting the vaccine into the hands of experts. My nerves started to jitter with excitement.

Evening was starting to fall when a building came into view up ahead. A small church. I hit the brake. Leo leaned forward as we both squinted through the windshield. Beyond the church was a squat concrete building with a windowed front, and the faces of several houses half hidden by the trees.

"This place isn't in the atlas," Leo said. "Too small, I guess."

There was no sign of smoke here, and no sound other than the low rumble of the tractor's engine. And we'd have to backtrack a couple hours to avoid the place.

"It looks abandoned," I said. "Let's just keep our eyes out."

As we drew closer, I made out the sign over the concrete building's windows, THE PINES CONVENIENCE & GROCERIES. The glass in the door had been smashed, but I still saw shapes on a few of the shelves.

"Maybe we should stop, see if there's anything we can use," I said.

"Might as well, now that we're here," Leo agreed.

I parked the tractor in front of the store and climbed out. "Stay put," I ordered Justin when he leaned out of the tent. "We're only taking a quick look."

Shards of glass crunched amid the snow under my feet as I opened the door by its battered handle. Leo came up behind me, and we surveyed the rows of shelves. A few bags of bread, the plastic fogged with green mold. A jar of pickles that had cracked open on the floor. In the long-dead freezer, a lonely pizza box that on further inspection turned out to be empty. Cartons of toothpicks scattered in an aisle. I grabbed two bars of soap that remained, and tucked them into my pocket, then pointed out a jug of laundry bleach near Leo. But it looked like any canned goods had been cleared out a long time ago.

"Well, we've got enough to last us already," I said, retreating. As long as we didn't get lost, or find the roads blocked up ahead, or have the tractor break down.

"Hey!" Anika said outside, with a squeak of panic. My pulse hiccupped. I dashed the last few steps to the door.

"Hello!" a bright voice called from beyond the trailer. A stout white-haired man was hurrying toward us along the road, waving his arm as if there was any chance we wouldn't see him. He grinned through his tangled beard, and then turned his head to sneeze. His nose was rubbed red. The snow was soaking the green plush slippers he'd walked out in.

"Don't go anywhere!" he said. "I need to talk to you. It's been so lonely—there hasn't been anyone by in a long time. Where are you from? Are you visiting for a while? I don't suppose you've heard anything about Mildred? I—"

He cut off his string of chatter to cough hoarsely into his bare hand, but he kept coming. "Stop!" I shouted. He was only ten feet away now. Ten feet from Anika and Justin. The two of them had ducked inside the tent, but any second now Justin would get some grand heroic idea, and a sneeze or a cough would carry. "Stay there!" I said, stepping forward.

"No, no, you don't understand," the man said, still hustling toward us. Totally unaware of how dangerous he was, of how he could kill a person just by breathing near them.

Like the guy who'd infected Gav.

My lungs constricted. Before I'd made any conscious decision, Tobias's pistol was in my hands.

"Stop!" I repeated, pointing it at him. My thumb fumbled for the safety. At the click of it sliding off, the man slowed. His face paled.

"Now then, you don't have to be that way. I was only—"

He sneezed again, and I stepped closer, my arms rigid. "Go away," I said. "Get away from us, *now*."

He drew to a halt a few paces from the end of the trailer. His fingers leapt up to scratch at his chin. His bleary eyes tracked the gun. "I just wanted to talk," he said, a whine creeping into his voice.

"Kaelyn?" Justin said, peeking out, but I didn't dare let my gaze waver.

"We don't want to talk," I said to the man. "We want you to leave us alone. Go back to your house." He just stood there, staring. A tremor passed through me. I took one more step, trying to make my face look menacing. *"Go."*

With a shudder, he scuttled backward. "It's not right," he muttered as he turned around. "A person can't even have a friendly conversation— shoot me, will you? Shoot *me*? I've lived in this town my whole life, and I can tell you . . ."

His rambling faded away as he veered onto the road beside the church and passed out of view. I exhaled in a rush, my arms falling to my sides, the gun almost slipping from my fingers.

"Kae," Leo said, and I flinched. When I looked around, he tilted his head toward the tractor. His expression was inscrutable. "Let's get going. I'll drive."

"Is he gone?" Anika asked from inside the tent.

"Yeah," Justin said. "Kaelyn scared him off. It was kind of awesome!"

I shoved the pistol back into my pocket and made myself walk over and climb in beside Leo. I didn't feel awesome. As he turned the key, a question rang in my head, so loud I was sure he had to be thinking it too.

What would I have done if that man had kept coming?

It wouldn't have come to that. Leo might have tackled him, or I would have. I hadn't *wanted* to shoot him. I was just doing whatever I could think of to get him to leave. It had worked. Everyone was safe.

So why did I feel *awful*?

Because pulling the trigger would have been so easy. Suddenly I could imagine all the things the people in the island gang could have been thinking, when they shot infected people in the streets. He was going to die soon anyway. I'd have been ending the danger completely. Stopping the virus right in its tracks, with a single twitch of my finger.

But that man hadn't been just the virus. He was a person too, a person whose only crime was being infected. And I'd pointed a gun at him without a second thought.

The road was completely cloaked in shadow now, the sun dipping below the tops of the trees. "We should stop soon," I said.

"As soon as we get some distance from that place," Leo said with a nod.

We drove in silence for about another hour, until the sky started to gray. Without waiting for confirmation, Leo pulled the tractor over to the side. When I got out, the faint trickle of running water reached my ears from somewhere in the distance. It sounded wonderfully peaceful.

"I'll refill the water bottles," I said. I scooped them up, along with our pot, and treaded through the crisp layer of snow amid the trees. Down a small slope, I found the stream, the first we'd come across that was deep enough that it hadn't frozen through.

I almost stepped in the water before I saw it, pulling back my foot at the creak of fragile ice. Kneeling on a mossy stone, I tapped a hole in the ice with a stick. Clear water burbled by underneath. I pulled off my mitten to dip my fingers in, and winced at the cold. It looked sparkling clean, but we'd use some of Tobias's water purification tablets on it all the same.

The simple motions had calmed me. I reached back to grasp the first of the bottles, inhaling the crisp air deep into my lungs. I was just about to lean forward and dip the bottle into the water when a movement upstream caught my eyes.

Some thirty feet away, blending into the shadows of the dusk, a lean gray-and-white form bent its head to the stream. Its conical ears twitched as it lapped water from a gap in the ice. I stared at it, afraid to blink, afraid it would vanish and I'd be left uncertain of whether I'd really seen it. Awe washed over me.

It was a wolf—larger and thicker-furred than the coyotes I used to study on the island. I'd never seen one outside of a zoo before. And down here in the States, from what I knew, hardly anyone had seen a wolf in the wild in decades. They'd been hunted almost to extinction.

It might not even be completely wild. There were sanctuaries—the employees might have opened the gates when the epidemic hit to give the animals all possible chance of survival. Still, having an opportunity to see it, to share this stream with it just for a minute, felt like a gift.

I shifted to keep my balance, and a twig snapped under my heel. The wolf flinched. Its golden eyes found mine through the trees. I held its gaze, my heart thumping, wanting to apologize for disturbing it. It considered me for a second, and then spun on its graceful feet and trotted deeper into the woods.

My fingers itched for a pen. I had to record this, every detail, every motion the wolf had made. As if I was going to forget.

Then I caught myself. Record it for who? Everyone still alive was too busy trying to stay that way to care what wolves or any other animal did.

How long had it been since I'd thought about the career I used to dream about before the virus? How long had it been since I'd thought about *anything* beyond making it to Atlanta?

What was the point when, like Justin said, for all we knew we weren't going to make it that far, no matter what I did?

Gritting my teeth, I plunged the bottle into the icy water, filling it quickly and turning for the next. But when they were all full and I stood with the bag of them over my arm and the pot in my other hand, my gaze wandered back to the spot where the wolf had stood.

Whether anyone else cared or not, whether I lived past the next few days or not, I was glad I'd seen it. A smile tugged at the corners of my mouth.

I was still smiling as I came up the slope toward the spot where the tractor was parked. Leo was building a pile of sticks several feet ahead of it, where we'd light a fire once it got completely dark, to warm ourselves and our dinner. He looked up at the sound of my boots.

The returning smile that crossed his lips didn't quite erase the wariness in his eyes. The way he watched me as I approached, I suddenly felt as if *I* were some elusive animal he'd never expected to see.

I'd let myself explain it away so many times, but here it was again—that sense that something wasn't quite right between us. I wasn't just imagining it. And I couldn't keep ignoring it, trying to avoid the disappointment or disapproval I was worried lay underneath. I remembered what it was like falling into that trap of refusing to talk. Our nearly two years of silence after that one immense misunderstanding. I'd hated it. If my best friend had a problem with something I'd done, I needed to know, now.

"Hey," I said, setting the bottles down by the campfire. "How're you doing?"

"Everything seems to be going all right," he said, straightening up. He glanced back toward the trailer, where Justin was cleaning the guns—one of the few jobs he could do without being on his feet—and explaining each part of the process to Anika. "I think we're going to have to look for more fuel soon, though. I refilled the tank as much as I could. The barrel's empty now. I'd guess we've got maybe half a day's driving left."

Half a day. I pictured the map. We could probably at least make it into Georgia. We'd just be coming down from the mountains, back into civilization, a little earlier than I'd hoped. Back into the hornet's nest. Michael would have more of his people watching the area around Atlanta than anywhere else.

Well, we'd deal with that when we had to.

"Good to know," I said, "but that's not what I meant. How are *you*?"

"Oh," he said. "I'm okay. As okay as anyone could be, given the circumstances."

"Yeah," I said. "I just . . . If something's bothering you, you'd tell me, right?"

Leo smiled again, but it faltered almost immediately. He tugged at the back of his hat. "It doesn't matter," he said. "Not really."

Even though I'd tried to brace myself for whatever was going to come, a chill rose up inside me. "*What* doesn't matter? Leo, just tell me."

"I don't want to—" He gestured vaguely as he grappled with the words. "I don't want to judge you. About taking all the gas that time, about breaking into the compound, about that guy today. You were doing it for all of us. Making sure we get through this. I know."

"But?" I said roughly.

His mouth twisted. "But you know how I feel about how I made it back to the island. I don't like seeing you get so . . . cut-throat, I guess."

He didn't like me, like this. My fingers curled into my palms as if I could hold back the sting of that admission. "Why should I be different from anyone else?" I asked.

"You were different, though," he said. "You were trying so hard to be better than them, even when people were trying to kill us."

"It's not like I've had a lot of choices," I protested.

"I know," he said, but he wouldn't even look at me. "It's just, I don't want the world to be like this, but I couldn't see how to get by and not be a horrible person, and it seemed like you found a way, like maybe it wasn't hopeless. But if even you can't . . ."

I blinked, fighting to keep my composure. "That isn't fair."

"I *know*. I'm not saying you're wrong. I'm not saying you're a horrible person now. I guess I don't really know what I'm saying."

Except maybe he was saying those things. Maybe I'd ruined this, our recovering friendship, somehow. How did I fix it? I couldn't magically revert back to being the optimistic, naive Kaelyn who'd believed I could keep us all alive without getting my hands dirty. But the thought of going on, with Leo looking like that every time I had to make a hard decision, made me cringe.

I crossed my arms, hugging myself. The things he'd said, they weighed on me, like a yoke snapped over my shoulders.

It *wasn't* fair.

"I want the world to be different too," I said. "I still think the vaccine can change it. But I can't be some perfect person." Emotions swelled inside me: prickling guilt and suffocating sadness, and the cold burn of regret. "If you're going to believe things can get better, believe it because you do, not because of me."

"Kaelyn," Leo started. He'd raised his head, but I couldn't stop, the words just kept tumbling out.

"The whole time we were heading to Toronto," I said, "and the whole time we were there, Gav didn't really think we'd find anyone, that the vaccine would do any good. The only reason he believed, the only reason he came, was because of me. And I couldn't save him. I couldn't even save *him*. Do you have any idea how hard it is to know that? I shouldn't have let him depend on me like that, and I can't do it again, Leo."

My voice choked off. I turned away, my cheeks hot with embarrassment.

But it was true, wasn't it? Gav had followed me like I was some kind of light in the darkness, but I wasn't. I was just me, and I made mistakes and got down in the muck and not every thought I had was kind. That was the real weight I'd been carrying: the knowledge that he'd left the island for me; he'd died for me. I couldn't stand carrying the responsibility of another person's choices too.

"Kae." Leo's footsteps scraped over the snow behind me. He touched my arm. I shifted toward him automatically, and he pulled me to him, his head bowing next to mine.

"I'm sorry," he said by my ear. "I'm so sorry. You're right. I know you're doing the best you can. I didn't mean to make you feel like it's all on you to save the rest of us. I'm sorry."

"I don't want to lose you too," I mumbled into the soft fabric of his coat.

"You won't," he said. "I'm not going anywhere—I never wanted to, I promise you. If I get freaked out about what we have to face, that's my problem. I'll deal with it."

The tension in me released. I let myself sink into him. His embrace was so warm and his body so solid and steady that I didn't want to let go. His pulse pattered where my jaw rested against the crook of his neck. Suddenly I was aware of mine, my heart skipping as he brushed his fingers over my hair, aware of his chin grazing my cheek. I'd hardly have to turn my head to be kissing him.

The impulse shot through me before I'd even processed the thought. It would feel good—it had felt good, when Leo had kissed me all those weeks ago, even if I hadn't wanted to notice. I hadn't felt like that in ages.

The notion passed through my head in the space of a second, and then my chest clenched up.

It was Gav I was supposed to be kissing. He'd died for me, and here I was considering taking Leo's affection in his place? Somehow that was even more awful than the idea of having betrayed Gav while he was alive.

Leo's hands dropped as I stepped back, out of his arms.

"It's okay," I said. I met his eyes, their brown so deep in the fading light, and then had to look away.

"Are you sure you're all right?" he asked. "I really am sorry, Kae. Nothing's going to change how important you are to me."

He was still watching me, with concern and caring and I didn't want to know what else. What had he been thinking of in that long embrace? What might he have been hoping for—and had I given him reason to hope? A different sort of guilt stabbed at my gut.

"It's okay," I repeated. "I just got a little overwhelmed. I'll be fine."

We stood there a moment longer, awkwardly. "I think we're going to need kerosene to get this going," he said, motioning to the pile of kindling. When I nodded, he headed toward the tractor. And I was left with a jumble of emotions I had no idea how to untangle.

TWELVE

With the needle on the fuel indicator sinking, we puttered down from the mountains in the middle of the following morning. I didn't want to delay our search for gas like we had with the SUV. We'd made it into Georgia, at least, about a hundred miles northeast of Atlanta, and we would have had to emerge from the forested slopes before much longer anyway.

As we returned to lower ground, the snow thinned, until we were driving on dry pavement. Sitting in the trailer with Justin, I unzipped my coat and he pushed aside his blanket, watching the trees pass by beyond the tent's open flap.

"Do you think the vaccine will be okay until we get to the CDC?" he asked.

"It should be." I'd packed the sides of the cold box with snow before the last of it had disappeared. On a flat clear road, I thought the tractor could cross a hundred miles in five hours. But that was assuming we found more fuel quickly. And that no one else found us.

Justin stirred restlessly. "Maybe we should scan the radio again," he suggested. "See if the Wardens are talking near here."

I doubted we'd just happen to stumble on a transmission at the right moment, but it'd give him something to do. It'd been hard for him, staying still to rest his leg during the long haul through the mountains. I could see the pent-up energy in the jerks of his movements.

"Good idea," I said.

As he set up the transceiver and started turning the dial, I watched the sky and the side roads, ears perked. The radio emitted only static, and the only motor I heard was our own. When Justin sighed and packed up the radio again, the forest had given way to yellow fields on our right.

"What do you think?" Anika called back, gesturing toward a barn up ahead through her open window.

"Let's check it out," I said.

Leo steered the tractor down a lane leading into the farm, stopping at a chained gate. We hopped out and clambered over the fence, leaving Justin guarding the trailer. The barn door hung open, but it held no vehicles and no fuel tanks, and the small garage nearby was equally empty.

We were just heading down the lane on our way back to the tractor when a rumble reverberated through the air. A helicopter was roaring into view from the south. I jerked to a stop. I hated to be separated from the vaccine samples, but the barn behind us was so much closer. Leo and Anika scrambled after me as I spun and dashed for the building. My breath was raw in my throat when I reached the barn. After the others joined me inside, I peeked around the doorway.

The helicopter whirred past a minute later without slowing. It was the same blue and white as the one we'd seen before, but I didn't know if that meant it was the exact same one or part of a matching set Michael had acquired. I glanced at the tractor. Justin had been smart enough to hide in the tent. From above, it would look like just another abandoned vehicle. As long as we'd managed to get to the barn before anyone had spotted us, I thought we were safe.

The chopper veered to the west. I waited, but it didn't circle back. When it had whirred out of view, I wiped the perspiration from my forehead and stepped outside.

"It's going to be a lot harder to go unnoticed now that we're out of the forest," I said as we hurried to the tractor. "Everyone keep your eyes and ears peeled."

"They just don't quit, do they?" Justin muttered, poking his head out of the tent when I climbed into the trailer.

"No," I said, "and I don't think they will."

Leo and Anika switched spots in the tractor, and the engine started with a sputter that seemed to echo across the fields. I winced. It settled into a low growl as we rolled on.

Leo leaned out the window. "This road passes through a town in a couple miles," he said. "It looks pretty small on the map. We could try to detour around it, but that might take a while."

The last thing I wanted to do was spend extra time out in the open on these roads. But my memory leapt back to the old man racing toward us in his slippers, snuffling and pleading for attention, in the last settlement we'd passed through. I shivered.

"What do you think?" I asked.

He hesitated. "I think I'd rather be spotted by some random strangers than whoever's in that helicopter, if those are our options."

"True," I said. "Okay, let's drive through."

I stood up by the front of the trailer to watch the buildings ease into sight. The place was bigger than that tiny hamlet in the mountains, but still little more than a main street dotted with the flat gray roofs of commercial-looking buildings and a few dozen roads of blue- and peach-shingled houses branching off from it. We were too far away to make out much, but no one seemed to be moving around. And as we crested one last hill, giving me a view over the entire town, I spotted a distinctive yellow shape in a wide parking lot.

"There's a school bus," I said. "Just a couple blocks off the main street. They run on diesel, don't they?"

"I think so," Leo said.

"So let's take a look," Anika said.

I nodded, and sank back down. Justin hauled himself out of the tent and leaned against the side of the trailer, peering at the thinning forest by the road. I studied the landscape on the other side. We passed what looked like an orchard, and a smaller farm where we stopped briefly but found only a rusted-out junker of a car and a house that looked—and smelled—like it now belonged to raccoons.

"Here we go!" Anika said as we passed the town's welcome sign. It had been bashed in half, leaving only the bottom section that announced a population of 2,630. The actual number was a lot smaller now, I was sure.

As we rumbled by a hardware store at the edge of town, I reached into my pocket, taking out Tobias's pistol. As uncomfortable as the confrontation in that other town had made me, the threat of the gun had worked.

"Turn left after a few blocks," I called to Anika. "The bus wasn't far."

The tires crunched over a tree branch that had fallen on the road. The wind rose, making the unlatched shutters on a store-top apartment flap open and closed. The shops were all dark, most of the doors hanging on loose hinges.

Anika turned a corner, the trailer rocking as it followed. The houses off the main street looked equally vacant, windows blank and paint flaking. A flicker of motion behind the railing on one porch made me flinch to attention, but I kept staring at it as we drove on, and nothing emerged. Maybe it'd been a bird or a squirrel or a piece of trash in the breeze. Maybe I'd imagined it.

We were approaching the end of the second block, watching for the parking lot and the bus, when the tractor jerked to a halt. "What's *that*?" Anika murmured. I leaned over the side of the trailer.

A dark form was stalking along the edges of the front yards, heading our way. For a second I thought it was an immense stray dog. Then it lumbered out of the shadow of a tree, and I saw the distinctive rounded face with its pale muzzle, the portly body that swayed as it walked on.

A bear. Not a large one as bears went, but even so I guessed it weighed more than twice as much as I did. Its sides were well padded, but its thick brown-black fur was matted in patches—patches that were hardened with what looked like congealed blood. It might have been driven out of the forests in a quarrel over territory and headed into town to see what the pickings here were like, now that the people had cleared out.

Anika kept her foot on the brake as the bear ambled by. Justin shifted forward, and its head twitched toward us. But it wasn't looking for a fight. It just eyed us for a moment and then continued on, stopping two lawns farther down to sniff at a tattered fast-food wrapper caught in the brambles of a hedge.

"You think we're okay?" Leo asked me.

"Black bears don't usually mess with people," I said. "As long as we don't bother it, it should leave us alone."

"I'm still glad we're going in opposite directions," Anika said.

We edged down the road. Just a half a block later, I caught a glimpse of a school sign.

"There!" I said, pointing.

We pulled up outside the two-story brick building. It was shaped like an L, bent around a small concrete area painted with schoolyard game lines. A lane led past the yard and building to the parking lot I'd seen from the hill, where the school bus stood. A heavy bar blocked off access from the road.

"You go check it out," Justin said, hefting the rifle. "I can protect our stuff."

I pushed the gun back into my pocket, grabbed the jugs and the siphon hose, and hopped out of the trailer as Leo and Anika climbed down from the cab. We ducked under the bar and hurried along the lane to the parking lot. Dead leaves wisped across the concrete, but otherwise the only sound was the rasp of our boots.

When we reached the bus, Leo took the tube from me as I worked open the gas cap. He fed it into the tank while Anika jogged around the school to see if there were any other vehicles around. She had just returned, shaking her head, when Leo yanked the other end of the tube away from his mouth and into the waiting jug. He spat onto the pavement. Dark liquid coursed down the tube into the jug.

"Go get the barrel!" I said to Anika, my spirits lifting. I readied the second jug so Leo could switch to it as soon as the first one filled. But the gas hadn't quite reached the top when the flow slowed to a dribble, and then cut out completely. Leo picked up the tube, wiped the end, and tried to restore the suction, but after a minute he lowered it with a frown.

"Well, it's a start," I said with forced cheerfulness. Anika had paused by the tractor, and I waved for her to stay there.

I considered the buildings around us as we walked back down the lane, wondering if we had any chance of finding another diesel vehicle here. Or a completely new vehicle, one that could cover a hundred miles in an hour instead of several. My mind was wandering off toward Atlanta when a sharp mechanical *snap* carried down the street.

Leo and I froze. Then I heard a growl, and a gasp, and the patter of racing feet.

I pushed under the bar and tossed the jugs into the trailer. Justin was standing up, and Anika hovered by the tractor door.

"Let's go!" I said.

Justin gestured at something beyond my view. "The kid—"

A scrawny boy who couldn't have been more than five years old pelted across the street and onto the sidewalk, heading straight for us. Then I saw why. The bear was loping after him, picking up speed with each stride, closing the distance effortlessly as another low growl rattled from its lungs.

The boy was staring over his shoulder, his face blotchy with fear. The toe of his sneaker caught on a crack in the pavement, and he shrieked as he stumbled to his knees. The bear gathered itself to spring. I started forward instinctively, but Leo beat me there.

He dashed in, scooped up the kid, and whipped around. In the same moment, the bear bounded onto the sidewalk between them and the tractor. Anika yelped, flattening herself against the door.

Leo's head jerked around, and then he was sprinting across the schoolyard, the little boy clinging to his neck. The bear whirled in pursuit.

Leo had trained in dancing, not running, but he was still fast. He'd cleared half the yard before I realized what he was aiming for. There was a large metal storage bin by the wall of the school, about the size of a Dumpster.

He reached it and yanked on the lid. When it refused to budge, Leo set the boy on top of the box and then heaved himself up after him, the lid clanging under their weight. He tugged the kid against the wall as the bear skidded to a halt. It looked up at them, and rose onto its back legs with a huffing sound. It loomed there in front of them, making a tentative swipe at their ankles and then shuffling to the side when they proved out of reach.

I stepped into the yard, my heart thudding. Going for the box would have worked if the bear had given up, but now Leo had trapped himself in a corner. He glanced up at the roof, at least fifteen feet over his head. Too high.

Justin clambered out of the trailer. He limped up beside me, but before I could say anything, other footsteps clattered on the sidewalk farther down the street. I turned, fumbling for my pistol.

A woman with the same red-blond hair as the little boy was hustling toward us, followed by an older man, a guy who looked to be in his early twenties, and a preteen girl. The girl was holding a gun that looked oddly plastic. Because it was plastic. A BB gun. Suddenly the snapping noise and the bear's pursuit of the boy made sense. He must have shot it.

The group came to a halt several feet from us, by the corner of the school building. The woman put her hand to her mouth when she saw the scene in the yard. "Ricky! My god . . ."

The younger man glared at Justin and me. "You should have stayed out of here," he said.

The comment seemed so bizarre that I gaped at him before I could find the words to answer. "It's not our fault he shot the bear," I said.

"He snuck out 'cause he heard your engine," the guy retorted. "He shouldn't have been outside the house on his own in the first place."

"Then maybe you should have been keeping a better eye on him," Justin said, returning the glare.

"That damn creature's been hanging around town three days. Only now that you came by it's been a problem," the older man muttered.

I opened my mouth, but whatever I would have said caught in my throat. The bear lunged closer to the box, swinging its front paws just inches from Leo's and the boy's legs. It dropped down again, pacing to one side and the other in a tight circuit, the muscles in its back and shoulders rippling. It might be able to jump right up there if it decided that was worth the trouble.

Leo pulled the boy close to him, eyeing the distance along the wall of the school. But I had the feeling the bear would be on them the second they leapt down.

"It doesn't matter why it happened," I said. "We've got to get them out of there."

"I'll shoot it, properly this time," the girl said, pushing back her dark curls and raising the BB gun.

"With that toy?" Justin said. He shifted forward, lifting the rifle from the ground, and I grasped his arm.

"You think it's easy to kill a bear with one shot? If you just hurt it, it's going to be even more upset." If Leo, with his hunting experience, hadn't thought it was a good idea to use his pistol, I didn't want Justin firing away.

"So what's your brilliant plan?" the young man snapped.

I didn't have one. All I knew was that even if this bear had lost some of its natural fear of humans, it wanted easy prey, small prey, weak prey. It wouldn't want to fight if it thought there was a real danger.

We had to convince it that we were dangerous, that it had to leave. If we came up beside it and made a lot of noise, all of us together— My thoughts stuttered as I glanced at the townspeople. For all we knew, one of them was infected. Justin and Anika had no protection from the virus at all, not even a makeshift face mask. And these strangers could turn on us the second the kid was safe.

Across the yard, the little boy whimpered. Leo murmured something to him, too faint for me to make out, and I remembered what he'd said last night. *I don't want the world to be like this.* I swallowed thickly.

I didn't want it to be like this either. I didn't want to have to feel like a criminal just for passing through a town. I didn't want to have to wonder who I might have to shoot. And I sure as hell didn't want to live in a world where we let two people get mauled and maybe die because the rest of us were too scared of each other to do anything about it.

My hands balled in my pockets. "We have to frighten the bear off," I said. "Act big and loud and threatening. Make it think it's not worth sticking around. Come on!"

I gestured to the four of them. The woman looked at the boy I assumed was her son and back to me, started to move, and then stiffened. The young man was scowling, the older man clutching the girl's arm.

Fine. We'd just have to show them what to do.

I nudged Justin and marched toward the side of the school without waiting to see if he'd follow. The rifle butt tapped along behind me as he hurried to keep up. I kept my steps as light as possible, sticking close to the brick wall, slowing as I came up parallel with the bear. It glanced over at us, then turned its focus back to Leo and the boy.

"Hey!" I yelled at the top of my lungs. I raised my hands and stomped one foot on the ground. "Hey, get out of here! Move it!"

"Take off!" Justin joined in, smacking the rifle against the ground and then waving it at the bear. "Go on, run for it!"

The bear lurched around to face us, backing up a few paccs. For a second, I thought we'd succeeded. Then it bared its teeth in a snarl.

"Hey, fur face, take a hike!" a voice hollered. The girl with the BB gun had come up beside Justin. She swung her arms in the air, flashing her own clenched teeth. Then the young man was with her, pounding the pavement with his running shoes and letting out a wordless bellow.

"Leave him alone, you monster!" the mother yelled, slipping into our midst. She clapped her hands against her sides, and I started stomping my feet again, and we all raised our voices in a cacophony of shouts and insults. The bear was watching us, braced, its hackles raised. I took one aggressive step forward, drawing myself up as tall as I could, and it whipped around. In the space of a blink, it had dashed across the schoolyard and was disappearing into the shadows down the street.

THIRTEEN

"Woohoo!" the girl cried, and the others started to laugh, the tension breaking. Even though my pulse was still pounding, I was grinning so wide my cheeks hurt. Leo handed the boy down to his mother and slid off the storage box. He walked straight to me and tugged me into a tight embrace.

"The unexpected benefits of having an animal-obsessed best friend," he said, but despite his joking tone, I felt a tremor ripple through his body. I hugged him back, and right then there was nothing awkward about it, just the immense gratitude that we'd all gotten through one more crisis okay.

"You did some pretty quick thinking too," I said. "If you hadn't raced in there, I don't know what it would have done to the kid."

"Yeah," he said, sounding almost startled, as if he'd forgotten how he'd ended up in the situation in the first place. "I probably should have handled it better, but the bear was coming at us so fast, my mind went blank. I just didn't want to make it angrier."

"Well, you managed that. And I don't think the kid's mom is complaining."

She was waiting nearby when Leo eased back from me, her son clutching her leg.

"Thank you," she said. "I—I don't know what to say. You saved his life."

A faint blush crept across Leo's face. "It was Kaelyn as much as me," he said, but his eyes had brightened.

"The bear will probably steer clear of this part of town from now on," I said.

"Good," the older man said gruffly, but then he added, "We'll know what to do if it causes any more problems, thanks to you."

"You look as if you've been traveling for a while," the woman put in. "Would you stop and have lunch with us?"

"Yes, you have to!" the girl said, bouncing on her heels and beaming at us. The older man inclined his head. The younger guy was still scowling, but he didn't argue.

A sort of exhilaration swept through me. We were standing here, talking like people used to, before the friendly flu and the Wardens. Not like enemies, not full of suspicion and threats, just like . . . human beings.

I'd almost forgotten what it felt like, to smile at a stranger, to invite someone to share a meal. It was so normal. And it was the most incredible feeling in the world.

This was what I wanted. I could survive without computers and malls and processed food. But what was the point in surviving if we could never go back to being regular people with one another? Working in harmony, sharing resources, accomplishing far more than we could have alone.

If you'd asked me a day ago, I wouldn't have been sure it could ever happen. It had seemed pretty much impossible. But right now . . . Right now I could see reason to hope all around me.

I let myself linger in that rush of joy for a few seconds longer, and then reality sank in. As much as I longed to stay here and keep the feeling of normalcy alive, we *did* still have the friendly flu and the Wardens to worry about. We had to get the vaccine samples to Atlanta while they were still cold.

But nothing said we couldn't come back, when our mission was complete.

"I wish we could," I told the woman. "But we're actually in kind of a hurry." I paused, hating that I couldn't say why and that if asked I'd have to lie. Protecting the vaccine trumped everything else, for now.

To my relief, the woman didn't ask. She patted her son's shoulder and said, "I'd like to do something. I can whip up some sandwiches quickly, for you to take on the road. I have a loaf of bread that just finished baking."

"That would be awesome," Justin said. I nodded, my stomach gurgling at the thought of anything fresh after the canned and prepackaged food we'd been eating for most of the last few months. We could wait a couple minutes.

The woman smiled and prodded her son ahead of her down the sidewalk. The older man followed them. His skin was as dark as theirs was pale, so I doubted he was related to them, but from the way he bent down to whisper in the boy's ear and the boy's answering grin, I guessed he'd taken on a grandfatherly role. When you lost your real family, you ended up making a new one out of the people you still had.

I glanced at the people who made up my family now. Leo shot me a smile and ambled a short ways down the road, checking the route the bear had taken.

Anika had sidled over to the young man and managed to crack his dour expression. He'd turned toward her, his eyebrows arched.

She flipped her hair over her shoulder with one of her artfully careless gestures and looked at him through her eyelashes.

"Yup," she was saying, tapping the hood of the tractor. "Right through the mountains. This thing's not really my dream car, but it did the job all right."

Beside me, Justin was watching them. Beneath his rumpled ponytail, the back of his neck had reddened. I bumped my elbow against his.

"Relax," I said quietly. "She's going to get to know him for all of five minutes."

The flush spread up to his cheeks. "I wasn't—" he started, and then dropped his gaze. "I know, I know."

Anika was certainly making good use of the time. In response to a question I'd missed, she gave the guy's arm a swat. "Oh, I could handle that. I'm tougher than I look. No, the only problem with it is the fuel. We've got to find diesel. That's why we went for the school bus, but it was basically empty." She shrugged, letting her face fall just slightly. I wasn't surprised when the guy jumped at the chance to play hero.

"Hey, you could head over to Murphy's place," he said, gesturing to the west. "It's just half a mile outside of town, over by the river. He was a trucker—I'm pretty sure his rig is still parked there, but he took off with some friends. Whatever he's left behind is free pickings."

As Anika murmured something demure about not wanting to take what he and the other townspeople might need and he eagerly denied any conflict, the girl with the BB gun cocked her head at me.

“Where’d you all come from, anyway?” she asked.

She looked hungry—not for food, but for information. Reassurance. She didn’t resemble any of the adults who’d come out, so I guessed what birth family she’d had was gone. These days, at eleven or twelve, maybe you had to *be* one of the adults.

“We came from up north,” I said, stumbling over how much I should tell her.

“Hmmm,” she said. “You must have been pretty cold up there. The winter wasn’t too bad here—we were okay when the gas ran out—but it wasn’t a lot of fun either.”

“Yeah,” I said. Anika guffawed at a comment the guy had made, and I wished I had her skill at chumming up to strangers. But what do you say to a kid who’s probably lost both her parents, maybe siblings, and all her friends, just in the last few months?

“It’s good,” I managed to continue, “the way you’re all sticking together. That’s how we got this far.”

“I guess,” the girl said with a skeptical frown, and then I didn’t have to worry about saying anything else, because the woman was hurrying back to us with a plastic shopping bag in her hands.

“Thank you so much,” I said, accepting it. She’d wrapped each of the sandwiches in parchment paper, but the smell of warm bread wafted through it. My mouth watered.

“It’s the least I could do,” she said. “I hope you all get to where you’re going safely.”

Anika waved to the guy and hopped into the cab. I handed off sandwiches to Leo and Justin, and then climbed in beside her.

“I take it you know where we’re going?” I said.

“Brendan was very happy to help,” she said, flashing a grin at me. *She did it for us*, I thought abruptly. She’d charmed the information out of that guy to get us where we, and the vaccines, needed to go.

Despite her protests three days ago, she did care. I hoped that meant her pledge to stick with us would hold, no matter what waited for us in Atlanta. She was starting to seem like a real part of our group. A part of this makeshift family.

We dug into our sandwiches together as Anika steered the tractor down the road and out the other end of town. The bread tasted faintly smoky, as if it'd been baked over a fire—which I supposed maybe it had. But it was crusty and chewy and filled with tuna salad, which was more filling than anything I remembered eating recently. And I'd forgotten just how wonderful mayonnaise could be. I finished, licking the crumbs off my fingers, just as a weathered wooden house appeared up ahead. Parked on a dusty stretch of earth between it and the river beyond was a flatbed transport truck.

We parked next to the truck and piled out. The breeze that greeted us was hardly wintery, but chilly enough that it tickled my skin under my open coat. Clouds were crawling across the sky, smothering the sun.

"Are the keys around?" I said, with a vision of speeding along the roads at regular car speed again. Justin glanced into the truck's cab and shook his head. I ordered him to stay with the tractor, which he agreed to with an exaggerated sigh, and the rest of us tramped through the bungalow. The place was unlocked and dusty with disuse, but either the owner had hoped he'd come back to trucking someday and held on to the keys, or he'd hidden them well. Our search turned up nothing.

It'd only be a few more hours anyway, I reminded myself as we hurried back outside. A damp wind had picked up, licking across our faces, and the clouds had darkened. Time to get going.

Leo took charge of the siphon tube again, and got the fuel flowing out of the truck's tank in a matter of seconds. After we'd filled the jugs, he started feeding it straight into the tractor. As he worked, Anika and I wandered around the yard to see if there might be a spare tank on the property. We found a shed that held plenty of repair tools, but no fuel. A rickety wooden dock stretched along the bank of the narrow gray river, with an aluminum rowboat bobbing by one corner, empty except for two wooden paddles. I crouched and dipped a hand into the river. The water was startlingly cold.

Anika poked at the rowboat with the toe of her boot. "Well," she said, "it looked like there was lots of gas in the truck."

"I think we'll have more than enough," I said.

Leo was still filling up the tractor when we returned. As I leaned over the side of the trailer, checking for empty water bottles I could fill, an odd squeaking sound reached my ears. I peered around the corner of the house.

A small figure on a bike was careening toward us down the road from town. I recognized the girl I'd talked to there. Her curly hair was billowing behind her. I stepped out to meet her as she screeched to a halt beside the house.

"Someone's going to come," she said, panting. "In a white Humvee. We were still outside, after you left, and they roared right in— They wanted to know if we saw some people in a tractor. We told them we hadn't, but they kept asking questions. I don't know if they believed us. So I thought I should tell you before they came looking. They kind of scared me."

She hadn't even finished speaking when I picked up the growl of an engine in the distance. A white blotch was traveling down the road the way she'd come. My heart stopped. If they'd mentioned the tractor—the people from the helicopter must have spotted us at the farm and sent another group our way.

"Thank you," I said to the girl. "Now get out of here before they come after you too!"

She nodded and shot off on her bike. "Let's move!" Justin said as I hurried back. He clutched the side of the trailer.

"Wait!" Anika said, her face paling. "We can't outrun a car in this thing."

"We don't have anything else," I said, but my pulse skittered. She was right. Could we just hide?

As I spun around, Leo hefted a bag out of the trailer and pointed toward the dock. "We do," he said. "The boat. They can't follow us on the water."

The roar of the Humvee's engine already sounded far too close. In the split second I had, I couldn't think of a better plan. I yanked out the cold box and a bundle of blankets. "Grab what you can and let's go!"

We fled across the yard to the river. I clambered into the rowboat, shifting to the side to make room for the others. The boat bobbed dangerously low as they scrambled in with what we'd salvaged of our supplies. Gravel rattled under tires on the other side of the house. I fumbled with the latch that hooked the boat's rope to the dock. It was caked with rust. Anika leaned over beside me and chopped through the cord with her hunting knife.

I let go. The boat swirled away from the dock, the current sweeping it past the end of the yard and into the shadows of the underbrush that lined the bank farther down. The sound of the engine cut out, and doors slammed. I gripped the edge of the seat. The yard and the dock vanished from sight an instant later as the river tugged us around the bend.

FOURTEEN

For a while I found it hard to do anything except scan the riverbanks. I wasn't totally convinced we'd actually managed to escape. The current whipped us around the humps of rocks jutting from the water's surface as we slipped past long stretches of forest. Bud-dotted branches rattled in the rising wind.

When the threat of the people in the Humvee finally felt far enough away that I could catch my breath, I started taking stock.

"What did everyone manage to bring?" I asked.

"The water bottles and the first-aid kit," Anika said from where she crouched in the bottom of the boat.

"Bag of food, rifle," Justin said, opposite her.

"The radio," Leo said, on the seat across from mine. He rested his hand on its plastic covering. "And the pack with the tent."

And I'd gotten the vaccine, and at least a couple blankets. In the warmer weather, we could make do without the sleeping bag, and the jugs of diesel fuel we'd filled wouldn't do us much good without the tractor. I glanced up at the sky, wondering exactly what direction the river was taking us in, but it was clotted with clouds, as gray as the surface of the water.

"We're going mostly south, I think," Leo said. "I haven't been able to keep track of all the turns."

We *had* left something important behind. The road atlas. It'd been sitting on the dash of the tractor—I could picture exactly where, but that didn't do us any good.

A drop of cool water hit my hair. I glanced up, and got another in the eye. As I wiped it away, a light rain began to patter down on us. Justin groaned.

"It figures."

I shrugged up the hood of my coat, even though its thick padding made me swelteringly hot, and the others did the same. The rain drummed the bottom of the boat. We were going to have to bail it out before too long. Or get out ourselves.

The sooner we got off the river, the harder it'd be for the Wardens to find us again. The thought of our close call made me shiver despite my coat. If the girl from town hadn't come to warn us, or hadn't come as soon as she had, we wouldn't have stood a chance.

I reached for one of the paddles that was leaning against the bow. "Let's find a spot where we can get off the river and regroup. We could end up drifting right past Atlanta at this rate."

"Here," Leo said, holding out his hand, and I passed him the other paddle. Turning to face ahead, I folded my legs under the seat and held the paddle over the water. Drips rolled off the edge of my hood.

For the next few minutes, we saw only trees. Then a clearing came into view on the right-hand bank, with a stubby dock poking into the water and a rusty swing set on the grass. I motioned to it, and Leo nodded. We dug the paddles into the river, pulling the boat toward the shore. At first the current resisted. My arms strained against it. But as we drew closer to the bank, the tugging eased. We pulled up beside the dock just in time for me to catch hold of the corner.

There was nothing to tie the boat with, so I held it in place as the others carried our supplies onto solid ground. "You figure we should just let it go?" Justin asked when everything was unloaded.

I considered the dingy vessel. The rowboat wasn't anything fancy, but it had served us well. And it was all we had right now. The thought of casting off our only method of transportation made me edgy.

"Let's keep it but hide it," I said.

Leo, Anika, and I hauled the boat out of the water and set it under the wide branches of a pine tree at the edge of the clearing, where nobody would be able to see it unless they were almost on top of it. Justin had already started toward the tall house on the other side of the overgrown lawn. We grabbed our things and hurried after him, ducking our heads to the rain.

The inner back door hung open, as if whoever had last been here had left too distracted to think of it, and the latch on the outer screen door snapped when Justin gave it a hard yank. We clustered in the mudroom, peeling off our soppy coats. Then we crept through the house, guns in hand. Only darkness and dust greeted us. There was a note on the fridge, scrawled in hasty cursive. *I've taken Bridget to the hospital. Meet us there. —S.*

A long empty driveway stretched away from the front of the house, through the forest, to some road beyond our view. I guessed whoever S had been writing to had followed his or her instructions, and neither they nor Bridget had come back home.

I perused the kitchen counters and end tables for any piece of mail that might give us a location, but the family had been too tidy to be helpful. The steel filing cabinet in the dining room looked promising, but its drawers were locked.

Justin sighed and stomped into the living room with his rifle. "Well, we know we have to keep heading south, right?"

"I'm not sure which way is south anymore," Leo admitted.

"If we had the road atlas," I said, and stopped. Regrets weren't going to help. "We just need to know where we are. The address, the nearest town, something. We can probably get a hold of the CDC on the radio, and they should be able to give us directions to Atlanta from here. Once we know where here is."

"There should be a mailbox at the end of the driveway," Justin said. "It might be locked too, but we can at least check. And if that doesn't work, there'll be signs somewhere down the road. I'll go take a look." He took an umbrella out of a stand in the front hall.

"Your leg—" I protested, and he grimaced at me.

"It's a lot better now," he said. "It should be, after doing nothing but sitting around the last three days. I'll be fine."

He looked so determined I didn't want to say no. Maybe it was better to let him burn off some steam. Who knew what crazy scheme he'd think up if he spent much longer feeling he wasn't contributing enough?

"None of us should go anywhere alone, right?" Anika broke in. "I'll go with him. Make sure he doesn't keel over. You two can keep searching the house."

"Right," Justin said, seeming emboldened by the gaining of an ally. He tapped the watch on his wrist. "We might have to walk a ways if we need to look for a sign, but we won't take more than an hour."

"All right," I said. "Just try to come back faster than that."

"And keep your eyes open," Leo added. "The Wardens know we're somewhere in the area now."

Justin gave us a quick salute. Anika went back for their coats, and when she returned he handed her a second umbrella. "No more than an hour," he repeated. "Hopefully a lot less." They headed out the door.

"Let's take a look upstairs," I said to Leo. I picked up the cold box, and paused, my palm warm against the plastic handle. So maybe it would be an hour before we were on the road again. Maybe it would be even more. And there was no telling when we'd find another vehicle, or if we wouldn't at all and we'd be stuck walking the rest of the way. How long would the snow I'd packed in there this morning last?

"Actually, give me a second," I said. I hadn't seen a basement entrance. Maybe there was a cellar doorway in the yard? Anywhere underground would be cooler.

I stepped into the mudroom and peered across the lawn. I didn't see any sign of a door amid the thick grass. My gaze strayed farther, to the rippling surface of the river. When I'd dipped my hands into it upstream, the water had been cold enough to sting. It was probably flowing down from the mountains, swelled by melting snow and ice.

Kneeling down, I opened the cold box just long enough to make sure Dad's notebooks were tightly wrapped in their plastic bag. Then I pressed the lid on, hooking the latches and testing them to make sure they were firmly in place. I didn't think water could leak in through the industrial-grade seal, but if it did, it shouldn't hurt anything inside.

I jogged across the yard to the dock. The water at the edge of the bank was only a few feet deep. I set the cold box in it, and it bobbed back to the surface. But the gap between the dock's wooden supports looked like just the right size. Wiggling the box back and forth, I wedged it between them, far enough under that it was mostly hidden by the dock. When I stood, it was nothing more than a pale sliver amid the rain-dappled water. I checked both ends of the river. No one was there to see my hiding place.

Still, my hands felt terribly empty as I hurried back to the house. This way the samples would stay cold, I reminded myself, and as soon as we had a plan of where to go, I could run back out and get them. The fish weren't going to steal them.

Leo was waiting in the kitchen when I came in. "I gave everything down here a second look, and nothing," he said, raising his eyebrows in question.

"I did what I needed to," I said, swiping my damp hair away from my face. "Let's see what we can find upstairs."

We poked through the bathroom and the three bedrooms on the second floor, checking cabinets and drawers and bedside tables. In the yellow room hung with posters of planets and nebulas, the garbage bin was overflowing with crumpled tissues. *Bridget.* I caught myself wondering how old she had been, and pushed that thought away.

The master bedroom offered a few pamphlets for Mexican beach resorts, but nothing local. Leo pointed out a trapdoor in the ceiling of the closet. "To the attic?" he said.

"I guess we might as well look," I said. "Maybe they stashed some old letters or tax records up there." And we'd covered every other inch of the house. I glanced around the room for a chair or something else I could stand on.

"Here, I can give you a boost," Leo said. "If we need to climb right up there to reach something, I saw a stepladder in the mudroom."

He backed up against the row of shirts and slacks, and braced one leg forward for me to step onto, offering me his hand. My skin warmed. Suddenly the closet felt twice as small. I made myself grasp his fingers without hesitating, keeping my eyes on the trapdoor. As I hopped up, he caught me around the waist. Ignoring the hiccup of my pulse, I pushed up the door and raised my head through the opening.

A waft of dust hit me. I sneezed, my eyes watering. What I could make out of the attic was no more than a crawl space, inhabited only by dust bunnies and cobwebs. With another sneeze, I hopped back down.

"Nothing there," I said as Leo straightened up. Some of the dust had sprinkled his dark hair. I brushed my hand over the top of his head. "Sorry."

"I'll live," he said. The corner of his mouth quirked up. "I should be used to it. You remember when you insisted we had to explore *my* attic?"

"Oh god." I covered my face at the memory. "You can't hold me responsible for that anymore. What were we, seven? Anyway, I think it was your idea as much as mine."

"No, no," he said, grinning now. "I kept telling you my parents said I wasn't allowed in the crawl space, but you were sure there had to be some animal living up there for us to discover."

"There was that scratching sound we kept hearing in your room!" I protested. "It was a reasonable guess."

"I don't think my mom bought that explanation when she found half her clothes knocked on the floor and us stuck in the ceiling."

"Well, I apologize for ruining your childhood," I said, swatting at his shoulder. He dodged out of the way, catching my hand before I could try again.

"Ruined?" he said. "I guess I'd have been bored a lot more without you."

The mischievous spark in his eyes took me back to that time, when we were younger, before arguments and silences and epidemics. When Leo had treated every challenge as an adventure, not a setback. I hadn't seen that spark very often in the last couple months, and I couldn't help smiling back. But as I did, his expression changed. An intensity came into his gaze that made my stomach flutter.

He'd looked at me that way before. In the garage back home, right before he'd kissed me.

I let go of his hand and stepped out of the closet, walking until I reached the end of the bed. Leo didn't move. But I could feel him still looking at me.

"I'm sorry," I said. "I just—"

"It's okay," Leo said.

It wasn't. We'd gotten past the awkwardness of not-quite-spoken crushes for a while, when we were on the road to Toronto. But I couldn't pretend anymore that it hadn't come back. I couldn't even pretend I didn't know why.

There had been Gav. And then . . . he was gone. But not entirely. My fingertips traced the edge of the strip of cardboard in my pocket.

"Maybe we should talk about it," Leo said. He rubbed the back of his neck, his voice sounding strained despite his lighthearted tone. "I'm not going to lie. You know how I feel about you. Nothing's changed. But I'd never push anything on you. I'm happy with friends. It's really not a problem."

"It's not you," I said, sitting down on the bed. "I'm the one acting weird."

"I wouldn't blame you, if you were angry," he said.

My head jerked up. "Angry—at you? For what?"

"For taking the vaccine, when Gav wouldn't? For surviving? I'd understand."

Fear jolted through me at the thought of Leo getting sick. "Of course I'm not angry about that," I said. "Do you have any idea how much more scared I'd be if I didn't know you were safe? I wish he *had* taken the vaccine, not that you hadn't."

He lowered his gaze, and his next words seemed to take a long time to come out. "But it's not just that," he said, haltingly. "I wanted to do more. When Gav was sick. He was a good guy. He made you happy, I could see that. And maybe I *should* have done more. I go over everything that happened and see where maybe I could have made a little difference. And then I wonder if there was a reason I didn't—"

I couldn't stand hearing him talk like that. "Leo," I interrupted. "Don't. You didn't make Gav get sick any more than I did, and after he got sick, there wasn't really anything we *could* do. I have never, even for a second, blamed you. I promise. Whatever weirdness is going on, it's got nothing to do with that. Things are just... complicated."

Part of me wanted to forget the complications and drive away the worry and guilt clouding his face. To put my arms around him and tell him I cared about him just as much as he cared about me. But another part, a bigger part, held me back.

My heart had been so beat up in the last few weeks—did I even know what I felt anymore? What was real? Was I drawn to Leo now because of that old crush reviving, or because he was here, comforting and supportive, and Gav wasn't, and I'd had no one else to turn to?

I didn't have to be with *anyone.* It was probably better for me to be with no one, while the memory of Gav's vacant body was still as vivid in my mind as if I'd taken that last look only moments ago. The knot of grief in my chest had barely loosened.

Even if everything I felt for Leo was real, I couldn't do that to Gav. If he'd known I'd forget him so quickly . . .

And then, in an instant, none of that mattered, because the sound of an engine rumbled through the wall.

I jumped up and darted to the window. A brown station wagon was turning the corner of the drive, heading toward the house.

FIFTEEN

The Wardens who'd come through the town had been driving a white Humvee. But that didn't mean another group couldn't be tracking us down. I bit my lip. Leo came up on the other side of the window.

"What do you want to do?" he asked.

"I don't know." We could have run for the boat again, but that would mean leaving Justin and Anika. Letting them come back to find us gone and the Wardens waiting for them.

I couldn't do it. I couldn't leave one more person behind.

"We have to defend ourselves," I said, bracing myself for Leo's response. "We can wait by the front door, and if they come in, hold them up. We don't have to hurt them, just barricade them in one of the rooms. If they don't fight back. If they do..."

"Then we do have we have to," Leo said with a nod. His eyes held mine unwaveringly. "Let's get ready."

A momentary relief washed over me, only to be swallowed by apprehension as I slid Tobias's pistol from my pocket. Not long ago, the thought of putting a bullet into one of the Wardens' heads had appealed to me. Now I only felt sick. But if someone was going to die here, I'd still rather it was them than us.

We hurried down the stairs and across the hall. Leo stepped

to the left of the door, his own gun in hand, his body tensed. I positioned myself against the wall on the other side. My fingers curled around the pistol. What if they outnumbered us? What if they'd already passed Justin and Anika on the road and taken them as hostages?

The engine growled to a stop. The car doors creaked open. Footsteps thudded across the paved driveway.

Then a familiar voice filtered through the door.

"I'm telling you, I could be a better driver than the rest of you put together. What do licenses even mean anymore?"

I let out my breath and lowered the gun. Leo was shaking his head.

Justin and Anika were coming up the front steps when I opened the door. Justin turned to me with a grin.

"Look what we found!"

"There's a road just a little ways past the bend," Anika said in explanation, gesturing toward the driveway. "About ten minutes' walk down that, there's another house—that's where we found the car. The key was in the house. It's got a half a tank of gas."

"Perfect," I said. My anxiety fell away. This was exactly what we needed. "Did you figure out where we are?"

"According to the signs, we're not too far east of some place called Clermont," Justin said as he limped into the house with his rifle walking stick. The butt of the rifle slid on the edge of the hall rug, and he started to stumble. Anika caught his elbow.

"*That's* why I didn't let you drive," she said, with a gentleness that made me look at her again. Her attention was totally focused on him, a smile curving her lips as he glowered at her halfheartedly.

"I guess I should keep holding on to you, then," Justin said, hooking his arm around hers, and she kept smiling. And for the first time, I wondered if her flirting wasn't just teasing anymore. Maybe age differences didn't matter so much when you weren't sure how many more days you'd be alive.

The idea hit me with a strange rush of sadness and a sharpened awareness of Leo standing on the other side of the hall.

"Clermont," I repeated, bringing myself back. I tried to picture the pages of the road atlas, the lay of the land around northern Georgia, but the name didn't click. I didn't know whether we needed to go east or west from here. And wandering around trying to figure it out would just use up the gas and give the Wardens more time to spot us.

"Let me try to get in touch with the CDC quickly," I said. "Dr. Guzman wanted us to contact her when we were close to Atlanta anyway."

The others followed me into the living room. Leo unwrapped the transceiver and set it on the coffee table. Outside, the rain had picked up again, drumming against the porch awning.

When I pressed the call button, the static fizzled more harshly than I remembered from before. But Dr. Guzman's voice cracked through it to answer my broadcast loud and clear.

"Kaelyn?"

"Yes," I said. "We're almost there. We've just gotten a little off track."

"What happened?" she asked sharply.

"We're okay," I said. "But the people who were chasing us, they almost caught us this morning. We lost our road atlas—we had to leave it behind. I think we're close to Atlanta. I just need some help figuring out how to get there from here."

"I can do that," she said. "You're all still all right? And the vaccine?"

"Everything's fine, other than us being lost," I said. "I think we should get moving soon, though. I don't know how close they might be behind us." Or whether they'd catch this transmission and soon have an even better idea of where we were.

"Of course, of course. Let me just get a map. . . ." There was a crackle as she stepped away. "Listen," she said when she returned. "I'm going to give you directions for how to approach the center once you get to the city, and you need to follow them exactly. When you're inside our walls, you'll be safe, but until then . . . Oh, I wish there was an easier way for us to send someone to you. But even if we could manage to take a vehicle out without getting overwhelmed, it would definitely be followed, and I don't know how well we could protect you if we led some of these people to you out in the open. We just don't have the means to spread ourselves that thin and keep the center secure."

Michael knew we were headed her way. He'd probably been expecting we'd arrive in Atlanta before now. "Has it gotten worse?" I asked. "You said there were people trying to break in?"

"It's—" She cut herself off with an indrawn breath. "It'll be fine. We'll get you here. They're all just hurting themselves in the long run. Where are you now?"

The memory of her comments a few days ago, about who would get the vaccine and who might not, made my skin prickle. But now wasn't the time to get into that. "We're just east of a place called Clermont," I said. "Near a river."

"Clermont . . . That's not far at all! You still have access to a vehicle?"

"Yes, and we're ready to go."

"All right. We may be talking face-to-face in just a couple hours. You'll want to go toward Clermont and get yourselves onto 129 heading south. From there on you should see signs for Atlanta. When you have a choice, stay on the—"

Whatever she said next was lost in the sudden *bang* of the doors slamming open. "Don't move!" a voice bellowed as we sprang to our feet. The mic slipped from my hand and dropped to the floor. Before I could grope for the gun I'd set on the couch beside me, two figures had barged into the living room from the front hall, another hustling through the dining room from the back, and I found myself staring into the mouths of a shotgun and two pistols.

The four of us froze. My mouth went dry. This was it. The moment I'd been afraid of for so long, and I hadn't been the slightest bit prepared.

"Kaelyn?" Dr. Guzman said through the radio's speaker. "Kaelyn, are you there?"

The larger of the two men jerked his head toward the other, a skinny guy not much older than me, who bent without lowering his gun and flicked the switch off. The woman moved behind Anika. Leo's hand twitched to his side, and the larger man—the group's leader, I guessed—tracked it. He stepped forward, yanked out the pistol Leo had stuck behind his belt, and then grabbed my gun off the couch. His black hair was dripping, his amber skin flecked with water. The face masks all three of them wore were drooping with moisture. They must have walked through the rain. That was why we hadn't heard them coming.

"Get that one too," the man said, motioning to the rifle by Justin's feet. The woman tugged it away with her heel and kicked it toward the dining room. Then she patted down Anika with her free hand, tossing aside the hunting knife before checking Justin. She arched an eyebrow at the flare gun she found in his coat pocket and chucked it after the knife. The other guy smacked his hands down Leo's sides, and mine.

When he was done, the leader shifted his shotgun so it pointed at each of us in turn.

"Where is it?" he demanded. "Where's the vaccine?"

Justin's gaze darted through the room and then caught mine. He didn't know. None of them knew, I realized. I'd only meant to keep the samples cold, but I'd effectively hidden them as well.

"We don't have it anymore!" Anika burst out. "These other guys took it from us. We barely got away from them."

She let out a squeak as the woman snatched at her hair and wrenched her head back, placing the pistol against her temple.

"Oh, really?" the woman said.

Justin's hand leapt toward Anika. The younger guy swung his gun toward him, his damp coppery hair dark as dried blood in the dim light. The leader poked me in the side with his shotgun, but his attention was fixed on Anika now.

"I'm finding it hard to believe you," he said. "Maybe if I fire a few rounds into your friends, you'll remember better?"

Anika quivered. I didn't think this was the response she'd been going for. Her lips parted, a shaky breath escaping over them, and in that moment I could see her searching for the words to give up the vaccine. But she didn't know how. And our captors had no clue. They could murder me to threaten her and never know they were killing the only person who had the answer.

My heart thumped. I could tell them that, but then they'd hurt the others to get me to talk. As long as they thought some of us were expendable—

Then we had to make them believe none of us were.

The idea had hardly formed in my mind before my mouth was moving. "You don't want to do that," I said. "You shoot any of us and you'll never find what you're looking for."

Three hostile pairs of eyes turned on me.

"What are you talking about?" the leader growled.

"There's more than one sample," I said, scrambling to put my thoughts in a coherent order. "And notebooks, with information on how to make more. Whenever we stop somewhere, we all take one part of the set and hide it without telling anyone else. You need all of us, or Michael's not going to be happy."

The copper-haired guy stiffened at the mention of their boss. The woman snorted. "Sounds pretty stupid to me."

"Maybe," Leo jumped in. "But it's true. You think we trusted each other enough to be sure that none of us would sneak off with everything if we could? We all want a piece of the reward."

"Yeah," Justin said. "I didn't want these guys skipping out and leaving me empty-handed. It was only fair if we each had something."

The leader eyed us one by one. I suspected it wasn't too hard for him to imagine distrusting his colleagues. "Check the house," he said to the other guy. "If they hid anything, find it."

As the copper-haired guy shuffled off, the woman tapped her gun against Anika's forehead. "And if we can't, we just rough 'em up until they talk. No big deal."

Anika cringed. "No way," I said quickly. It was one thing for her to have played along with our team, and another to withstand torture for us. But Anika had as much to lose as me or Justin or Leo. "We're not that stupid. As soon as you get what you want from us, you'll kill us. Hurt me all you want, but I plan on staying alive."

"I didn't come this far to die for nothing," Leo said, quietly but firmly.

"Me neither," Justin added, jutting out his chin. Anika looked at him, and her shoulders squared.

"I'd rather die than tell you assholes anything," she said.

The woman whipped back her pistol and cracked Anika across the head, grabbing her when she staggered. All Anika let out was a muffled gasp. Her hands balled into fists at her sides. Justin's face had tightened, his eyes seething.

"Hold it, Marissa," the leader said as the woman raised her gun again. "Let me think." His forehead had furrowed. I guessed he'd expected us to be easily intimidated. He didn't know what we'd already been through to get this far.

"Last we heard, there were six of you," he said after a moment. "Where are the others?"

Gav and Tobias. I kept my mouth pressed shut.

Marissa sighed and reached back to squeeze some of the rain-water from her long brown braid. "One of them was sick, the report said, right? He's probably dead now."

"And the other one?" the leader said, glowering at us. We all stared back at him, silent. His jaw clenched. Good. Let him worry about that instead of finding the vaccine.

God, I wished Gav and Tobias *were* here. Or rather, somewhere outside the house, strategizing a way to overpower these thugs. They'd known how to fight. I'd kept the four of us alive, but I didn't know how to get us out of this. Even if one of our captors made a mistake, gave us an opening, I didn't think any of us had the skill to disarm them and get the upper hand.

We'd just have to wait, and see what opportunities we got. As long as we were alive, we had a chance.

"Well, this is fun," Marissa said drily.

The leader turned his glare on her. "Let's see what Connor turns up. If we find the vaccine, we don't need them to talk."

But when the other guy trudged back downstairs a few minutes later, of course he'd found nothing. From the dust streaking his windbreaker, it looked like he'd even crawled into the attic.

"I don't even know what I'm looking for, Chay," he said. Unlike the other two, his voice rolled with a southern drawl—a local recruit, presumably. "Maybe I should take one of them with me."

"They'd probably get the drop on you the second you're out of our sight," Marissa sneered.

"Go look outside," Chay said. "And hurry up."

Muttering to himself, Connor stomped off. I struggled to keep my expression calm as the back door thumped shut behind him. Would he think to look under the dock? I focused on breathing evenly, in and out, as the seconds ticked away.

"Why don't we shoot them all in the kneecaps, see how brave they're feeling then?" Marissa said, after we'd been standing there for what felt like an hour.

"And if they don't talk?" Chay said. "They'd bleed to death, and Michael'll kill us. Fucking hell."

"So let him figure out what to do with them, then," she said. "We did our job; we tracked 'em down. It's not our fault they're crazy."

"You want to call him and explain that?"

"Let's bring 'em in. Then they're his problem. One of those useless doctors can probably figure out how to torture them 'safely.'"

"And he's really going to like that," Chay snapped. "Just shut up, all right?"

Despite my fear, a tiny spark of triumph lit inside me. They had the guns, they had the strength, but they hadn't overpowered us. As long as they didn't find the cold box, we were the ones in control.

Connor pushed back into the house through the front door, thoroughly soaked.

"There's no vaccine, there's no notebooks, there's no nothing," he said. "You want to take a look?"

"Maybe I should," Chay said. "Get over here. And don't do anything stupid." As Connor drew out his pistol and took Chay's place, Chay stalked off. A minute later, furniture started toppling upstairs, the thuds echoing through the ceiling. He marched back down and began ripping everything out of the kitchen cabinets, pots clattering and dishes smashing. Then he too headed out the back door.

When he came back, I knew from the way the door smacked shut that he'd been equally unsuccessful. He stepped into the living room, his expression dark.

"Fine," he said. "You want to play games, you can come play with Michael. We'll see how much you enjoy that."

SIXTEEN

Every muscle in me balked. Here in this house we might have gotten some slight advantage. On Michael's home turf, we'd be ten times as screwed.

And leaving the house meant leaving the vaccine too. I thought I'd wedged it under the dock securely, but what if the current jostled it free? What if someone else came by and spotted it?

Our captors were still debating the details.

"Are they all going to fit in the Humvee?" Connor asked.

"They've got a car out there we can take," Marissa said. "A station wagon sounds about your speed, Connor. Who's got the key?"

She held out her free hand into the midst of our group. None of us moved. I squeezed my fingers into my palms in an effort to stop my arms from trembling.

"Look," Chay said, "it works like this. You give us the key and you can sit comfortably in the back. You don't, and we throw you in the trunk of the Humvee. Your choice."

"What if we want to stay here?" Justin said. "Michael wants to talk, he can come to us."

Chay's gaze flicked to Connor. "Go get the cuffs."

Connor ducked out the front door, and returned a moment later with a canvas bag I guessed they'd left on the porch. I could tell from the light in his eyes that he was probably grinning under his face mask. He pulled a pair of steel handcuffs out of the bag and tossed them to Chay. Before I had time to process what was happening, Chay had already snapped one side around my left wrist.

My body reacted automatically. I yanked away from him, whipping my other arm out of his reach. As he wrenched me around by the shoulder, Leo lunged at him. In that instant, I thought we might have a chance.

Then Chay slammed the butt of his shotgun into Leo's face. Leo stumbled back, clutching his nose as blood streaked over his lips and chin. Justin made a dash for us, and Connor caught him with a kick to his bad leg, ramming his elbow into Justin's back as Justin fell. Anika gave a little cry, but as she shifted forward, Marissa yanked her head back.

I swung my foot out at Chay. He dodged, twisting me around and snatching my other wrist. Before I could blink, he'd jammed on the second cuff and shoved me onto the armchair with a painful jolt, my arms locked behind my back.

"You're all coming one way or another," Chay said, sounding not even a little out of breath. "Anyone want to reconsider how?"

A stark certainty settled over me. We couldn't fight them. And if we were going, I wanted to at least be able to see *where* we were going. But I didn't want to make it even more obvious that I was the leader of the group by speaking up yet again.

I raised my head, trying to catch Anika's eye. Marissa had spun her sideways, snapping another set of cuffs onto her wrists. My gaze leapt to the others. Connor was crouched over Justin on the floor. Leo, who had raised his sleeve to his face to staunch the blood, caught my desperate glance.

"Give them the key, Anika," he said, his voice ragged with pain.

A maroon bruise was already blooming across his right cheekbone, and his nose looked slightly crooked. Rage coursed through me. If Chay had really hurt him— Then what? I was going to kick his ass like I'd completely failed to do a minute ago, when I'd still had the use of my hands? I closed my eyes, my anger deflating as quickly as it had come. We were alive, but we were pretty much helpless. The best we could hope for right now was to avoid provoking them into hurting us even more.

"I can't," Anika said, the cuffs clinking as she jiggled them. "It's in my front pocket."

Marissa pulled the key out. "You ride with Connor," Chay told her. "I think I can handle two of these kids on my own."

Connor hauled Justin to his feet. Justin staggered, trying to keep all his weight on his uninjured leg. His eyes were wild. Dangerously wild. I squirmed around so I was sitting up and tapped his good ankle with my toe.

"Hey," I said. *Stay cool*, I wanted to add. Or, more to the point, *Don't get yourself killed.* This wasn't a moment when attempted heroics would do us any good.

He looked at me, and my expression must have said it for me. His fury faded, as if he was just realizing what I'd already figured out. The only way we could help ourselves right now was to play along.

"If you two are so chummy, why don't you stick together?" Connor said. He nudged Justin forward and gestured for me to get up. I swayed to my feet without argument. Chay cuffed Leo.

"Take their stuff," he said to the others, picking up our radio. "Michael will want to see everything."

They scooped up our bags and ushered us out into the rain.

Chay motioned Leo and Anika in front of him with his shotgun, directing them down the drive. Marissa unlocked the doors of the station wagon and pushed Justin and me into the back. Justin winced as his foot hit the floor awkwardly, but he didn't make a sound.

"Michael's not going to like this," Connor commented as he took the wheel. Marissa plopped into the seat beside him, angling herself so she could keep an eye on us in the back.

"That's their problem," she said, giving us a sharkish smile.

A short distance around the bend in the driveway, we caught up with the white Humvee. Chay raised his hand in acknowledgment and drove on ahead of us. Connor followed him onto the narrow road Justin and Anika must have walked down less than half an hour ago.

I stared out the window, watching for signs, landmarks. We needed to know how to get back here. When I glanced over at Justin a little while later, he appeared to be doing the same thing.

Good, I thought as I turned back. Two sets of memories to help us find the house and the cold box again. As long as I had something to focus on, it wasn't as hard to ignore the panic screaming in the back of my head. The imagined possibilities of all the ways Michael might find to pry the information he wanted out of us. Out of me. Because I was the one it would come down to, if the others broke and admitted *I* had hidden everything.

Despite my best efforts, my stomach started to churn. How long did we have before none of this even mattered anymore? The river water had felt freezing cold, but it wouldn't stay that way as the weather warmed. The samples might be okay for a few days—a week? Could I hope for longer than that?

My arms were aching in their cramped position behind my back. The minutes ticked away from us. Eventually, the forest gave way to a scattering of small towns, one leading into the next with only brief stretches of farmland in between. Connor kept close behind the Humvee. Chay was driving fast. I wondered how Leo was holding up. What kind of complications could result from a broken nose?

We passed a series of untended fields, then another town and two farms. Chay took a left and then a right. The rain eased up, but the sky was still too gray for me to make out the sun.

It felt as though at least a couple hours had gone by before the Humvee finally slowed. It veered onto a winding road off the highway and drove on until it reached a gate in a chain-link fence. Beyond the fence, a lane curved between lawns of patchy grass to a cluster of brick and concrete buildings. A woman with a two-way radio at her hip hopped down from the booth outside the fence and talked to Chay for a moment before opening the gate for us. Connor followed the Humvee inside.

A sleek red convertible, gleaming like it'd just been waxed, roared down the lane toward us. The driver brought the car to a halt when he saw us coming, abruptly but so smoothly the tires didn't even squeal.

"Nathan," Marissa grumbled. "Show-off prick."

Connor rolled down his window to listen in. The guy in the convertible was leaning toward the Humvee, his mahogany-brown hair slicked to one side and a smirk stretched across his boyish face.

"Coming in with your tail between your legs again?" he said to Chay. "You're early—are you sure you even tried?"

The edge in Chay's voice suggested he didn't like Nathan any more than Marissa did. "More than tried," he said. "We caught the little fugitives. Bringing them to Michael right now."

Nathan's narrowed eyes cut along the side of the Humvee to the station wagon. I shifted out of view behind the driver's seat, the iciness of his gaze making my skin crawl. Suddenly I knew there were worse ways we could have been caught. Worse people we could have been caught by.

"You've got the kids," Nathan said, turning back to Chay. "How about the vaccine?"

"They're going to lead us to it, one way or another," Chay said. "What have you brought Michael lately?"

He rolled up his window before Nathan could respond, and gunned the engine. As we drove on toward the buildings, the convertible whipped into reverse, spun around, and raced past us, cutting Chay off to pull into the parking lot. We turned in after Nathan, coming to a stop amid an assortment of vehicles that included three transport trucks and, oddly, several police cars.

"What the hell is this place?" Justin said. He didn't sound as if he expected an answer, but Connor obliged him anyway.

"Regional police training center," he said. "Michael knows how to pick good digs."

"Shut up, Connor," Marissa said. His shoulders tensed, and he shut off the engine and pocketed the key in silence.

They prodded Justin and me out at gunpoint while Chay did the same with Leo and Anika. Leo sidled next to me.

They hustled us toward the nearest building, a wide two-story structure of dun concrete. Nathan slipped in ahead of us. In his slim navy suit, he looked like he should be arriving for a business meeting, not to consult with the continent's new warlord.

"We do all the work, and he runs to tell Michael first," Marissa muttered as soon as the door had closed behind him.

"Michael's not going to care who tells him," Chay said. "He's going to care that we found them while Nate was busy polishing his hubcaps."

"Would have been better if we'd gotten the vaccine too," Connor said.

"Thank you," Chay replied in a voice laced with acid. "I hadn't thought of that."

A man and a woman, both with rifles slung across their backs, looked up from their conversation when we came into the foyer. "Hey, whatcha got there, Chay?" the woman said, raising her eyebrows at us.

"First-class delivery for the boss," Chay replied. "You'll want to come see this, I think. He in the usual place?"

"As far as I know."

The two of them tagged along as we continued into a wide hall. The woman ducked into a few of the rooms that branched off from it. Beyond the doors, I glimpsed a row of tables scattered with ammunition in the process of being sorted, the glint of hanging pans in what looked like a kitchen, a line of shelves stuffed with fabric that could have been clothes or bedding. Each time the woman emerged, a couple more figures joined our group, murmuring to one another. A few of them looked to be around our age, but they all eyed us as if we were some alien species. One said something that must have been a joke, because the others laughed, with a warm sort of camaraderie that would have reassured me if I hadn't known that we *were* the joke.

An odd, salty-slick smell hung in the air, like gravy laced with machine oil. As we were marched deeper into the building, I noticed artificial light gleaming in the panels on the ceiling. They had electricity here. And they were smart enough to conserve it. Only one out of every three panels shone, dimly.

From what Anika had said, Michael couldn't have settled in here very long ago. He clearly knew how to get things organized fast. I wondered how many of these people had traveled from up north with him, and how many he'd recruited from nearby areas in just the last few weeks.

Chay pushed ahead of the group to shove open a set of double doors. "In you go," he said.

The sound of our boots hitting the wooden floor echoed through the huge room, almost as loud as the pounding of my heart. We'd come into a gymnasium. In the corner, a pair of guys was dodging each other as they sparred. Pipes crisscrossed the high ceiling around motionless fans. And at the far end of the room, beneath the blank scoreboard mounted high on the wall, stood a broad oak desk. A man sat in the leather chair behind it, bent over to study something spread on its varnished surface.

This had to be Michael.

Chay propelled us toward the desk. Justin stumbled, and Marissa grabbed his arm, dragging him onward. As we drew closer, the man in the leather chair looked up from what I could now see was a map.

If Nathan had run ahead to share the news, Michael must have known who we were, but his manner was blandly casual. It chilled me. What was a life-or-death situation seemed to be no more than a momentary distraction to him. As his dark eyes contemplated us, he rubbed his thumb over the trim beard covering his jaw, the hair there the same gray-speckled sandy-brown as the waves that curled across his forehead. Then he leaned back in his chair and folded his hands on his lap. The sports jacket he wore obscured the shape of his upper body, but I could tell from the way he held himself that any bulk on him was muscle. He moved like a lion.

I hadn't expected the desk. I hadn't expected that detached control. But after seeing the disciplined and coordinated operation he'd been orchestrating all the way across this country and ours, maybe I should have.

The appearance of civility didn't comfort me. A revolver with a wooden grip lay on the desk—off to the side, as if to remind anyone approaching that he had it, and that he didn't need to keep it in his hand to be ready to shoot you if he decided to.

It wasn't until Connor jerked me to a halt about five feet from the desk that I registered Nathan leaning against a white metal shelving unit to our right, by the gymnasium wall. His lips were twisted into a smile that looked tightly amused. The shelves behind him were lined with thick hardcover books.

He wasn't the only figure hovering nearby. Two men with handguns holstered on their belts stood behind the desk by one of the corners of the room, and on the opposite side leaned a young woman with what appeared to be a submachine gun slung over her shoulder.

Wardens continued to follow us in, a small crowd gathering around us. They gave us a wide berth, and no one strayed past the red gymnasium line that marked the floor in front of the desk. Not even Nathan. It was as if Michael's "office" had invisible walls.

Leo bumped his shoulder against mine gently. When I glanced toward him, my heart nearly stopped. Beyond him, in the midst of the spectators watching our capture play out, my gaze snagged on a familiar face.

Drew. My lips parted, but I caught the name before it slipped out, yanking my gaze away from my brother's worried eyes. I couldn't give away that I knew him. He'd helped us escape from the Wardens twice. If Michael found out, I couldn't imagine what Drew's punishment would be.

But why was he *here*? When we'd last spoken, Drew had been in Toronto. Had he spent the last ten days helping the Wardens track us down?

Michael seemed to have finished his assessment of us.

"What's this about, Chay?" he asked. His voice was low and cool.

"This is them, Michael," Chay said, stepping forward. "The bunch with the vaccine. We caught them down the river, like I figured we would."

Michael regarded him steadily. "I don't remember asking you to bring me the kids," he said.

"Well . . ." Chay's eyes flicked past us, I guessed to Marissa. Apparently getting nothing from her, he drew himself up straighter. "We haven't been able to find the vaccine yet. They say they split up the materials, each of them only knows where part of it is, and none of them will talk. I'm not sure it's even at the house where we caught them—Connor and I both searched the place and turned up nothing. I thought you'd want to handle things from here."

Michael's expression didn't change much—a twitch of his eyebrows, a slight tensing of his mouth—but I got the feeling what he would have wanted was for Chay to figure out how to find the vaccine on his own. His gaze slid over us again.

"And even in the new world, it's teenagers making most of the trouble," he said. Then, to Chay, "There were only four of them?"

"We figure the sick one must have kicked the bucket somewhere along the way," Marissa piped up. I had to suppress a bristle at her flippant mention of Gav. "No sign of the tall white guy."

Michael tapped his lips with his thumb. "If I'm not mistaken, Huan's team took down a 'tall white guy' around the place they got their tires slashed."

I couldn't control my reaction to that information. Tobias would have been alone, unarmed, in the woods, maybe already drugged up on sedatives—and the Wardens from the Jeep must have shot him like an animal. I cringed, trying to shut out the image, and when I opened my eyes, Michael was nodding at us.

"Do you really want to keep dragging this out?" he said. "You've only seen the beginning of how unpleasant I can make things for you."

"Bring it on," Justin said. "You're not getting anything out of us."

Even though Justin was the one who spoke, Michael's attention zeroed in on me. Maybe Justin had glanced toward me. Maybe we'd tipped off Michael that I was in charge somehow before then. He leaned forward with his elbows on the desk, his eyes locked with mine.

"These are your people, aren't they?" he said. "You brought them here. Anything I have to do to them, any way they suffer, it'll be on your head."

My skin felt tight. I fought to keep my voice from shaking. "It'll be on my head if I give up, so you can just kill us," I said. "We're not stupid."

"*This* is stupid," Nathan sneered, pushing himself off the makeshift bookcase. "Why are we even standing around talking about it? Get a knife, a cigarette, some pliers, and get to work. Look at them." He stalked past us. Up close, I could see lines at the corners of his eyes and mouth that indicated, despite his boyish features, he was several years older than any of us. He brushed his forefinger along Anika's jaw, flicked Leo's chin, and swept around to face Michael. "Five minutes, maybe ten, and they'll be foaming at the mouth to spill every secret they ever had."

"Thank you, Nathan," Michael said evenly. "I'll take your advice into consideration."

"What's there to consider?" Nathan said. "Let me at them right now, and I'll have the vaccine before the sun's down."

Michael didn't answer right away. His expression shifted from cool to cold and calculating. It occurred to me that unlike Nathan, Michael had been incredibly vague in his threats so far, as if even he wasn't sure what he was going to do. Maybe he'd never had to arrange a torture session before. Anyone else who'd gotten in his way, who hadn't bowed to his bribes or threats, he could have ignored or had killed. We might be the only people he'd faced who had something he couldn't get anywhere else.

But as sick as Nathan's proposal made me feel, it seemed like the obvious answer. And Nathan's words had held a challenge. If Michael rejected the suggestion without another plan, he was going to look weak, indecisive. As he stood up, still matching glares with Nathan, I braced myself to hear him agree.

SEVENTEEN

I never found out what Michael would have said right then. Because before he could speak, a childish shriek carried in from the hall outside. Every head in the gym turned, including mine, in time to see a tabby cat scamper past the open door. As it darted along the wall, a gangly girl with a pale bushy ponytail burst in after it. She skidded to a halt when she saw the crowd gathered in front of the desk, her cheeks flushing. A gray-haired man came running after her, panting for breath. The cat paused by the shelving unit to peer back at them. Its tail whipped back and forth, fur bristled.

The girl walked carefully toward it, but her eyes were fixed on Michael. She pushed a curl that had escaped from her ponytail behind her ear. "Sorry, Dad," she said, in a voice that sounded too calmly mature for her age, considering she looked only nine or ten years old. "I know you're working. I didn't mean for her to get out of the room—she's really fast."

Dad. I found myself staring at Michael, as if there was any doubt about who she meant. His lips had curved into a crooked smile.

"I'm in the middle of something right now, Samantha," he said with a gentleness that surprised me even more. "The cat won't go anywhere. Why don't you go back to your room with Nikolas, and I'll come get you when it's a better time?"

Samantha edged a little closer to the cat. "She might get out of the building," she said. "What if she runs into the parking lot? Someone will hit her."

"It's my fault," said the gray-haired man, who I assumed was Nikolas. "Camille found the cat on the grounds and brought it in for Sam. We weren't expecting it to bolt like that."

Samantha took one more step, and the cat dashed away. It squeezed under a rack of basketballs. The girl crouched down, gazing at it longingly. "I'm not going to hurt her," she said. Her voice quavered. "Why won't she let me look after her?"

For the first time since Chay and the others had burst into the house, I saw a problem I could fix.

"Get her some food," I said, before I could second-guess the impulse. "A can of tuna or salmon, if you have it. But you'll have to let her come to you if you want her to trust you."

Samantha straightened up, regarding me with large brown eyes. I felt her take in our handcuffs, the awkward way Justin was standing, Leo's bruised face. Her brow knit.

"Who are they?" she asked her dad.

"Some people it's very important I talk to," Michael said as Nikolas rested his hand on Samantha's shoulder. "Go check the storeroom—we've got to have some canned tuna. And then *wait*, until I say it's a good time. The animal must be even more scared now, with all these people around."

She bowed her head. "Okay."

When Nikolas had ushered the girl out of the room, Michael turned not toward us, but to Nathan. Mr. Slick had visibly deflated with the appearance of a child in the room. He raised his sharp chin.

"So? Are you going to deal with them?" he demanded.

"I'm going to let them cool their heels and consider their options for a while," Michael said. Nathan opened his mouth to argue, but Michael cut him off. "You know what you get with the kind of torture you're talking about? Unreliable rambling from people who can't even think, they're so desperate for you to stop. We've waited weeks to get our hands on the vaccine—I'm not going to lose it because of your impatience. We'll find out what we need to know.

"Chay, Marissa, Connor, take them to the jail room," he went on. "I want a rotating guard, two at a time, switching off every four hours. If one of them decides they want to chat, radio me immediately. Otherwise, I'll be by when I'm ready." He swept his arm toward our audience. "The rest of you, get back to work. I know you've all got something to do."

I'd hardly comprehended that our interrogation was over before Connor started tugging me away. He pushed me and Leo ahead of him, Chay stalking along beside Anika, and Marissa resuming her grip on Justin's arm. I had the urge to glance back, to find Drew again amid the crowd, but I squashed it as quickly as it rose up. I didn't know why he was here, I didn't know what he'd been doing since we last spoke, but he was the best chance we had of finding a way out. I couldn't jeopardize that.

Chay's group marched us down a flight of stairs, into a drab beige basement hallway even more dimly lit than the hall above. We turned a corner to face a row of three barred cells, each of which held nothing but a plastic wastebucket.

"The girls in one, the boys in the other," Chay said. Marissa and Connor hustled us forward.

"Should we leave the cuffs on them?" Connor asked.

"Cuff 'em to the bars," Chay said. "One at a time!"

My arms were so numb I couldn't have put up much of a fight anyway. Connor detached the cuff from my right wrist and snapped it against one of the vertical bars that formed a wall between the cells. When we were all similarly restrained, Chay locked the cell doors with a key he then shoved into his pocket.

"You and I'll take the first shift," he said to Connor. "Marissa, you grab one of your friends and be down here in four hours."

They all stepped back into the hall. Marissa's shoes tapped against the concrete floor as she strode away. But I could see the edge of Chay's shoulder through the doorway. They were giving us the illusion of privacy while staying within hearing range.

"Well, fuck," Justin said, slumping down on the rough floor. His cuffs clanged against the horizontal bar at waist height, forcing him to keep one hand raised. He propped his elbow on his knee. I rolled my shoulders, trying to work the pins and needles out of the muscles. Trying to focus on that rather than the possible horrors Michael might be planning for us right now.

Leo was cuffed to the opposite side of the same wall as me. He leaned his head against the bars, his bruised cheek tipped away. I could reach just far enough to brush my fingers over his.

"Are you okay?" I asked.

"I guess nothing's broken," he said. "I can still breathe all right. So it could be a lot worse. Hurts, though." He raised his free hand to his cheek. "I'll have to avoid smiling for a while."

"There isn't much to smile about anyway," I said.

"I don't know. I'm pretty happy to have that Nathan guy nowhere near us. And . . . with what I saw in the gym . . ."

Drew.

Leo looked up at me, and lowered his voice. "We all just have to wait for the right moment."

"Yeah," I said, even as I started to choke up. The right moment? Even with Drew on our side, this situation seemed hopeless. We were restrained and behind bars, surrounded by dozens of people who'd have gleefully watched us die if not for the information they believed we had. It wasn't just one chance we needed; it was several. All in a neat row. And we needed them before Michael broke us down.

I blinked hard, clutching at the forced calm that had kept me going so far. "Hey," Leo said. He shifted closer to me, crossing one arm over the other so he could clasp my hand. "It's not all on you. We're in this together."

A hysterical laugh bubbled up my throat. "That doesn't make me feel much better. You must wish you'd stayed back on the island."

"No," he said quietly. "I'm glad I came."

"How can you say that?"

He paused. "You know I was in a bad place when I got home. I was so caught up in feeling guilty about the crap I'd had to do to make it back. . . . But I've had a lot of time to think now; a lot of time for things to sink in." His grip on my hand tightened. "I saved a kid's life this morning. Just like that. Maybe that starts to balance out all the awful things we've been through. We have chances to do something like that, something good, all the time. You got one when you talked to Michael's daughter. We're going to get more. I'm not giving up yet."

"Right," I said, my despair receding a few inches. Drew had come through for us before. I had to believe he could again. Or that we could find a way to get ourselves out of this disaster like we had so many already. If we weren't going to believe there was a chance, we might as well give up right now.

"What do you think Michael's going to do?" Justin asked.

"I don't know," I said. Although my imagination had come up with lots of unpleasant possibilities. Across from me, Anika sank down with her back against the bars, pulling her knees up in front of her. "Do you have any idea?" I asked her.

"Only that it won't be good," she said. "Look at this place—look at how many people he's brought on board. I told you, he knows how to get what he wants." She shuddered. "And I'm with Leo about Nathan. I wish someone would shoot *him*."

"Michael kind of looked like he wanted to," Justin remarked.

"Maybe," Leo said. "But if you get rid of all the people who want to do the dirty work, you have to start doing it yourself."

I wasn't convinced that Michael planned to keep his hands clean. He'd pursued us across an entire continent to get the vaccine—there was no way he was backing down now.

I settled onto the cold concrete and tried to let go of those thoughts. To relax, as much as I could, so I'd be stronger when Michael did appear.

As time slipped past, the light in the basement didn't change. I had no concept of how long we'd been down there until footsteps tapped along the hall and our guards exchanged a few words before switching off. Four hours. My stomach pinched and gurgled, reminding me that I hadn't eaten since the sandwich that morning. Anika licked her lips.

"Hey," she called through the doorway. "I need to talk to someone, just for a second."

Marissa poked her head into the room, scowling. "What?"

Anika got to her feet, stepping as close as she could to the front of the cell, but keeping her head low, her shoulders slumped, unthreatening. "I just wondered if we could get a little water?"

"You're asking for favors now?"

"I get that we're not supposed to be comfortable," Anika said, in the same appeasing tone she'd used on me when we first met, after she'd stalked us back to our apartment in Toronto. "And obviously you're going to do your job. I just thought it might be better for Michael too if we're not completely dehydrated."

Marissa's scowl didn't budge. She pulled back into the hall without another word. I thought Anika's gambit hadn't worked, until a minute later a crackle of radio static carried through the wall. A new set of footsteps joined our two guards, and Marissa ducked back in with a small bottle of water.

"This is all you get until tomorrow," she said. "For all of you. I hope you know how to share."

She smacked the bottle down just inside the bars and marched out of the room. Anika groped, and then resorted to using her foot to slide the bottle into reach. She opened it and took a long gulp that made me feel just how parched my own mouth was. When she twisted the cap back on and passed it over to me, still mostly full, she was smiling.

"Thanks," I said with honest gratitude.

"Thank you," she said, meeting my eyes and then looking away. "I mean, for jumping in, when they started in on me at the house . . . I don't know what I would have done."

It sounded like an admission of guilt. I sipped the water, but my gut had clenched.

The only thing keeping her and the rest of us alive was staying quiet. I could only hope she'd remember that, no matter what Michael had in store.

EIGHTEEN

Just after the second guard change, the hall lights dimmed even more. Sleep seemed like a lost cause. My legs were sore against the hard concrete, and my arms still throbbed from being cuffed. My stomach was a knot of hunger. But at some point exhaustion overwhelmed my anxious thoughts and pulled me under. I woke with a start to the sound of shoes scraping over the floor just outside the cell.

Two figures had come to a halt by the cell door. I looked up blearily and snapped fully awake. One of them was Drew.

My pulse leapt, but I forced myself to gaze aimlessly at the wall where Anika was hunched in sleep, as if I didn't care what was happening outside. I watched them from the corner of my eyes. My brother was facing the Warden who'd come in with him, a stocky guy with freckles who looked to be about the same age as Drew. In the neighboring cell, Leo stirred.

"I'll be fine," Drew said, touching the other guy's arm. "Give me five minutes."

The guy frowned, but nodded before he headed out. I heard him stop beyond the doorway and murmur a few words to someone there. Drew turned toward the cell. I pulled myself to my feet in front of him. My head swam.

It had been four months since I'd last talked to Drew face-to-face.

Looking at him, I could almost believe it'd been four years. He'd turned nineteen earlier this month, but the weariness in his eyes made him look much older. He was thinner too. The sweater he wore hung loosely off his narrow shoulders, and his cheekbones jutted from his lean face. His light brown skin had turned sallow.

"You almost made it, Kaelyn," he murmured. "You were so *close.* I did everything I could."

Any doubts I might have had about his allegiances vanished. I ached to hug him through the bars. I'd gone without my real family for so long—it felt like a miracle having him there, alive if not perfectly well. But the handcuffs held me back. And if we had only five minutes, there wasn't time for a real reunion.

"Can you get us out?" I asked under my breath.

"Not right now," he said, stepping closer to the bars and keeping his voice low, "but I'll try. It's going to be complicated. I've got a lot of logistics to figure out."

"We don't have much time. The vaccine samples—I'm not sure how long they'll stay cool enough, where I left them."

He nodded. "I wondered about that."

"And Michael . . ." I trailed off, not finding the words to express how frightened I was under the stoic front I was trying to maintain.

"I have to figure things out," Drew repeated. "It's more than just getting you out of this room. You'll need a car to get away in. And something to stop anyone else from following you right away. I think I can make it happen, but it'll take some planning."

I hadn't even thought that far. If he got us a car, we could drive back to the house, pick up the vaccine, and head to Atlanta in a matter of hours.

Atlanta, where Michael probably still had Wardens posted around the CDC.

"Our radio transceiver," I said. "The people who brought us here took it. We'll need a way to reach our contact at the CDC. She was going to tell us how to get to them safely, but she didn't have the chance."

"That won't be too hard." He smiled crookedly. "I'm kind of the main radio guy around here. It's because I'd shown off my tech skills that Michael approved me coming down, when he heard you were heading this way and called for more support. I just wish I could have stopped this from happening at all."

He fell silent, and for a moment, all we could do was stare at each other. He was really here. I'd known he was alive from the first time we'd talked over the radio, but it hadn't seemed completely real until right now.

"Drew," I said, "you'll come with us, won't you? If we can make it to the CDC, we'll be protected there."

Drew hesitated, and his gaze darted toward the doorway. Toward the freckled guy who was making the other guard chuckle at some joke. My brother's expression was so familiar, and yet it took me a second to place where I'd seen it before. On Justin's face, and Tobias's, when they looked at Anika.

On Leo's, sometimes, when he looked at me.

"Oh," I said.

A flush spread across his face. "Zack's a good guy," he said. "He wouldn't be with the Wardens if Michael hadn't 'conscripted' his mom—she's a doctor. He transferred down here so we could stay together. He even lied for me to get me in here."

"Does he know what you're really talking to me about?"

"No."

"So you're picking them," I said, straining to stay quiet. "You're sticking with Michael and the Wardens instead of coming with me? You won't need them anymore, Drew. Once the CDC is making the vaccine, whatever power Michael has won't matter so much." I could almost understand why Drew had joined up with them to begin with, how it had helped him survive and keep track of what was going on, but how could he stay now?

"He's not going to give up that easily," Drew said. "What if you need my help here again? And I can't just run off on Zack, Kae. I don't know if I could have kept going this long if I hadn't had someone who makes me feel the way he does."

I couldn't argue with that. I remembered with painful clarity how one fond look from Gav had been able to buoy me through an entire horrible day.

"Okay," I said. "I—I'm glad you found someone."

The someone in question peered around the doorway, his eyebrows raised. When Drew held up a finger, Zack ducked back out.

"I've got to get going," Drew said. "But listen. Keeping you, and Dad's vaccine, safe—that's still my first priority. That's why I lied to Zack, even though I think he'd understand. That's why I'm going to do everything I can to get all of you out and on the road again. I swear."

"Thank you," I said, and then, before I knew the words were coming, "I missed you."

"Same here." He reached between the bars to quickly squeeze my hand. "Dad would be proud, you know."

He was just stepping away when brisk footsteps echoed down

the hall outside. Drew stiffened, and then strode toward the doorway. He was almost there when he had to dodge to the side to make way, as the last person I wanted to see swept into the room.

Nathan paused, slicking back a strand of his dark hair. He considered Drew and then us prisoners. I edged backward, hugging myself as if Drew had been harassing me rather than reassuring me. It was easy to pretend. Nathan's pointed gaze was already making me feel queasy.

In the other cell, Leo sat up. I wondered how much of my hushed conversation with Drew he'd heard.

"This is quite the party," Nathan said, his glib voice bouncing around the small room. Anika jerked awake, and Justin raised his head, rubbing his eyes. But Nathan turned back to Drew.

"What are *you* doing here?"

Drew shrugged. "I had an idea I thought might get them to fess up. It didn't work." He shot us a feigned glare.

"Really?" Nathan said. I shrank farther into the shadows at the back of the cell, hoping in the dim light he wouldn't notice the family resemblance between Drew and me. We were hardly twins, but side by side, it might be noticeable.

Thankfully, it appeared Nathan had other things on his mind. "Trying to impress the boss, or figured you'd grab the vaccine for yourself?" he went on. "I'm not sure which is more stupid."

"It doesn't matter," Drew said. "Like I said, it didn't work."

"I'm not surprised," Nathan said. "You're never going to *talk* anything out of them. Maybe Michael's too much of a bleeding heart to see it, but it's going to take a few cuts and jabs to open them up, so to speak."

He strode closer to the cells, his smirk so wide it made the hairs on my arms rise. I clamped my mouth shut, suspecting any protest would only encourage him.

Unfortunately, not all of us had a fully developed sense of self-preservation. "I've been shot, and that didn't break me," Justin retorted. He clambered to his feet near the cell door.

"You heard Michael," Drew said to Nathan with an edge in his tone. "No torture. Not yet, anyway. You're planning to go against his direct orders, and you call *me* stupid?"

"If I bring in the vaccine, Michael's not going to care how I got it." Nathan clapped his hands together. "I think I'll start with that one," he said, nodding to Justin. "He'll be fun. Where are the keys?"

"I have them." The guard Zack had been talking to entered the room with his burly arms crossed over his chest and Zack close behind him. The older man didn't bother to hide the disapproval in his frown. When Nathan held out a hand, he shook his head.

"I follow Michael's orders."

"And you really think they're good ones?" Nathan sneered. "We're babying these vermin. Give them one good ass-kicking, and you know they'd give it all up. Watch."

With no other warning, he sidestepped and snatched Justin's wrist through the bars. Justin jerked away, not fast enough. With a twist of his hand, Nathan flipped Justin's arm upside down and wrenched it forward, so sharply Justin gave a pained gasp. I lunged toward them before I could catch myself, as if I could do anything to help with the cell wall between us. Gripping the bars, I braced myself for the sound of bone cracking.

"Hands off!" the guard hollered. When Nathan didn't immediately let go, he hauled back and slammed his fist into the younger man's face. Nathan staggered against the cell door, releasing Justin's arm to cup his wounded cheek. Justin lurched backward, his face white and his jaw clenched tight. Then he sprang at Nathan. At the same moment, Nathan swiveled away from the cell, whipping a flip-blade knife from his suit jacket pocket.

"I could kill you," Nathan snarled at the guard. In that instant, the rabid fury in his eyes reminded me of the bear chasing Leo and the boy, and I believed he would. But as Zack and Drew flanked the guard, that fury faded into hostile disdain. Nathan flicked the blade back into its handle.

"You're going to regret doing that," he said, and then glanced at us. "And I'll be back, with Michael's permission or the keys. So give it a little thought, whether maybe you'd like to spill your secrets without the pain first."

He shot one last glower at the guard and stalked out of the room.

The guard was scowling. "Can't wait for the day he pushes too far and Michael puts a bullet in his brain, like the last dozen guys who got too full of themselves," he muttered as soon as Nathan was out of earshot.

"Don't think I protected you because I like you," he added, toward us. "If Michael gives him the okay, you're all Nate's."

He headed back into the hall, with Zack trailing behind. Drew hesitated, looking as if he wanted to say something comforting. But I was pretty sure there was nothing comforting that could be said. He bobbed his head to me, and then the four of us were alone again in the darkened prison room.

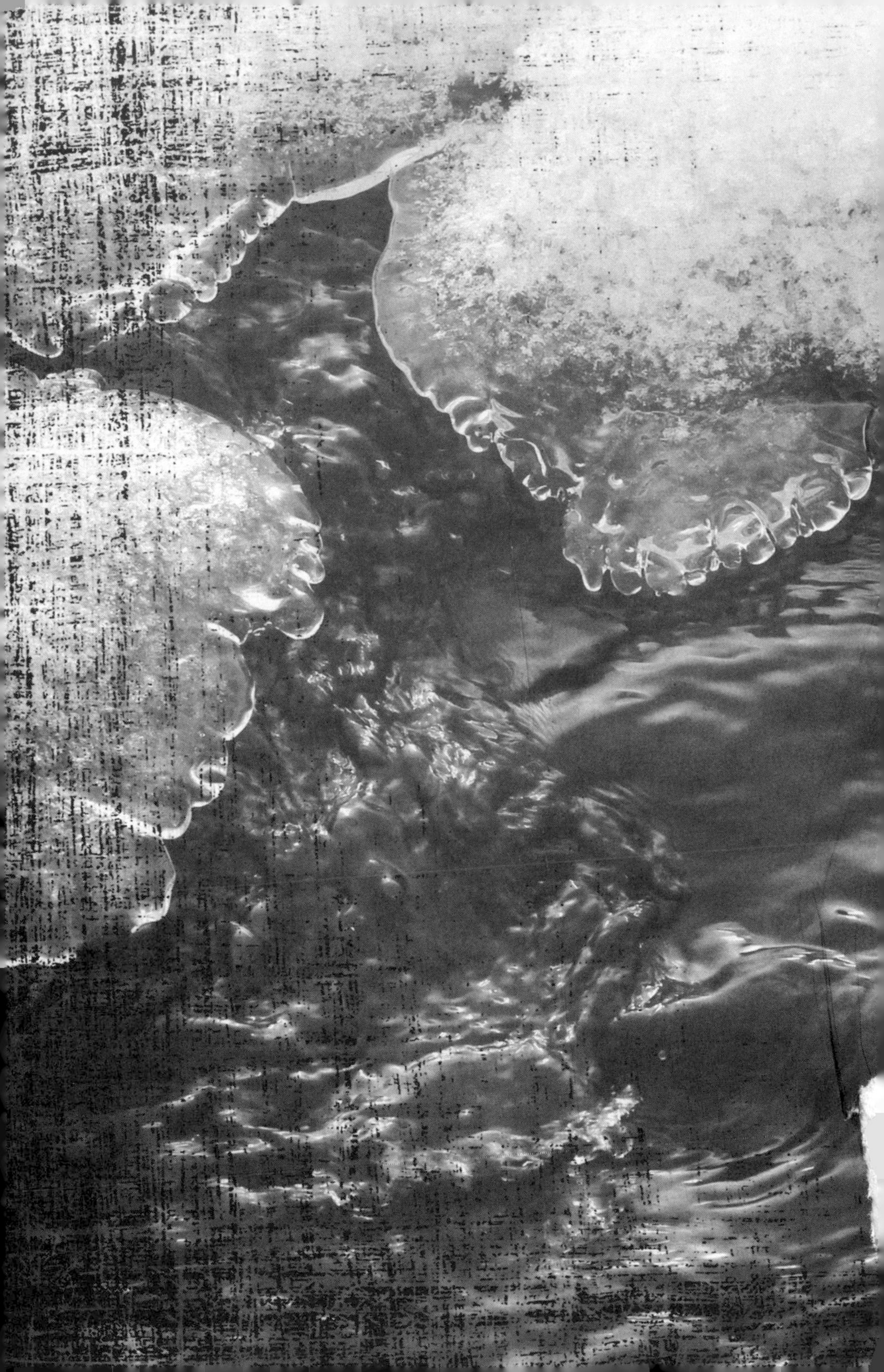

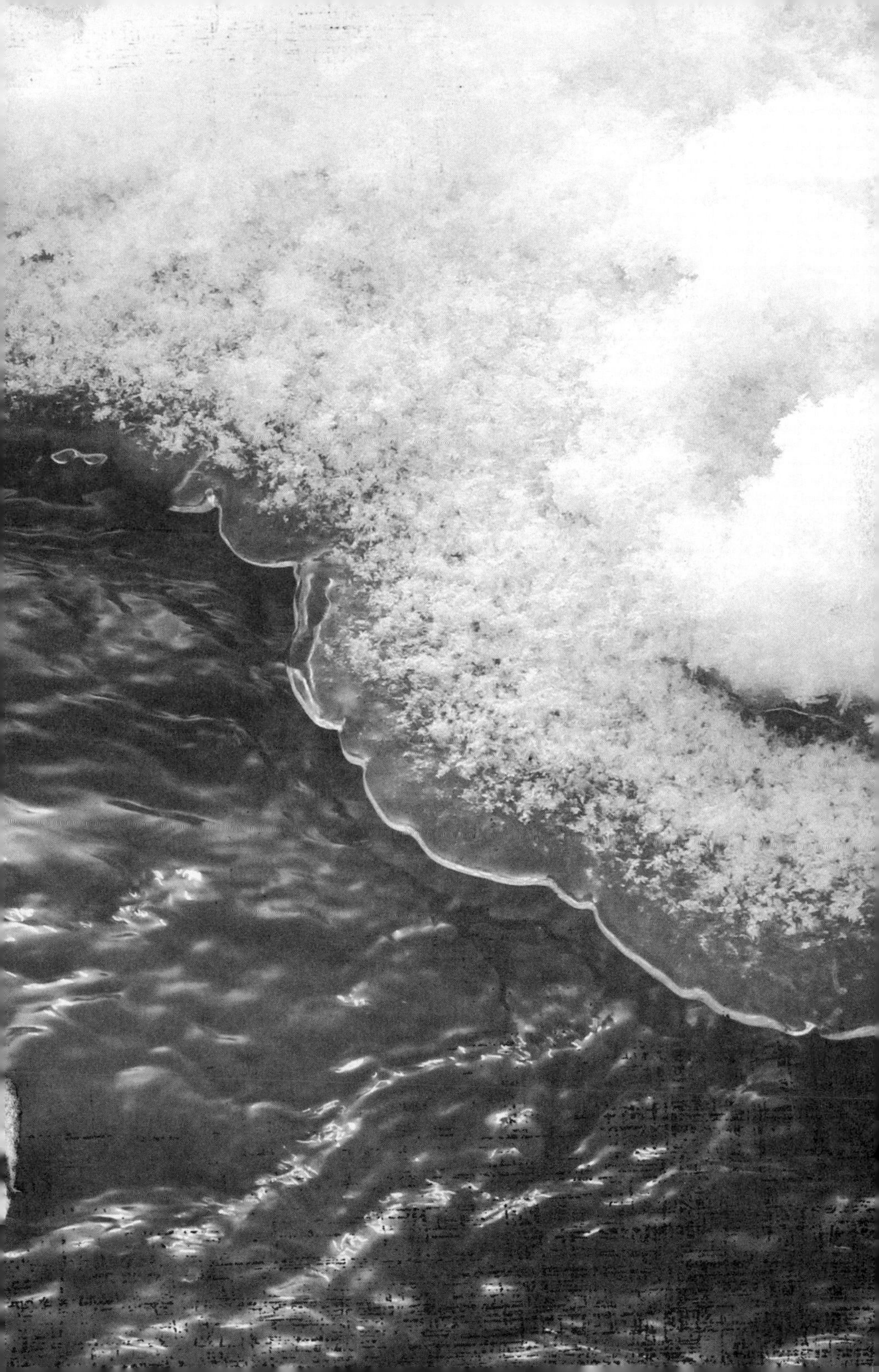

NINETEEN

Through the rest of the night, every time my mind started to drift, some sound would yank me back into consciousness, my pulse tripping with the certainty that Nathan had returned with his knife and a key. But it wasn't until a while after the hall lights had brightened for the morning that more visitors arrived.

A guy I didn't recognize came in just long enough to toss a box of crackers into my and Anika's cell. They were crumbly and stale, but I gulped down my share so quickly I hardly tasted them. It was only a couple handfuls, not nearly enough to dull my hunger.

I had just passed the last of the water over to the guys when Chay strode in with Connor lurking behind him. "You," Chay said, pointing at Leo. "You're first."

"First for what?" Justin demanded as one of our guards unlocked the cell door. Chay ignored him.

The second he stepped into the cell, Justin took a swing at him. "No!" I said. Chay caught Justin's fist easily and shoved his arm against the bars, blocking Justin's legs with one of his own at the same time. Justin winced. His wrist was mottled with purple splotches where Nathan had grabbed him yesterday.

"Cuff his hands behind his back again," Chay said to Connor, jerking his head toward Leo. "I don't want any more of this clowning around."

"Asshole," Justin muttered. Leo bowed his head as Connor escorted him out, looking as though he was biting back harsh words of his own. Chay released Justin and followed.

I stepped closer to the door, watching them prod Leo into the hall and then off to the right. There was nothing we could do. I tugged at my cuffs again, as if they might have gotten looser overnight, and the metal pinched my wrist. The pain was only a slight distraction from the fear stabbing through me.

"Sorry," Justin said to my surprise, his voice hollow. "That was dumb. Last night too." He leaned his head against the bars. "'Pick your battles,' my dad used to say. I know I probably couldn't take that guy even if I had both my hands. I just really, really want to."

"Me too," I said. "But if we get out of here, I don't think it's going to be by fighting. I don't want you ending up more injured, okay?" We needed him able to walk, able to run, if Drew could pull off whatever he was working out.

"Yeah," Justin said. He twisted his own cuffs, looking miserable. If it had driven him around the bend having to sit in the trailer those three days, I couldn't imagine how crazy this imprisonment was making him. But then he added, quietly, "I won't go at them again. Not unless it's really going to help us."

Anika was staring off toward the doorway where Leo had vanished. "What do you think they're going to do to him?" she said.

"I don't know," I said. "But whatever it is, the best thing *we* can do is say nothing."

Her gaze flickered back and forth between me and the guards standing beyond the doorway. Her voice dipped to a murmur. "That guy yesterday. You knew him."

So she'd noticed that last exchange between Drew and me. My

shoulders tensed. I'd never mentioned my brother's involvement with the Wardens to her; the last time we'd spoken to him, she hadn't joined up with us yet. Now it was dangerous information.

"You said you had—" she started, and I cut her off. I didn't know how carefully the guards were listening.

"Please don't say anything about that, either."

Anika lowered her eyes. "Okay," she said. And then, "I *hate* this."

It didn't feel like much time passed before they came back, without Leo, and dragged Justin out. Anika sat silently against the wall, but the color had drained from her face.

"They're trying to freak us out," I said. "They could just be sticking them in some other room and leaving them there, for all we know."

But it was working. I was freaked out. Maybe they weren't hurting Leo and Justin, but probably they were. How far would Michael take it, at the start?

Not too far, I pleaded inwardly. *Let them be okay.*

When Chay and Connor came for the third time and marched Anika out without a word, a new thought made my heart seem to sink down to the soles of my feet.

What if Nathan was involved in this? Had he talked Michael into going along with his brand of torture after all? I'd have thought he'd be in here smirking at us as we were led to our doom, but maybe he was enjoying keeping us in suspense.

I had to be prepared for anything. Brace myself for the worse I could imagine.

I waited for a long time alone in my cell. Much longer than it had taken Chay and Connor to come back before. After a while, I forced myself to sit down and focused on just breathing. None of the others could give away where the vaccine was hidden, because none of the others had any idea. And if they'd given away *that*, surely someone would have come for me.

So Michael was still trying to convince them to talk. Not exactly reassuring.

When Chay finally appeared in the doorway once more, I was almost relieved, for about a split second before fear choked me. He recuffed my hands behind me, and he and Connor ushered me out of the jail room.

In the hall, we turned left instead of right. I tried to glance behind me, toward the direction they'd taken the others in, but Connor swatted my head.

"Just walk," Chay growled.

They brought me up to a side door that led into a paved yard beside the main building. One of the police cars was waiting by the curb. Michael leaned against the hood, his eyes hidden behind bulky sunglasses. The panes reflected the pasty blue sky.

He straightened up as Chay prodded me over. The holster that held his revolver shifted against his hip.

"Uncuff her," he said. "I'll take the handcuffs and the key."

If Chay thought there was anything unusual about his boss's request, he didn't show it. With a click, the pressure around my wrists fell away. Michael opened the front passenger door of the car. I stared at him.

"Get in," he said tersely.

Was he taking me back to the house where Chay had caught

us? Maybe one of the others had let it slip that the vaccine had to be there. I hesitated, but at the tightening of his mouth I ducked into the car. The inside smelled faintly of cigarette smoke.

"I'll radio when I need you again," Michael told Chay. He walked around the front of the car and got in beside me. I didn't know where to look, so I studied my hands. The cuffs had rubbed my skin raw in patches around my left wrist, the one that had been restrained overnight. But the marks didn't look half as bad as the ones Nathan had left on Justin.

"Where are my friends?" I asked.

"Where I want them to be," Michael said. "Put your seat belt on."

When I had, he leaned past me to grab a bandanna from the glove compartment. "Turn your head," he said.

I stiffened. "Why?"

"Because I'm going to cover your eyes. Unless you'd rather ride in the trunk?"

I turned toward the window. He pulled the bandanna over my face and tied it behind my head. A sliver of light peeked around the edges, but otherwise I was blind.

"You uncuff me and then you blindfold me?" I said, not really expecting an answer.

"I don't need you cuffed," he said as he moved away. "When you've spent twenty-one years as a cop handling real criminals, you don't feel too scared of one teenage girl. If you make the slightest move out of line, I *will* shoot you somewhere it'll hurt very much. I figure you'd prefer to avoid that, and you'll be more comfortable without the cuffs. I'm trying to be reasonable. But I can't let you see where we're going." He paused. "Do you think I should put the cuffs back on?"

"No," I said quickly. Even if I thought I could outmaneuver him, what would that accomplish? An accident in which I could be just as hurt as him? Getting myself stranded in the middle of nowhere with a wrecked car and nothing else?

"I am trying to be reasonable," he said again, "so maybe you'll do me the favor of being reasonable too."

He started the engine, and the car rolled forward. I tried to relax into the seat, but the blackness before my eyes was unnerving. I flinched as we swayed around a curve I couldn't have seen coming.

The rest of what Michael had said sank in as he drove. He'd been a police officer? One of the people who should have been protecting us?

My hands clenched in my lap. Obviously he'd given up that commitment the second things got bad. His comment about real criminals—what did he think *he* was now? What had his associates—Nathan, and Chay, and Marissa—been in their former lives? Probably not kindergarten teachers.

I couldn't think of anything more unreasonable than what he'd ordered done in the last few months. Chasing down a group of teens, stalking them with the intent to kill. Looting all the hospitals and rounding up the surviving doctors, when it would have taken only one to maybe save Gav. Shooting Tobias, who still could have been cured, unarmed and alone in the woods. Chaining the rest of us in those cells.

Gav's body wrapped in that pale blue sheet. The bruises on Leo's cheek, Justin's arm. What part of that was *reasonable*?

By the time the car eased to a stop and Michael jerked up the parking brake, I was seething under my terror.

"You can take off the blindfold," Michael said. "We're getting out now."

I shoved the rough fabric away from my eyes. Michael had parked in a small lot outside a single-story building with walls of gray aluminum siding. There was nothing else around but patches of forest on either side.

Michael seemed to be waiting for me to move, so I stepped out onto the asphalt. He locked the doors after he'd followed and directed me toward the building.

"What are you going to do to me in there?" I asked, trying to sound defiant and not as panicked as I felt.

"I'm going to make you look at some things," Michael said. "Let's go."

I didn't know what to think of that. When he gestured again, I forced myself to start walking. At the building's door, he pulled a key ring from his pocket. Inside, a flashlight sat on a small table at the far end of a hall. Michael picked it up, and unlocked the second door there. As it swung to the side, he flicked on the flashlight.

"I've outfitted this place with three generators," he said. "Two for backup. And I've stockpiled enough fuel to keep them running for years. But I'm not wasting it on show-and-tell."

I lingered in the front hall as he stepped farther inside. Part of me wanted to bolt. But bolt to where? He'd put a bullet in my leg before I made it two yards.

Cautiously, I approached the doorway. As my gaze followed the flashlight's beam, my breath caught in my throat.

The room looked like Dad's laboratory, expanded tenfold. Glassware and microscopes and dozens of machines I didn't know the names for lined the counters. A shelving unit in the corner held rows of filtration masks and what looked like folded biohazard suits. Five industrial-sized fridges gleamed by the opposite wall.

"I started looking for a place to set this up as soon as I heard a vaccine prototype existed," Michael said. "It's been outfitted with the advice of my virologist and the two doctors with me who have experience with vaccine manufacturing. We just finished putting it in order two days ago. With this equipment, we're capable of close to mass production. We have nine other doctors here to assist, and I can call down more from up north if necessary. The materials we need that have to be refrigerated, we're holding at the training center until it's time to use them."

"Why are you showing me this?" I said, as if the sight hadn't sent a shiver of excitement through me. I could picture scientists moving around this lab, processing vial after vial of the vaccine, until we had enough that the virus could never kill another person. It felt so real. So within reach.

"I want you to know that I'm not some goon who just hijacks anything that sounds valuable," Michael said. "I want you to know that if the vaccine found its way to me, I'd have the means to make more—I might even have a better setup here than those cowards in the CDC do. It wouldn't be in bad hands."

I'd wondered if he'd planned to replicate the vaccine, but I'd never guessed he'd be this ambitious, that he could have pulled off an undertaking of this scale. And yet uneasiness was already trickling through my amazement.

"That depends on how you define 'bad,' doesn't it?" I said. "What would you do with it, after you made more? What would people have to do *for* you to get it?"

He switched off the flashlight and nudged me back toward the hall. "People don't value what they can get for free," he said. "And they don't respect the person handing it out, either."

"So being respected is more important to you than saving lives," I said. Now that the lab had vanished back into the darkness, the momentary excitement fell away in the wake of my anger.

"Keeping the vaccine out of my hands is more important to you than making sure *someone* is able to use it?" he retorted.

I swallowed. It could come to that, couldn't it? Every day we resisted was another day's chance the samples would be lost, or spoil.

"It's not just up to me," I said.

Michael studied me, expressionless, before saying, "I think it is."

I made myself frown with what I hoped looked like confusion. "What are you talking about? We all—"

"You all hid part of the puzzle. I heard the story. And I've seen the four of you, and I've talked to your friends. You don't spend as much time on the streets as I have without learning how to read people. And developing an ear for bullshit. There is no puzzle. *You* know where everything is. You could hand it over right now if you wanted to."

"Well, you're wrong," I said, ignoring the skip of my heartbeat. "I guess you don't read people as well as you think."

"You can say that all you want," he said, "but every day my people go out into this world and risk infection, and the doctors and nurses who examine them risk it too, and as long as they don't have a vaccine to protect them, some of them will get sick. And die. That's on you. Do you honestly believe the CDC is going to be a hero here, offering vaccinations to anyone who asks, with no price to pay? That the people there are so special it's worth taking the chance of losing the vaccine completely? It doesn't matter what their job titles are; they're still human beings. And there aren't any laws left except the ones we're making for ourselves."

His insinuations pricked at me, reminding me of Dr. Guzman's hints about withholding the vaccine. Yes, maybe they'd have their own criteria for giving it away. But it wasn't the same.

"They haven't tried to murder us," I said. "How many people have died, not because of the virus, but because of *you*?"

Finally, I provoked a reaction. A spark flashed in his eyes. "Believe me, I've saved enough lives too. I've done what I had to."

"And what are you going to do to us if we don't talk?" I demanded. "Let Nathan carve us up? That's how it works, isn't it? You get to sit behind your desk like you're some kind of CEO, making other people do the awful parts so you can pretend it's not on you—so you can pretend to your daughter that all you do is paperwork. You're even *worse* than the rest of them."

The words came out in a burst of rage, but the instant I finished speaking, a chill washed over me. I was practically asking him to go ahead and torture me himself.

Michael opened his mouth and then seemed to bite back whatever he'd been going to say. Something in his expression softened with what looked like sadness, or regret. His face stiffened again so quickly I almost couldn't believe I'd seen it. But I had.

"I do what I have to do," he said again.

Even if he didn't like it, I realized. He was working with the kinds of people he'd spent most of his life putting behind bars. How *could* he like that? This was his preferred strategy, right here. Showing me the lab, trying to persuade me that it was in my best interests to go along with him. He hadn't laid a hand on me.

Maybe I'd hit closer to home than I'd known. Maybe that desk and that shelf of books were his wall between him and the reality of what "his" people really did to get what he wanted.

"I can be reasonable," Michael went on, gathering himself, "but I can be unreasonable too. I need that vaccine. You *will* tell me where it is. If you haven't decided to cough up the information by tomorrow, I'll have to switch to a more painful approach. And I know much more effective techniques than Nathan does."

There was nothing but ice in his gaze now. I had no doubt he'd do it if he had to. Whatever it took.

Some distant part of me even understood. No one had to tell me how important the vaccine was. How many awful things had I done to protect it myself—and to protect *my* people? I wasn't sure any of the decisions I'd made getting here could've been much better. But maybe that was how it seemed to Michael too, no matter how much more horrible his actions were.

"We'll think about it," I said.

He walked me back to the car and put the blindfold on me. As we drove away from the lab, I stewed in my thoughts.

When Anika had first told us about Michael, I'd gotten the idea he'd been a sadistic criminal mastermind all along, but obviously that wasn't true. How did a random cop end up here? How far had he traveled between his old life and the one he was living now?

I guessed he'd have gotten to know people, working on the street. The kind of people who were used to getting out of dangerous situations. Who weren't afraid to take desperate measures to stay alive. It would be useful, if you were trying to survive, to protect your daughter, to have those kind of people on your side. He certainly knew how to keep them in line.

"I heard you came from out west," I said. "BC."

Michael hesitated so long I thought he wasn't going to bother answering. Then he said, "Vancouver."

"And there wasn't enough for you there?"

"I don't know if you've noticed," he said, "but the friendly flu doesn't care how many people you have on your side, how much food you stockpile, how many vehicles you can keep running. I can't stop until I can stop *it*."

Which was why he'd been stockpiling doctors and medical equipment too. Why he'd headed south to stake out the CDC, Drew had said, before he'd heard about our vaccine.

"And then?" I asked. "What would you do, if you got the vaccine, after everyone who could pay your price had taken it?"

"Keep sitting behind my desk, I'd imagine," he said with an edge of sarcasm.

I tried to picture it: a world where Michael controlled the vaccine. Maybe there wouldn't be much else he could do but keep on this way. He'd still need food and shelter—and protection. Nathan couldn't be the only one hungry to take his place.

And so he'd keep shaping this world into one where strength through violence ruled and your only choices were to be the victim or the perpetrator. A world I suspected he didn't even like.

The car rolled to a stop sooner than I expected. But when I raised the blindfold, we were back at the training center. As we drove past the gate, Samantha looked up from where she was crouched on the lawn by the fence. Nikolas stood beside her, and the cat she'd been chasing yesterday was prowling through the grass at the end of a leash. Samantha must have caught a glimpse of me through the car window, because she waved eagerly and pointed to the cat. I guessed the tuna trick had worked.

"It's for her too, you know," Michael said as he turned into the parking lot. "Not just people like Nathan and Chay. She could be exposed by accident any day. You could be condemning her along with the rest of us."

I didn't know what to say to that.

He got out of the car. Marissa and a guy I hadn't seen before were striding from the main building toward us.

"I can see you're a smart young woman," Michael said to me. "I'm hoping you'll make a smart decision."

Then Marissa was snapping the cuffs around my wrists, and Michael stalked off toward the building without looking back.

TWENTY

When Marissa hustled me back to the jail cells, Leo, Justin, and Anika were already there, in approximately the same spots as before.

"Are you okay?" I asked as soon as Marissa had ambled off, keeping my voice low. "What did they do to you?"

"Just talked," Leo said quietly. "Brought us into a room with Michael, he asked a bunch of questions, and then they stuck us in a different room to wait." He paused. "Mostly he asked about you."

"We didn't tell him anything," Justin jumped in. He glanced toward the doorway, and dropped into a whisper. "I even managed not to tell him to go screw himself. And that was hard."

"He's so creepy," Anika murmured with a shudder. "The way he just sits there with that look on his face like he doesn't care whether you even answer him or not. Like whatever you say, he'll just know what's really true. Now I get why everyone in Toronto talked like he might be listening over their shoulder."

Michael couldn't read minds, but he'd known enough. I remembered what he'd said at the lab—*There is no puzzle.* You *know where everything is*—and had to suppress a shudder of my own.

"What happened to you, Kae?" Leo asked. "It looked like they were giving us all the same treatment, one by one, but when they finished with Anika, they brought the three of us back here together, and you were gone. For a while."

"He drove me to a lab he's set up," I said, sitting on the floor. "To try to convince me that we should hand over the vaccine." I didn't want to mention why he'd focused on me. If he was sure I had all the information he needed, that meant the three of them would be expendable in his eyes, didn't it? Was that how he'd try to get to me: by hurting them, punishing my silence with their pain? I pulled my knees up to my chest, hugging them with my free arm.

"Did he say anything about what he's going to do next?" Anika said.

"Only that he'd come back tomorrow," I said. "I don't know what'll happen then."

He could change his mind and show up earlier, but I didn't think he would. I got the feeling he made a point of keeping his word.

We lapsed into an uneasy silence. The guards outside changed, and then changed again. Anika called to them, cajoling them for more water, but they didn't even acknowledge her. She slumped back against the wall.

Michael had told them to ignore us, I guessed. To remind us that he had complete control over us now, down to whether we ate or drank. The morning's stale cracker breakfast felt like it'd been years ago. My thoughts kept creeping to the glimpse of the kitchen I'd gotten upstairs, the salty smell in the air. The gnawing in my stomach expanded into a steady ache. My mouth felt grittier every time I swallowed.

We each drifted off for moments here and there, exhausted after the tense and uncomfortable night. Once, I woke from hazy sleep at the sound of footsteps, and my mind immediately leapt to, *Drew!* But it was only another pair of guards taking over.

The lights dimmed. Night had fallen. Our time was slipping away.

I could hardly expect Drew to come again so soon. He might *never* find a way to get us out. How could we possibly get the entire distance from these cells to the front gate without someone catching us?

If it really was impossible, what was left for us to do? Stay here, holding out, until . . . what?

Maybe Michael had been smart to let me stew this over.

"I think we should talk about our options," I said quietly.

"What options?" Justin asked, and covered a yawn. Anika shifted around to face me.

"The options we have to choose between if we're stuck here," I said. "If we don't get a chance to escape."

On the other side of the barred wall, Leo lowered his head. "You're not sure how long the vaccine will last, where it's hidden," he said. His expression was solemn. He knew where I was going with this.

"I think a few days should be all right," I said. "But more than that . . . I just don't know."

"So we could go through hell here to save a vaccine that'll be ruined anyway," Anika said.

"So what?" Justin said. "There's no way we're giving it to these pricks. Right?"

"That's what we have to figure out," I said. "Wouldn't it be better for them to have it than for *no one* to have it?" Especially if the lives of the three people staring at me could be on the line too. Expendable meant Michael could go as far as killing them to make me talk. I drew in a breath. "Their lab looks good. I think they could replicate the vaccine pretty quickly."

To my surprise, it was Anika who protested first. "You know what they'd do with it? Hold it over the heads of everyone who didn't want to join up with them, or wasn't smart or strong enough for them to use. Like they've been doing with everything else they have. They're bad enough already!"

"Would you still say that if giving it to them was the only way you'd get vaccinated?" I asked.

"I turned it down before, didn't I?" she said. "I never let anyone push me around before the friendly flu came along, and I was a lot happier then."

"Yeah!" Justin said, and quickly lowered his voice again. "If we give up, they'll just keep running things; nothing's ever going to get better. Gav and Tobias *died* so we could get here. We can't let them down. Or everyone else who's not with the Wardens."

My throat tightened, but I managed to say, "I think we'd be letting them down more if we let the vaccine get ruined completely."

"Kaelyn's right," Leo said. "It's not that simple. I don't want to live in a world where the Wardens decide who gets the vaccine and who doesn't. But I don't want to live in a world where the virus rules, either."

Of course, even if we did manage to escape and bring the vaccine to the CDC, it'd just be a different set of people deciding for us. I trusted Dr. Guzman far more than I trusted Michael, but if she had the vaccine, that might mean condemning Samantha, and Drew, and Zack, and anyone else who'd gotten caught up in Michael's schemes out of necessity rather than greed and cruelty.

It wasn't simple at all.

"I don't want to do it," I said. "I don't want to give up. I don't want the Wardens having that power. But I also don't want to be the person who stops the rest of the world from getting that vaccine, you know?" I paused, rubbing at my bleary eyes. "But we don't have to make up our minds now."

"Right," Justin said. "You said we've got at least a couple more days. I'm ready. Let Michael bring it on."

Michael would. That was what I was afraid of.

Leo shifted along the wall and reached between the bars to squeeze my shoulder. I leaned into his touch, taking a small comfort in the warmth of his fingers. How was I supposed to choose when the only options I could see both felt wrong?

Leo turned his hand to cup the side of my face, his thumb skimming my cheek. "We've made it through a lot," he murmured. "We'll make it through this too."

I twined my fingers around his. In that moment, I didn't care what this gesture meant or what the exact nature of my feelings was. I just ached to feel his arms around me. This was as close as I could get.

"Thank you," I whispered.

We sat like that for a long time. I dozed with his breath grazing my skin, until a nightmare whirling with knives and blood and a face that shifted back and forth between Nathan's and Michael's jerked me awake, my nerves jangling. The jitters stayed long after the room around me had come back into focus. Letting go of Leo's hand, I stood up and stretched my legs.

"Come on," Anika called toward the doorway, with a hoarseness I didn't think she was putting on. "Just a little water. Please?"

I couldn't see the guards, but the low muttering of their voices told me they were still there. No one responded to her plea. I sat back down.

My nerves were just starting to steady when a new set of footsteps echoed down the hall.

"Time to switch off," the newcomer said. My head jerked up at the voice. It was Drew.

"Where's your partner?" one of the guards asked.

"He said he'd be down as soon as he's grabbed something from the dorms," Drew said. "We can wait if you want. But I'm pretty sure I can handle standing here by myself for a bit."

"Well, let's give him a minute."

I held myself completely still, straining to hear over the thumping of my heart. The seconds ticked by, and the guard who'd spoken sighed.

"To hell with it. This has got to be about the most boring job around—you'll survive on your own." There was a clink as she handed off the keys. "Just make sure you call for someone if the guy who was supposed to join you doesn't turn up soon. You've got a two-way, right?"

"Of course," Drew said.

The other guards walked off. The door at the end of the hall squeaked open and shut. I got up again, stepping closer to the front of the cell, and the others roused at my reaction. Drew waited the space of two of my breaths, and then ducked into the room.

"Okay," he said, fumbling with the keys. "We don't have a lot of time."

"What are we doing?" I asked as he opened the cell and reached to unlock our handcuffs. "Where do we go from here?"

“Up the stairs to the left, out the door, and around this building to the right until you reach the parking lot,” Drew said. “As quickly and quietly as you can. I think I’ll be able to distract the people who’ll be watching the doors, but if anyone spots you, there’ll be trouble. I managed to pick up your radio transceiver, and a little food—stuck them in the fastest car we’ve got.”

He pressed a car key on a steel fob into my palm after releasing my wrist. “Nathan’s going to be pretty pissed.”

The image of the shiny red convertible popped into my head. It wasn’t the most discrete of vehicles, but that didn’t matter at night, and it *did* have quite the engine on it.

“Sweet!” Justin said. “That’ll teach him to mess with us.”

I slipped the key into my pocket. “How did you get it?”

“The cars are supposed to be shared,” Drew said as he freed Anika and then moved to the guys’ cell. “So Michael makes people leave the keys on a rack in the foyer. Nathan put word around that if anyone touched ‘his’ car he’d slice and dice them, of course, but it’s not as if you’re going to let anyone catch you.” The corner of his mouth curled with the start of a smile.

“So we have to just hope we can outdrive the others?” Leo said.

Drew shook his head. “I poured water into the gas tanks of the other cars here. That should make the engines stall—right away, or a little ways down the road. You just have to keep ahead of them long enough for it to kick in.”

My skin went cold. “They’re going to know you helped us, aren’t they? Forget Nathan—what will Michael do to you when he finds out? You have to come with us.”

“It’ll be fine,” Drew said. “I think I’ve made it look as if it’s all someone else’s fault. Except this.” He tapped the door of the cell. "So I'll need a little help. They have to believe I just made a mistake."

He stepped back, having released the guys, and spread his arms wide. "Take a swing at me, Leo."

"What?" Leo said, his eyes widening.

"They've got to think I put up a fight," Drew said. "Or else it'll be obvious I was in on it. Just a couple good punches should do it. I'll live."

When Leo hesitated, Justin pushed in front of him. "I'll do it," he said brusquely. "You want it in the face, where they'll see it?"

Drew nodded, his body tensing in anticipation of the blows. I looked away as Justin let his fist fly, cringing at the *smack* of knuckles against skin. Drew swayed to the side, grabbing a bar for balance.

"Good," he said, a little roughly. "One more. How about here?" He pointed to his jaw.

After, he sank down on the floor and spat a little blood onto the concrete beside him. "Okay," he said. "Get going. I'm going to buy you your window of opportunity now."

"Drew . . ." I said. He waved me off when I stepped toward him. *"Go."*

If it had been just my life I was risking, I might have taken a second to hug him. But it was his and the others' too. So I hurried with Leo, Justin, and Anika through the doorway and down the hall. As we left Drew behind, I heard the crackle of static as he faked a deep voice into his two-way.

"I think I saw someone running by the south fence. There they are! Can I get some backup? They're heading east now. . . ."

We fled up the stairs and paused outside the first-floor hallway, but the lights there were dim, and I saw no one patrolling. We darted to the nearest exit. If Drew's ploy hadn't worked, if there were Wardens standing right outside, I wasn't sure we could outrun them. Justin was still limping.

But it appeared everything was going to plan. We slipped out into the night. Somewhere beyond the neighboring building, flashlights flickered and someone shouted. I didn't stop to listen. We hustled around the corner toward the parking lot. Justin started to drift behind, his bad leg wobbling, and Anika fell back beside him. I slowed enough so that we didn't lose them completely.

A single pale light shone on one of the fence posts around the lot. I caught the crimson gleam of Nathan's convertible, top up, partway down the second row. Motioning to the others, I veered toward it.

"Hey!" a voice bellowed, so close my stomach flipped over. "Stop right there—one more step and you're dead!"

As if we wouldn't be dead if we stayed. I bolted forward, and the others followed. Our boots thudded across the pavement, but there wasn't any point in trying to be quiet now. The convertible was just a few car-lengths away.

I dug out the car key with shaky fingers. We could still make it.

A shot crackled through the air. Anika let out a startled gasp. I glanced back to where she was running next to Justin, who was staggering now as he tried to keep up, his face contorted. Anika had glanced back too. I saw her flinch, and then she lunged at Justin.

"No!" The word broke from my throat before I had a chance to process what was happening. The idea flashed through my mind that she was betraying us after all, using Justin to save herself.

Then, as she hit him and shoved him to the side, the gun thundered again.

Justin stumbled between two cars. Anika lurched and tumbled forward. Her hands didn't come up to break her fall. Her head hit the pavement with a sickening crack, the impact rippling through her body. And then she was still.

TWENTY-ONE

"Anika!" Justin yelled. A dark blotch was spreading across the back of her sweater. Her head had twisted to the side, and her eyes stared blindly. She didn't so much as twitch. A little cry filled my throat, but in the same moment I saw the figures rushing at us from the edge of the parking lot. Justin threw himself at Anika, and I threw myself at him.

Leo met me there, the two of us grabbing Justin by the elbows. An iron taste was seeping through my mouth where I'd bitten my lip, and a sharp ache filled my chest. But the rising shouts drowned out everything else.

Anika was dead. And the rest of us would be too, if we didn't get out of here *now*.

Justin stumbled with us the last few feet to the convertible. I yanked open the driver's-side door while Leo leapt for the back. The key jarred against the ignition and then slid in. I took a quick glance around to make sure Leo and Justin were inside, and then I pressed my foot to the gas.

Nathan obviously knew how to pick a car. The engine responded instantly. The convertible roared forward, swerving around the other cars as I jerked the steering wheel. We had only a twenty-foot run down the drive to the locked gate.

A Warden stood on the other side of the gate, raising a gun. Drew hadn't said anything about this part of our escape, but I couldn't stop. So I jammed my foot down harder. The engine thrummed, and the car ripped over the pavement toward that narrow chain-link square.

I tensed, fighting the urge to close my eyes, as we barreled straight into the gate. The convertible's hood crashed into the metal links, and the gate's hinges wrenched open with a shriek. The guard on the other side dove out of the way, his shot going wild. The gate clattered against the concrete curb, and we were out, tearing down the road.

The lights of the training center fell away behind us. I became aware of the raspy hitching of my breath, the sweat that was now cooling on my arms and neck. I wiped my damp bangs away from my face.

In the back, Justin was staring out the window, moisture glinting in his eyes. Leo leaned against the front passenger seat.

"You know the way back to the house?" he asked softly.

"I think so." I tried to dredge up my memories of the drive here in the back of the station wagon, and my thoughts blurred together. I was hungry and dehydrated and sleep deprived, running mostly on adrenaline. And a cool haze of shock was creeping over me. The image of Anika hitting the ground flitted through my mind. I clenched my jaw against a sudden rush of nausea.

She'd been one of us, in the end. A real part of our makeshift family. And I hadn't protected her any better than I had Gav or Tobias.

I'd done even worse by her. Right up until the last moment, I hadn't totally trusted her not to give us up somehow, whether strategically or out of weakness. And then she'd sacrificed herself for us, for Justin.

Maybe she'd seen that niggling uncertainty in me. Maybe I'd made her feel she hadn't done enough after all, like she still had to prove her loyalty. Would she have been so quick to throw herself in front of a bullet if she'd really felt accepted in our group?

I couldn't ask her now. I'd been so incredibly wrong, and there was no way I could ever tell her that. All I'd done for her was leave her body to the Wardens—the people she hated the most.

"I'm sorry, Justin," I said, my voice cracking.

He turned and swiped at his eyes. He looked as sick as I felt. My own eyes welled up.

"Why did she *do* that?" he said. "I never asked her to. . . ."

"She was protecting you," I said. "You didn't have to ask her. No one made her. She just wanted to."

He exhaled. "You don't think—could she still be—"

I remembered the limpness of her body as she'd fallen, the blood on her back, her unblinking eyes. A fresh wave of nausea rolled through me. "No," I said.

"Fuck," he said. "God fucking damn it." He hit out at the car door, his elbow and fist smacking the window, and then kicked it for good measure. I stayed silent, letting him have his rage. It was all I could give him.

The road we were following curved into a town, and my gaze caught on the welcome sign. I recognized that name. Connor had turned here. There'd been an ice-cream shop by a corner. I spotted the posters in the store window just in time, and took a right. I thought we'd kept on this new road for a while. Maybe a whole hour? But I was driving faster than Connor had been.

There'd been no signs of pursuit behind us. I hoped that meant Drew's trick with the water had worked, and not just that the Wardens were taking some other route to cut us off.

The headlights lit the unmowed grass along the shoulder an eerie yellow gray. We sped past the twisting branches of a patch of forest and the vacant buildings along the main street of another small town. This one's name didn't jog my memory. I blinked hard and stretched my arms, one and then the other. The haze in my mind receded only a little.

"Justin," I said, and hesitated. "I don't want to ask this, but—I'm not sure I'm going to recognize all the landmarks on the way. Do you think you could climb up front and tell me if I miss anything you remember?"

"Yeah," he said after a moment. "I can do that."

He clambered between the seats and slumped into the one beside me. Leo fumbled with something in the back.

"There's water," he said, passing a bottle forward. "And some snack bars. We'll do better if we're not starving."

I choked down one of the bars and a half a bottle of water, passing it back and forth with Justin. He pointed to a sign we whizzed past, that advertised a cottage resort fifty miles ahead. "We take a left when we get to that place."

"Thanks," I said, and he gave me a stiff nod.

None of us spoke again until the turn, and afterward only to confirm the next few adjustments of our course. I could feel the empty space in the car that should have been Anika's weighing on all our minds. There were practicalities we maybe should have been discussing, but it seemed, at least to me, that we owed her that period of silence.

When we finally reached the long driveway that curved through the trees toward the house by the river, my pulse kicked up a notch. I slowed, watching the high beams light trunks and bushes and the empty lane ahead of us. No other vehicles were parked there, or in the yard around the house. Still, I didn't want to spend a second longer here than we had to. I eased the car to a stop, jumped out, and ran down to the river.

For a moment, in the darkness, I thought the cold box had vanished. A broken sob burst from my lips just before my groping hand touched the smooth plastic surface of the lid beneath the dock.

The water was just as icy as before. By the time I'd hauled the cold box onto the bank, I was shivering and the skin on my arm had numbed. I hoped that meant the last batch of snow I'd packed in there had stayed frozen well enough to last the rest of the way to Atlanta.

When I got back to the car, Leo was sitting in the driver's seat. "I figured you could use a break," he said. Justin had moved to the back again, so I got in beside Leo, setting the cold box by my feet.

"What do we do now?" Justin said.

"We get to Atlanta as fast as we can," I said. "And then we call up Dr. Guzman and find out how to get to the CDC in one piece."

Leo shut off the high beams as we turned the car back down the driveway. In the thin glow of the regular headlights, the world became a ghostly landscape of muted shapes and shadows.

"You know which way to go?" I asked.

"Toward Clermont, and then onto the 129 south. Keep an eye out for signs, okay?"

"Go right when you get to the end of the driveway," Justin put in. "That's the way we went when we saw the sign for Clermont."

He tipped his head against the window. Remembering walking this way with Anika, I guessed. That was the last time he'd had with her before the Wardens came. I wanted to say something hopeful, but I couldn't find any words that would make what had happened the slightest bit better. And who was I to talk, after the way I'd misjudged her?

A short distance down the road, we turned onto a highway. Leo started to speed up, straddling the middle lanes. Several minutes later, we merged onto a freeway heading south.

We drove around a broken-down Greyhound bus, and later a stalled van. I scanned the darkness whenever we passed an exit, watching for lights. The cars in the training center's parking lot might have been temporarily useless, but Michael had other allies in Georgia, people he could have sent our way by radio. We were hardly in the clear yet.

We were only a couple miles from the city limits when something glinted up ahead. "Stop!" I whispered, as if anyone would be able to hear us from that far away. Leo pressed the brake, bringing us to a quick but quiet halt. I stared into the blackness, and then rolled down the window. No sound reached my ears. But a moment later, I saw the glimmer of lights again. Someone was on the freeway down there.

"Time to move onto the smaller roads?" Leo suggested.

"Looks like it," I said.

He turned the car around and drove back to the last exit we'd passed, which wound down into a suburban neighborhood. The houses were set so far back on their treed lawns that I could barely make out their silhouettes in the dark. The roar of the convertible's engine echoed in my ears. The night around us was too quiet for comfort.

"If they're just sitting and waiting, they'll still be able to hear us when we get close to where they're staked out," I said. "And the farther we get into the city, the more people Michael might have in position. We should ditch the car. I think it'll only be a few more miles to the CDC buildings. If you're okay to walk?" I glanced back at Justin.

"I'll manage," he said shortly.

Leo drove the car up one of the long driveways, pulling it onto the lawn behind a row of spruces that would hide it from the road. For the first time, we opened the trunk. Tobias's transceiver sat there, still in its plastic case. My heart leapt with gratitude for Drew. He'd also left a bag with more of the snack bars and some juice boxes, and a couple of the two-way radios the Wardens used.

I wished I'd thought to ask him for some sort of map. But I couldn't feel disappointed looking at how much he'd managed to accomplish right under Michael's nose.

"Hold on," Leo said as I turned away from the car. He squirmed under it on his back and fiddled with something underneath. A thin stream of liquid pattered onto the grass.

"Emptying the oil," Leo explained as he scrambled back out. "If the Wardens find the car, they won't be able to drive it far."

"I'd like to smash the whole thing," Justin muttered. He settled for smacking one of the doors with his knee. Then we left the car behind, stalking across the vast lawns.

The trees and shrubs provided almost as much shelter as if we'd been wandering through a forest. I sent a silent thank-you to the

Atlanta suburbanites for their fondness for greenery. The world around us was still except for the murmur of our feet over the grass and the rustling of leaves overhead. Justin found a narrow branch that had fallen by the base of an oak and turned it into a cane, adding a soft *thump* to the sound of our passing.

A thick-leafed vine crawled across the faces of most of the houses, looking like dark splotches of mold in the moonlight. The air was crisp, the breeze chilly. I started to hunch inside my sweater, missing my coat.

We'd made it four blocks from the car when a breathless shout broke the quiet. "Is anyone there? Is anyone—is anyone out there? Hellooooo!"

I jumped, and Leo grasped my arm. A string of harsh coughs carried from wherever the shouter was, somewhere behind us. My fingers tightened around the handle of the cold box. One more person the vaccine was coming too late to save.

We walked even more carefully after that. An engine rumbled by somewhere to our left, and we went right for several blocks before continuing south. Justin limped along at a steady pace, but I could tell from the wobble in his steps that he was getting tired. And we were losing the cover of night. A faint glow tinged the sky to the east.

It was time we figured out exactly where we were going.

I was studying the homes on our side of the street when a low growl reverberated through a hedge up ahead. I edged across the lawn and peeked over.

Several thin, furry bodies were pacing around the lawn on the other side. Dogs. As my vision sharpened in the dim light, I saw that most of them were gathered together in a pack, facing a lone husky that stood over a lumpy shape on the grass. It took me another second to recognize the thing they were fighting over. My gaze caught the bend of a knee, the flesh torn down to the bone. I grimaced, swallowing down the bile rising the back of my mouth.

It looked as if the husky had found the body first, and the other five dogs had come across it and wanted dibs. As I watched, a ragged mutt and an Irish wolfhound charged right up to the corpse. The husky's growl deepened. It snapped at them, even though it should have known it was outnumbered. Its coat was matted and its body gaunt. When had it last found such an easy "meal"?

The dogs circled around, and then all five of them rushed at the husky. One sank its teeth into the husky's shoulder. The husky rolled out of reach, blood spurting over its pale fur, before springing back at them. I looked away as the wolfhound grabbed it by the throat. The husky let out a pained squeal, and then there was the sticky, liquid sound of tearing flesh. Paws drummed the grass as the entire pack fell on its victim.

I turned, my lips clamped tight. "I think we'd better backtrack," I said. Leo nodded, looking equally sickened.

As we hurried back the way we'd come and took a left at the first intersection, the images of the fight—what I'd seen, what I could easily imagine from what I'd heard—echoed through my head. The pallor of dead limbs, the angry pink of ripped flesh. Fur-clotted blood splashed across the grass. As red as the blood that had streaked Leo's face after Chay had hit him, as Anika's blood on her back, on the pavement of the Wardens' parking lot.

In that moment, I couldn't see the difference. That was what we'd become: packs of dogs fighting over a world that was already mostly dead. Maybe Michael had forced us to his level, or maybe we could have found a way to rise above it—it didn't matter now. We'd stolen and threatened and killed, and I hated it. I hated so many things of the things I'd done these last few weeks.

What was the point in being human, in having brains that could develop vaccines and organize people across a continent, if all we did was behave like animals? This world, where all that mattered was being in the strongest, biggest pack—it wasn't a world I wanted to save.

But that was all we had, wasn't it?

My legs quivered, and I stopped. Leo and Justin stopped beside me. I closed my eyes, trying to picture us walking through the CDC's gates and everything turning right again. But the scene felt like something from a movie, overbright and silicon hollow.

I knew what happened today wouldn't stop Michael from wanting the vaccine. Once the CDC had it, he'd just send his Wardens after them in even greater force. How were the doctors going to get the vaccine to anyone who needed it, with Michael's people waiting to steal it the moment they left their buildings? It would just keep happening, this spiral of violence and fear, on and on.

"Are you okay?" Leo asked, pulling me back to the present. I looked into his worried eyes, lit now by the rising dawn. We had to keep moving.

"Yeah," I mumbled, and made myself start walking. As we meandered past another row of ruined houses, I tried to remember when I'd last felt truly hopeful.

In that town near the river, after we'd chased off the bear. We'd helped those people, and they'd helped us. For a few fleeting moments, we'd been able to enjoy the company of strangers. That had been my proof. We didn't always have to be fighting, even now.

That was the world I wanted, one where we battled the threats that faced us together. Why wouldn't Michael prefer a world like that over the one he was creating—for his daughter, if no one else?

Maybe he would. Maybe he just didn't see how he could get it.

If that was the world I wanted, maybe *I* had to find a way to make it happen.

I almost laughed at the thought, it seemed so ridiculous. Me? Then the weight of the cold box shifted in my hand, and I glanced down at it, and suddenly my heart was pounding.

I was the person who had the vaccine right now—the one vaccine in existence as far as we knew. If that wasn't power, what was?

A nebulous sense of purpose I couldn't quite wrap my mind around rose up inside me. We had to talk to Dr. Guzman. If I could talk to her, if I knew exactly what she and the rest of the scientists at the CDC were planning, then I could decide . . . whatever exactly it was I needed to decide.

At the next intersection, I checked the street signs and started trying the doors of the houses as we headed down the block. The third hung ajar, the doorknob broken. Our quick sweep turned up no sign that anyone had come through recently. From the half-empty closets and the bare tabletops, I guessed the family who'd lived here had grabbed their most valued belongings and run for it.

We set the transceiver on the dining room table. A brief worry flitted through my head, that the Wardens might have stumbled on the CDC's frequency when we'd broadcasted before. But if Drew was the main radio guy, he'd have known if they'd been listening to us, and he'd have told me. We'd just have to be quick, in case they were scanning the airwaves now.

I switched the radio on and lifted the mic. Every nerve in my body hummed. I didn't know what I was going to say. Well, I'd have to figure that out as I went.

"Hello?" I said. "I'm attempting to contact Dr. Guzman or anyone else at the CDC. If anyone from the CDC can hear this, please respond."

We waited, poised around the table. The static fizzed. I repeated the message. A minute passed, and not a single clear sound emerged from the speaker. The nervous anticipation seeped out of me. I set down the mic.

"No one's there."

TWENTY-TWO

"It's really early in the morning," Leo said. "We don't know how many people are still at the CDC—they probably have to take breaks from monitoring the radio."

I looked outside, at the pinkish light spreading across the sky, and squashed down the feeling of desperation that had started to claw up through my chest.

"Right," I said. "We'll try again in an hour."

Justin pushed his chair back and limped into the kitchen, where he pawed through the cupboards. Then he stepped back into the dining room, his arms folded in front of him.

"I can't just sit around here waiting," he said. "I'll go check the other houses, see if I can find a map of the city."

He'd only just finished speaking when he swayed on his feet and had to snatch at the door frame to catch his balance.

"Justin," I said, "you need to rest. You've put enough strain on your leg already. And we don't know how hard it's going to be just getting from here to the CDC."

"I have to *do* something," he said, his voice ragged. "I've been so useless, and I'm not—I can't—"

He trailed off, looking as if he'd lost the thread of what he wanted to say. Looking just plain lost.

"You are *not* useless," I said. "You've done ten times more than most people could have with both their legs working properly. And I *need* you to be okay so you can keep being useful when we head out. I'm not letting you take some stupid risk when we're lucky any of us are here at all."

He ducked his head. "It wasn't luck. It was Anika. I should have been the one looking after her, and she— It should have been me."

He swayed again, and Leo caught him.

"It shouldn't have been anyone," Leo said. "Anika must have done it because she wanted you to be alive. Let her have what she wanted. If you owe her something, it'd be that."

Justin glanced from Leo to me, and his jaw tensed.

"Leo's right," I said before he could argue more. "And if you don't go lie down on your own, we're going to tie you to the couch. You can hardly stand up, Justin. I don't care how else you spend your time, but I don't want you moving for the next hour. Got it?"

He glowered at me the way he always did when I refused to let him do something stupid. It occurred to me that it'd been a while since we'd really been at odds. The standoff didn't last long. He closed his eyes, and a miserable resignation came over his face. Sighing, he pulled away from Leo's grasp.

"Fine," he said. He hobbled over and threw himself down on the couch, propping his head against the padded arm. It was only a few seconds before his eyelids drifted shut again.

I set my hands on the table, trying not to look as if I needed them to hold me up, even though I pretty much did. My own head was heavy and my body exhausted, but my mind was whirling. What if no one answered the next time we called the CDC? What if no one answered all day? It had sounded as if they were well protected, but if the Wardens had gotten in, what hope did we have left?

I pushed myself upright, as if I could walk away from those worries. At least there were a few things I could control.

"I'm going to bring the cold box down to the basement," I said to Leo. "It'll stay cooler down there."

He came with me down the stairs that led from the kitchen, into the wide white-walled room below. A few dents in the walls revealed the crumbly drywall under the paint, and the laminate floor gave way under my feet where it had started to warp. Cobwebs clustered around the corners of the small, high windows. A plush futon stood off to one side, in front of an old TV surrounded by floor-to-ceiling particleboard shelves. They were stacked with dozens of DVDs and hundreds of CD cases. As I set the cold box down beside the stairs, Leo wandered over to the shelves. He blew the dust off a boom box sitting beside one stack of CDs and pressed a couple of the buttons.

"Still some juice in the batteries," he said. "I wonder if they have any decent music." His fingers skimmed over the cases, sliding some out and then nudging them back into place. I sat down on the arm of the futon, relaxing just fractionally into the soft fabric. For a moment, despite the dust and the cobwebs and the vaccine we couldn't deliver, I was able to let myself pretend that everything was normal. We were just a couple friends picking the right tunes to chill out to.

"Hey!" Leo said. He opened one of the cases and popped the disc into the boom box.

"What?" I asked, straightening up.

"Listen."

He skipped through the tracks, turned the volume down, and pressed play. A shimmer of strings soared through the speakers. Then a horn joined in, forming a playful melody that jolted me back eight years in one instant.

It was a waltz. Like the waltz Leo had practiced to for months, with me as his awkward partner, when we were kids. When life had seemed so simple.

I couldn't imagine being as happy as I'd been back then again.

Leo cleared his throat. When I opened my eyes, he was watching me, his mouth slanted crookedly, his fingers hovering over the controls. "I can turn it off," he said.

"No," I said around the lump in my throat. "There are a lot worse things I could be thinking about."

He let his arm drop. The music drifted through the room.

"Do you remember the steps?" he asked.

I hesitated. "One two three, one two three?"

Moving toward me, he offered his hand. "We can work with that."

I could see in Leo's uncertain smile, in the flicker of his eyes, the same sort of desperation I'd heard in Justin's voice, the same I'd felt in myself when the radio had failed. It wasn't a dance he was asking for so much as a temporary escape from here and now. An escape we both needed. So I stood up and folded my fingers around his.

He placed his other hand behind my back, and mine rose to his shoulder automatically. Apparently something from all those months of practice had stuck. All at once we were only inches apart. A jittery heat washed over me, and I might have panicked if Leo hadn't bent his head next to mine at exactly that moment.

"Left foot first," he said. "Back, side, together."

I stepped back, staring at Leo's shoulder, and he followed, his feet matching my pace. After a few stumbles, I started to find the rhythm. We moved faster, Leo turning us as we neared the wall, the patter of our feet almost drowning out the music. He spun us around, and around again, and a laugh jolted out of me. I was following him now, my feet strangely light in my boots, as if I might float right off the ground. My fingers tightened around his. Maybe he could dance us right out of this place, back into the lives we once had.

But then the music faded, and we came to a halt in the middle of the same dreary basement. I inhaled shakily, catching my breath. Another song began, low and soft.

"I definitely don't know how to dance to this one," I said.

Leo paused. "There's always the school-dance shuffle, if you promise never to tell anyone I called that 'dancing.'"

I rolled my eyes, even as my cheeks flushed. "I've got more practice at the waltz than that," I admitted. "Actually, I don't have any school-dance practice at all. I kind of avoided them."

And now I'd probably never have to again. I could hardly see the high schools reopening any time soon.

"Perfect opportunity to learn," Leo said, his tone light. "I'm a good partner. No groping."

I laughed, and suddenly my reluctance seemed silly. It was just me and my best friend, and another way to keep our minds off the silent transceiver a little while longer.

"Okay," I said. "Why not?"

I shifted closer, raising my other arm so my hands met behind Leo's neck. His slid around my waist. We started to shuffle in time with the music. After a few rotations, I let my head sink down to rest against his shoulder. The warmth of his body encircled me. When the music stopped, for good this time, we stopped too, but I didn't let him go. I had the urge to sink right into him, to see how far away I could get from everything waiting outside.

Leo eased back, but only slightly, to look down into my eyes. He traced the line of my cheek. My pulse stuttered and my lips parted in an instinctive protest, but he just tipped his face forward so our foreheads touched.

"I believe that things can get better," he said. "We've gone through so much, and we're still here. But even if they don't, I'm glad at least I was here with you."

I wanted to say I was glad to have been with him too, but I'd lost my voice. All I could feel was the thumping of my heart, his skin soft against mine, his shoulders firm beneath my hands. It felt good, being this close to him. It always had, hadn't it? As my initial nervousness faded, a longing welled up inside me. A longing for him to do what I'd thought he was going to do, to close that last small distance between us and kiss me.

But he didn't. He stood there, one hand at my back and the other at my cheek, motionless. I could feel his pulse too, drumming against my fingers.

Well, why would he take the chance, when I'd pushed him away so many times already? He was waiting for me. Letting me choose.

So what was *I* waiting for?

I loved him. As a friend, and much more. I knew that. The second I opened my mind to the idea, the truth of it shone through me. I'd put the feeling aside, and then buried it under grief and guilt, but I knew it. And this might be my last chance to do something about it. We had no idea what lay ahead of us. I could lose Leo or he me as easily as we'd lost Anika. In an instant, at the crack of a gunshot.

My thoughts leapt to Gav, and my heart wrenched. I still had his last message in my pocket. The message that had told me to keep going.

Because Gav was gone. He'd known he wouldn't be around much longer when he wrote that. Would he really have wanted me to spend the rest of my life loving no one but his memory?

No, I didn't think he would.

I lifted my head. Leo sucked in a little breath as my lips brushed his. He returned the kiss as cautiously as I had offered it. It wasn't nearly enough.

I slid my fingers into his hair, and pulled our mouths closer together. I wanted, I *needed*, so much I was suddenly dizzy with it, as if he were water and I was parched. A faint groan hummed through him as I kissed him even more deeply, and he drew me in so my body pressed tight against his. We kissed again, and again, until nothing else was real.

I came back to the world only when Leo stepped back, gripping my arms and breathing hard. My hands slipped from behind his head to rest against his chest. His eyes searched mine.

"This isn't—" he said, and swallowed audibly. "You're okay with this, right? It's not just— Everything's been so crazy, we've all been freaked out—"

I touched his mouth to silence him. "Leo," I said, "I've wanted to do this since we were fourteen years old."

He stared at me for a second. "Okay," he said, and laughed. "Okay." His head dipped back down, his lips finding mine again.

And neither of us said anything for quite a while after that.

It was only a temporary respite, of course. We were sitting on the futon, my legs across Leo's lap, his arms still around me, when the intensity of the moment started to fade. I dropped my head from a kiss to lean against his collarbone, feeling the rise and fall of his breath drift over my hair. As we cuddled there, the rest of reality crept back in. My gaze flicked through the room and caught on the blank face of the digital clock perched on top of the TV.

"Do you think it's time to try the radio again?" I asked.

Leo kissed my temple. "It can't hurt," he said. "Those doctors have slept enough."

I smiled at his jovial tone. "Pleased with yourself, are you?"

"Of course," he said. "I always knew dancing was going to get me a girl someday."

I snorted and swung my legs off him. He followed me to the stairs, grinning. As I reached for the railing, he caught me and tugged me back against him, his lips grazing the back of my ear in a way that sent a tingle down my neck.

"For the record," he said, "the only girl I really wanted to get was you."

I turned in his embrace, and we lost another few minutes I was happy to give up. But the nagging uncertainty of what awaited us upstairs didn't let me go this time.

We made our way back to the dining room. Leo's good humor dimmed as we checked on Justin, who was fast asleep, a faint snore rasping over his parted lips, his limbs tucked around to his body as if to shield himself.

"Should we wake him up?" Leo asked doubtfully.

"Leave him," I said. "He needs it."

I hoped if Justin was dreaming, it wasn't about last night.

When we sat down at the table and I called out into the transceiver's microphone, all we heard was the same static as before. I broadcast our message three times, and then turned the radio off again, not wanting to waste the battery.

"We'll just keep trying," Leo said.

"Yeah."

He scooted closer to me. I leaned into him, part of the tension easing out of me. It was funny, and sad, that I'd spent so much time resisting being with him like this, when now that it had happened it felt like the most natural thing in the world.

Without moving away from him, I started flipping through one of Dad's notebooks. I'd read Dad's account of the first few months of the epidemic enough times that coming back to these scrawled notes was comfortingly familiar. I could hear the echo of his voice in the words he'd written. He'd been so smart figuring out the vaccine, experimenting with both the first, not-so-deadly version of the virus and its current mutation, finally constructing the samples we now carried by combining bits of both. If he hadn't died, he could have handled all this himself. We wouldn't have had to leave the island, to worry about Michael's motives or the CDC's.

But he had, and now it was up to me.

I'd reached the day when Dad had injected himself with the prototype when Justin rolled over with an inarticulate mutter and rubbed his eyes.

"Hey," he said, and then yawned so wide his jaw creaked. "You get a hold of anyone yet?"

I shook my head. "Still waiting. I guess we might as well try again."

He limped over to the table with his rough walking stick as I switched on the transceiver. The sun was beaming now, casting a golden glow through the window behind him and filling the house with a thin warmth. In the back of my mind, I saw the snow in the cold box disintegrating into slush.

I sent out our call twice, waiting a minute after each one. I'd just given it one more shot, my heart heavy, when Dr. Guzman's soft drawl warbled out of the speaker.

"Kaelyn! Thank god. You were cut off before—I didn't know what had happened."

The relief that rushed through me was so overwhelming it carried away my words. "We . . ." I started, and realized I couldn't quickly summarize what we'd been through in the last two days. "We ran into some trouble," I improvised, "but we're all right now." All of us except Anika. I forced myself to go on. "We're in Atlanta. In the suburbs up north. Can you give us directions? We'll be coming on foot from here."

"Of course! Let me get the map."

Leo grabbed a pen and a piece of paper off the kitchen counter and brought them to me. When Dr. Guzman came back on, I gave her the street names from the intersection I'd noted nearby, and sketched a rough map as she walked me through the best route to the CDC.

"There's a fence around the complex, with one main gate," she said. "The militant types have made it their main focus, and there's an even larger crowd of them out there than we had a few days ago, I'm afraid. But we do have a smaller gate around the back that's securely barricaded, with a detachable section we've kept hidden that allows people to move in and out. No one outside seems to be paying much attention to that spot. If you work your way around to the south end and come along Houston Mill Road, and be cautious, you should be able to make it close unnoticed. We have a military presence here with us—I'll ask for two or three of the soldiers to be sent out to meet you and escort you the rest of the way. How should I tell them to recognize you?"

"I'm wearing a purple sweater and jeans," I said. "And I'll have the cold box with me."

"Excellent. And you're clear on the route?"

"I've got it." Based on her directions, I didn't think it'd take us much more than an hour to get there.

Not long ago, I would have been overjoyed that our journey was almost over, that we could finally set everything right. But from the moment I'd started speaking with her, my gut had been twisting, because I didn't really believe that anymore. Her earlier remarks, Michael's insinuations, and my own worries were tangling together in my head. I couldn't do this right until I knew for sure where she stood.

"Dr. Guzman," I said, my hand tensing around the mic, "when we were talking before, you said something about—the people who've been attacking the CDC, who've been harassing us—that they'd lose out on the vaccine."

"Don't bother yourself about that," Dr. Guzman said firmly. "The delinquents will just have to deal with the beds they've made for themselves."

I shifted in the chair, and an edge of cardboard dug into my hip. A thought I hadn't known had been niggling at me until that instant spilled out.

"It's just, there was someone, a guy in our hometown," I said. "He grabbed all the food that was left in the stores, and then was deciding who would get what. . . ."

I trailed off, trying to find the best way to explain what Gav had done, and Dr. Guzman jumped in.

"You won't have to deal with anyone like that anymore," she said. "The people who've crossed the line, they're going to find there are consequences now."

"Right," I said. So it was as easy as that? She'd use just a few incomplete thoughts to judge whether a person was worthy of saving? "But there are some people who might have done things that weren't the best, just because they didn't know how else to stay alive. I mean, it's a hard line to draw."

"I'm sure we can work out the specifics once you're here with the vaccine," Dr. Guzman said, a note of impatience entering her voice. "Oh—you will be bringing your father's notes, won't you? You haven't lost them? You said you had them with you."

"I still do," I said, my throat raw. She wasn't really listening. She was just saying whatever she thought she had to, to get me and the vaccine there. Which meant I couldn't have trusted her answer even if she'd given a real one.

"Good. It's unlikely we'll be able to replicate the vaccine without his exact instructions, even with samples. I should let the soldiers know to be prepared for you. I'm looking forward to meeting you, Kaelyn. Be safe."

"Yeah," I managed, and switched off the radio.

Justin gave me a puzzled frown, but Leo's expression was knowing. "Kae," he said, "she didn't hear the whole story."

"She didn't want to," I said. "All she cares about is getting the vaccine. Do you really think they're going to take the time to find out the whole story, for everyone like Gav? What do you think she'd say about Drew?" How would they react to half the things we'd done getting down here, if they hadn't been more concerned about us bringing them the vaccine than anything else?

"I don't know," Leo admitted.

"It's still better than giving the vaccine to that prick Michael," Justin said.

"Yeah," I said. "Yeah." I looked down at Dad's notebook, thinking of the dogs tearing each other apart over a corpse. Of the way the girl from the town by the river had raced to warn us, because we'd helped her neighbors. Of Tobias's panicked comrades dropping missiles on our island in some warped act of vengeance, and Tobias, risking his life to rescue us—a bunch of strangers. Of Michael, sending his followers to storm the CDC, the soldiers shooting back, the bodies that would pile up before anyone outside this city so much as saw the vaccine.

A vaccine that was still in my hands.

The sense of purpose I'd felt before flooded me, twice as strong. For such a long time, the responsibility of carrying the samples had felt like a burden. But it was actually a gift. I'd spent all this time intending to just hand it over to people with more authority than me, but I didn't have to. It was up to me. I didn't have to let them —Michael and the Wardens, the CDC's scientists and soldiers, any of them—decide how the world should be. I could at least try for the world *I* wanted.

I had to.

As I smoothed my fingers over the indentations left by the pressure of Dad's pen, months ago, the threads of thought that had been winding through my head started to meld into an actual plan. These notebooks didn't just hold a record. Dr. Guzman had referred to them as Dad's "instructions." They told every protein that needed to be cloned, every procedure that needed to be followed, every bit and piece that needed to be intertwined.

Because the vaccine wasn't just one thing. It was made of many parts, working together.

"We need another pen, and a bunch of paper," I said.

"There was a desk in one of the bedrooms," Leo said, standing up. "I think I saw some there. What are we doing, Kae?"

"I'm still figuring that out," I said. "But I think it's going to be good."

TWENTY-THREE

My plan required that Justin part ways with us early. "You don't have to worry," he told me, when I went with him to the door. "I'll stick to the script."

"I know," I said. Justin had come a long way from the hotheaded kid who'd joined us a month ago. "I wouldn't have asked you to do this if I didn't know that."

He smiled, pleased but nervous, and gave me a brief salute before shambling down the street with his stick.

It took me and Leo a little more than an hour to finish our frantic copying of Dad's notes. Then we left too, heading south. The neighborhoods between the one we'd holed up in and the Centers for Disease Control fit the same leafy, suburban mold. We walked through the yards hand in hand. Leo held the cold-storage box, and I had the strap of a soft-sided cooler we'd found in the house's kitchen over my shoulder. We'd split the mushy snow that had remained in the cold box between the two. To make things as equal as possible, I'd filled a syringe with half the contents of one of the vials, so we each had one and a half samples of the vaccine. And a slightly differing set of copied notes. Dad's original notebooks we'd left behind, wrapped in the plastic bag to protect them from damp and wedged into a gap under the basement stairs, out of view to anyone who didn't know where to look for them.

As Leo and I approached the university grounds the CDC sat in the middle of, we had to duck behind fences and hedges three times at the sound of car engines. One of those cars drove directly past us while we hunched by a vine-strangled shed. The Wardens were gathering. My heart thudded as we hurried on. We'd know soon whether Justin had delivered our message unharmed.

We'd know whether Michael was truly as reasonable as he'd said.

When I spotted the taller buildings that Dr. Guzman had said would mark the end of the residential area, we halted. I turned to Leo. The bruise on his cheek was starting to fade, purple red blending into brown. I touched the skin beside it gently and rose on my feet to meet his lips when he tipped his head toward me.

He drew out the kiss, as if maybe we could just never stop, never have to face another moment of danger. When we finally eased apart, I had to catch my breath before I could speak.

"You'll stay out of sight?" I said. "Until I call you?" I patted the two-way radio I'd hooked to one of my belt loops.

Leo nodded. "And if you don't call after a couple hours, I'll go to the CDC myself."

Now that we were so close to our goal, now that I had to leave him, the doubts I'd managed to suppress before were bubbling up inside me. If any part of this plan went wrong, it would probably mean at least one of us dead.

But then, not trying might mean that too.

"Hey," Leo said, and squeezed my hand. "Whatever happens, I'll be right behind you."

"And if something happens to me?" I said.

"Then I'll keep at this until everyone in the world is protected, or I've died trying. Justin and I know where the notebooks are—we'll make sure *someone* knows how to make the vaccine. Kaelyn . . ." He waited until I met his eyes. "I'm here for you, but I'm here for me too. Because I believe we're doing the right thing. If something happens to *me*, that's not on you. You know that, right?"

I'd thought I did, but hearing the words released something inside me. I kissed him again, hard, wishing I could convey everything I was feeling from my lips to his. Leo set down the cold box and pulled me into an embrace.

"I love you," he said by my ear.

"I love you." I tightened my grip on him until tears crept into my eyes, and then I let him go.

"No more than two hours," I said.

"You'll be calling before that."

I took one last look at him, and then headed down the street.

After another block, the cover became sparse. I edged past a large building that looked like some sort of Gothic mansion, darting from pine tree to pine tree. The houses on the other side of the road had given way to office buildings and weedy lawns. I hesitated on the brink of a wide intersection, scanning the roads and listening. This was the street Dr. Guzman had told me to take. Where was the military assistance she'd said she'd send?

An engine gunned to my left, and then cut out. Footsteps thudded ahead of me. I dropped down behind an overgrown shrub as two men in civilian clothes hurried around the corner.

When the men had disappeared down the street, I dashed across the intersection. I was just coming up on the grassy slope beside the sidewalk when a couple soldiers stepped out from behind a tree made fat by loops of vine. Both of them carried rifles. The taller one, a square-jawed man with lightly tanned skin, waved me over.

"Kaelyn Weber?" he said under his breath. I nodded. "Where are the others?"

"It's just me right now," I whispered, and patted the cooler to indicate I had the vaccine. He frowned, but he gestured for me to follow him and his companion.

We jogged past the scattered trees and mounds of vine that covered the slope. A fence lined the opposite sidewalk, made of wrought-iron bars that rose from a brick base. It had been fortified with sheets of plywood and corrugated steel that blocked the gaps between the bars, and topped with curls of barbed wire. Up ahead, a lane branched off from the road toward the fence. What had once been a gate there was blocked with boards and battered furniture and more steel and wire. The barrier looked completely solid, but the soldiers went straight to it, scanning the street as we hustled across.

The moment our feet hit the sidewalk, one of the boards was wrenched aside, creating a narrow gap in the barricade. A hand reached through it. The guy behind me nudged me forward. I took the hand and let the person on the other side pull me in. My shoulders bumped against the sides of the gap, and then I was stumbling out into a wide uncluttered lane.

The soldiers who'd come to meet me ducked through after me. One shoved the board back into place and secured it while the woman who'd helped me through hopped back onto her post beside the gate. Another soldier perched across from her, rifle at the ready, watching the street.

The square-jawed man gripped my elbow, ushering me up the lane toward the buildings that loomed ahead.

"We expected you earlier," he said curtly. "What happened? Dr. Guzman said there should be four of you."

We hadn't told her what had happened to Anika. I grasped the strap of the cooler to steady myself. I couldn't let this situation slip out of my control.

"I need to go to the front gate," I said. "Which way is that?"

The soldier's frown deepened. "Dr. Guzman is waiting for you. If your friends went to the front gate, the maniacs out there have probably already caught them."

"I need to go to the front gate," I repeated firmly, "or I won't be able to give Dr. Guzman what she wants."

"I think you'd better talk to the doctor about that."

"Then let her come down here."

He was still frowning, but he pulled a walkie-talkie from his belt. "The girl's here," he said. "She wants Guzman to come down. Let's have the doc sort things out."

We strode past a building of red brick and another of pale concrete set with rows of high windows. "That's the front gate," the soldier said, stopping and motioning down another lane to a spot where a single sheet of steel stood amid the plywood-and-furniture barricade covering the fence, about twenty feet away. Two more soldiers were stationed there. The sound of murmuring voices carried through the wall, and then the rumble of a car sweeping past.

When my escort stayed where he was, I marched on toward the gate. I was halfway there when he caught up with me, yanking me to a halt.

"What are you doing?"

"I need to talk to someone," I said.

"Do you have any idea—"

He paused as a door whined open on one of the nearby buildings. A stout woman with round-paned glasses hurried over to us, swiping her short black hair away from her eyes. Another woman and a man, both wearing lab coats, trailed behind her.

"You must be Kaelyn," the first woman said. "I'm Sheryl Guzman." She held out her hand for me to shake, and her gaze dipped to the cooler at my side. "You have the vaccine in there? Why didn't the others come with you? What's going on, Sergeant?"

"Apparently they came around front," the soldier with me said. "She thinks she's going to talk to them."

"No," I said. "I need to talk to someone else. If you'll just listen to me we can get this over with, and everyone will have what they want."

Dr. Guzman's brow knit. "I don't understand."

"I'll explain everything in a minute," I said. "Believe me, if you want to be able to make the vaccine, I need to do this."

The sergeant looked at Dr. Guzman. She pursed her lips, and then shrugged. "After all this time, I can't see how another minute will hurt." But she hadn't stopped eyeing the cooler.

I stepped away from my escort and walked right up to the corrugated steel sheet that fortified the gate. "Hey!" I shouted, and kicked the metal so it rang out. "Is Michael there yet?"

My question was met by a momentary hush, and my heart sank. If he wasn't there, if I hadn't given Justin enough time, I wasn't sure how long I could convince the scientists and their soldier allies to wait.

Then a familiar dry voice carried through the barrier. "I'm here."

I exhaled. "And Justin's with you? No one's hurt him?"

"I received that part of the message too."

"I'm here," Justin's voice called out. "They've been all right."

"Then you know you're not getting anything until he's in here safely," I said to Michael.

"I'm ready when you are."

I turned back. "We need to open the gate," I said. "Just long enough to let one person in."

"Kaelyn—" Dr. Guzman started.

"If you want the vaccine, that's what I need," I said. "It's not all here." I raised my voice so it could be heard on the other side of the fence. "And Michael's people know that if there's one shot fired, they're not getting what they want either."

"That's right," Michael said. "For the moment, we're here to talk."

"You can't trust them," the sergeant said.

He could have been right, but I'd already committed to taking that risk. "If you're worried, stay out of the way," I said.

"Just open it," Dr. Guzman said.

"Sheryl, I'm not sure—" one of the doctors behind her broke in, and she cut him off with a glare.

"We decided I would call the shots on this one," she reminded him.

He and the other doctor moved to the side, out of range of any guns beyond the gate. Dr. Guzman stayed where she was, a few feet behind me, her hands on her hips.

The sergeant looked to his colleagues at the gate. "Be ready," he said.

When the others nodded, he bent to shift the concrete blocks that propped the steel sheet in place. Then he slid the sheet a couple feet to the right, revealing the vertical iron bars of the actual gate. A dense cluster of vehicles and people stood on the other side, with Michael at the front of the crowd. A few of the Wardens jerked forward instinctively at the sight of the opening, and someone let out a hoarse shout. Michael's arm shot into the air, signaling them to stand down. The crowd settled, but I could see the muzzles of several pistols and shotguns glinting in its midst.

Justin left Michael's side and ran up to the gate as fast as his bad leg allowed.

"He's the one we're letting in," I said to the soldier. "He's with me."

The sergeant grimaced, but he unlocked the heavy chain that held the gate closed. As soon as he'd eased the gate open, Justin squeezed inside and ducked around behind the wall. The sergeant jerked the gate shut the second Justin was through. No one else had budged. Michael watched me, his eyes hard.

When the sergeant reached to pull the steel sheet back into place, I said, "No. Leave it. I'll be fast." I needed to see Michael, to evaluate his expressions, his body language, before I could make the final decision about whether to go through with this.

"This is the deal," I said, glancing at Michael and then at the doctors. "This is what everyone wants." I set the cooler on the ground in front of me, knelt down, and unzipped the lid just long enough to grab one of the vials—the one that was only half full. As I held it up, the amber liquid caught the sunlight. A murmur rose on Michael's side, movement rippling through the crowd. Michael motioned them silent.

"Millions people are dead because of the friendly flu," I said.

"This vaccine will mean we can finally stop being scared of the virus, but I don't want to keep watching the rest of us trying to kill each other. We should be working together to survive. I don't think we're *going* to survive if we can't stop fighting. No one should be forced to do things they don't want to in order to get the vaccine." I fixed Michael with a stare, and he glowered back. Then I turned to the doctors. "And no one should be told they can't have it because of what they've done to stay alive. No one deserves to be infected.

"The vaccine was made with two different sets of proteins," I went on. "So I've brought half my dad's samples for the CDC, and a copy of his notes that includes instructions on how to clone and treat only one set of the proteins. If we can all agree, then I'll call someone to bring the other half, and a copy of the notes that includes instructions on handling the other necessary set, for you." I looked back at Michael. "The vaccine's not going to work with just one set or the other. So at some point you'll have to get together to combine them, and to figure out a way for you both to distribute the finished product. I don't think one group of people should be making all the decisions anymore."

The second my voice fell, I was bombarded with accusations from both sides. "Who the hell do you think you are?" one of the Wardens snarled, and another hollered, "Screw that, we're taking it all!" and the doctor who'd spoken up before started gesticulating wildly, saying, "You're crazy, you can't give any of it to them! It's because of people like them we've had to lock ourselves in here," and Dr. Guzman, in a kindly patronizing tone that made me angrier than everything else, murmured, "Kaelyn, I don't think you've thought this through."

As if I'd had much to do in the last six months other than think, while I watched my neighbors and friends and family die.

"Stop it!" I said. "We can only talk if you'll listen."

The crowd behind Michael pushed forward, guns flashing, and the soldiers by the fence stiffened, aiming their rifles. "This is ridiculous," the ranting doctor said. He gestured to the sergeant, who stepped toward me as if to drag me away. So I used the only power I had.

"I said stop!" I shouted, and threw the sample vial I was holding at the ground.

The glass shattered instantly. The vaccine I'd spent so long trying to keep safe puddled on the asphalt. And everyone went still. The voices fell away. I placed one of my feet on top of the cooler, letting it dent the soft lid. My heel couldn't break the remaining vial, not through the empty syringe case I'd secured it in, but no one else knew that.

"I don't see any point in having a vaccine at all if we can't even talk to each other for five seconds," I said. "You've got problems with my suggestion, I'll listen. To Michael and Dr. Guzman."

I just needed one of them to agree. If one said yes, and the other resisted, I could threaten to hand the whole thing over to the first group, and I suspected the other would fall in line rather than risk losing all control over the vaccine. And if only one was willing to compromise, well, then I'd know who deserved my faith.

A man near Michael lunged toward the gate, and Michael caught him by his shirt collar, jerking him back and smacking his revolver against the man's temple.

"Stay where you are," he growled. And then, to me, "You expect me to trust these government lackeys? You think the second they have any advantage, they won't turn the tables on us?"

"I don't think there's much of a government left," I said. "And I think if you're both smart, no one's going to get an advantage. You're going to need each other. If you screw that up, well, that's not my fault."

"How are we supposed to trust *them*?" Dr. Guzman said. "If we have to combine what we've both produced—I mean, we aren't just going to hand over what we have to them. And I'm guessing they're not going to want to do the same with us."

"Maybe you do an exchange," I said. "They give you some of theirs, you give them some of yours, and you each make your own final product. Maybe you take turns—a little batch here, a little batch there, until you've proven to each other than you can handle this. I don't know."

"They're never going to let it lie," she said, shaking her head. "You haven't seen—"

"You have no idea what I've seen," I snapped, and paused to collect myself. "You could be right. They could try to overpower you, or you overpower them, so you can control the whole process. But I'm pretty sure that'll just mean more people dying and more time lost while people out there are still getting infected. Is there anyone here who really wants that? Don't you think having a vaccine at all is more important than being the only people who have it?"

Between them, there shouldn't be a single person in the world who wouldn't have access to the vaccine. Even if both groups kept to their own rules, anyone who'd broken too many laws to earn the CDC's sympathy should be able to buy from Michael. And if one group did turn on the other, we'd deliver Dad's notebooks to whoever had kept to the deal, and the playing field would be equal again. But I hoped it wouldn't come to that.

When I turned back to the gate, Michael's face was its usual impassive mask. "Do you really think Samantha will ever be safe if you're the one guy making the decisions about the vaccine?" I said to him. "How many people do you know who are already itching for the chance to take that power from you?

"And how much vaccine could you make in a day, or a week?" I asked Dr. Guzman. "How many people do you have who could distribute it? Michael has doctors and scientists working for him—he's got a network of people all the way up to Canada. The faster we get everyone vaccinated, the sooner the virus is gone for good. All you have to do is cooperate with each other."

They both stared at me in stony silence. I lifted the two-way from my hip.

"What do you think? Can I make this call? Or would you rather just fight it out? Seriously, if you can't even manage to try, then one of you might as well shoot *me*, because I don't want to live in whatever world you're going to make."

In the crowd beyond the fence, I heard the click of a safety switched off. One of the soldiers tensed his finger on the trigger of his rifle. Michael shifted toward the gate, just a few inches from the bars. Dr. Guzman hesitated, and then came to meet him, matching his glare.

My breath stuck in my throat. I braced myself for one of them, or one of the others, to make some move that would dissolve all of this into a hail of bullets. But then Michael's lips formed a thin smile, and he stuck his hand between the bars.

“To a partnership beneficial to the both of us,” he said.

“Sheryl,” the other doctor protested, but Dr. Guzman ignored him. She accepted Michael’s hand and shook it once.

“We’ll be watching you closely,” she said.

“Believe me, we’ll be keeping an eye on you too,” he retorted.

As he pulled back, his gaze flicked to me. “I hope you didn’t think I was going to thank you.”

“Not for a second,” I said. “But I think you should.”

He didn’t answer, but his smile widened, just fractionally. And right then I believed that this might all work out the way I’d imagined.

I brought the two-way to my mouth. “Leo,” I said, “we’re good to go.”

TWENTY-FOUR

I half expected Dr. Guzman and her colleagues to run us out of the complex after Leo arrived, to make us join the criminals we'd shared our loyalty with. I might not have blamed them. But when Michael had inspected the cold box and passed the sheaf of notes to a fidgety woman from one of the cars, he waved Leo toward the gate, and the soldier who'd escorted me in opened it once more. Michael gathered his troops and sent them all packing. He gave me a brief, cryptic nod before heading to his police car. The soldiers guarding the gate gaped as the entire crowd dispersed, leaving the street outside quiet and empty.

"Well, hell," one said, with a startled laugh.

Leo had come straight to me after he'd hurried inside. He wrapped his arm around my waist, and I slumped against him. I felt as though I'd spent the last ten minutes sprinting at full speed rather than just talking. Dr. Guzman dashed forward to grab the cooler. Justin sidled over to us and said under his breath, "You kicked *ass*." And a grin broke through my exhaustion.

It might not be enough. Tomorrow the CDC could be at war with the Wardens, and I wouldn't be able to stop it. I'd done all I could do, and now I had to hope that the world I'd caught glimpses of in the last couple months, a world that was more about living than dying, would appeal to everyone else enough to keep them cooperating.

As Dr. Guzman and the other woman disappeared into one of the buildings, I turned to the man in the lab coat. "Justin was shot in the leg a few days ago," I said. "We've done our best to look after it, but he should really have it seen by a doctor."

"Fine," the man said. "He can come with me. I suppose you can take these two to your living area," he added to the sergeant, and then stalked off with Justin limping after him.

The sergeant sighed and motioned for us to come with him. He led us into the building across the lane and down to the basement, where his unit had set up a sort of dormitory. "This one's been empty, so you can have it to yourselves," he said briskly outside a room full of cots. "And the washroom's down here. The docs say the water's still drinkable."

I could have cried at the sight of the clear water gushing from the tap. Leo and I showered in turn and then crashed on the cots. The lumpy pillow felt like heaven.

When I woke, having caught up on a little of my lost sleep, a dim light that could have been mid-evening or early morning was streaking through the narrow windows. Justin was sprawled on one of the other cots, looking dead to the world. A set of crutches leaned against the wall nearby, and the bottom of a fresh bandage poked from beneath the cuff of his pant leg.

I crept out, and immediately took another shower. For the first time in weeks, I felt completely clean. I'd just slipped back into the room when Dr. Guzman appeared in the doorway. Leo was sitting up, stretching his back. He nudged Justin with his toes.

"I thought it might have been a while since you've had anything to eat," Dr. Guzman said. "Join us in the cafeteria?"

"Hell yes!" Justin said, springing upright.

As we followed Dr. Guzman up the stairs, I wondered if I should broach the topic of how I'd handled the vaccine. But she started to chatter as if it didn't matter anyway, so I decided to let it rest for now.

"We've done all right for food and practicalities," she said. "We received quite a large shipment of canned and dry goods before the emergency proceedings completely fell apart. The only thing we're low on is medical supplies, but we've been strict about quarantining. No one here has gotten sick in the last month."

"You have what you need to make more of the vaccine, don't you?" I said with a flash of panic.

"Oh!" she said. "Plenty. We stockpiled the standard materials before the first vaccine was even finished, so we'd be ready if we needed to help with production. They've just been sitting there waiting for us. Bernice and Todd are working on cloning the proteins right now."

We stepped into what looked like an office kitchen. The other woman doctor who'd come outside yesterday was seated at one of the three small tables with a young man I hadn't seen before, discussing something between bites of their meal. A rich spicy smell wafted through the room, setting my stomach gurgling.

"Chili is one of our standbys," Dr. Guzman said, going to a large pot on the stove. "The spices help cover the not-entirely-pleasant taste of the canned turkey."

We all filled bowls and sat around one of the other tables. I had some idea of being polite, but as soon as the food was in front of me, I was scooping it into my mouth so quickly I didn't realize I'd reached the bottom until my spoon was scraping it. When I glanced up, wondering if it'd be rude to ask for seconds, the young man at the other table stood and came over.

"You must be Kaelyn Weber," he said, beaming at me as he offered his hand.

I hadn't expected anyone to give us a friendly reception after the way we'd arrived. "I—Yes," I said.

"I spoke with your father a few times," he said. "In the early stages of the pandemic. I was always impressed by his insight. Naturally he was the one to solve the vaccine problem in the end. I've read the notes you gave us—really quite brilliant. I assume the part the other fellow's got is too."

"Why hadn't you guys figured it out by now?" Justin demanded. "I thought you were supposed to be the experts."

The man's cheeks turned pink. "Well, yes," he said. "Believe me, we tried. There are only five of us still working here, and, well . . ." He looked away, rubbing his chin. "It seems we had the means all along and simply didn't know it. The original virus, before its deadly mutation—we received a sample via Halifax nearly two years back. We have it in storage. But with all the different channels of communication between different agencies and different people at them, it was never made totally clear to us that *that* virus was connected to the one we were fighting."

I remembered Dad's constant frustration, his complaints about dealing with all the strangers dropping in and out of the hospital with their conflicting agendas, and couldn't find it in me to be surprised. So it'd been the same story from the beginning: everyone so focused on what they wanted for themselves that they weren't really collaborating. How much sooner would we have had a vaccine if making one had been more of a priority than controlling information and following their conflicting policies?

"At least we have a vaccine now," I said.

"Yes," he agreed, his smile returning. "Yes, we do."

"Ed," Dr. Guzman said, "you should probably take a look at both of these young men. Todd neglected to give Justin a blood test yesterday, to make sure he hasn't been exposed, and I understand Leo was vaccinated . . . how long ago?"

"About a month," I said.

"Yes," she went on. "So an examination to ensure there've been no undetected ill effects would be worthwhile." She looked at me. "And Kaelyn, I was hoping you would take a walk with me."

I tensed, but all I said was, "Okay." I managed not to take too many longing glances at the chili pot while I washed my bowl and spoon.

The young doctor took the guys down the hall in one direction, and Dr. Guzman set off in the other. I meandered along beside her, looking out the broad windows onto the road below. Soldiers were still staked out by the gates, and a few were patrolling the line of the fence in the deepening evening shadows.

"You've had to defend this place a lot?" I asked to break the silence.

"I don't know if it's been worse than any other medical facility," she said, and then paused. "No, I suppose it would have been. We were on the news a lot, down here at least. Some people were convinced that if they showed up they'd be first to get a cure. And then they got violent when they realized we didn't have one. But that subsided. Over time."

As most of those people died.

"Most recently we've been dealing with more organized groups," she went on. "I suppose mainly people sent by this Michael. A few will yell and bang on the walls, but many just cruise around and watch and wait, and pry at the barricades until the soldiers catch them and scare them off. Which is actually more unnerving than the yelling and banging. But we've been fine as long as we stayed inside the walls."

"It's even more unnerving when you don't have that option," I said, my mind dredging up every close call, every moment crouched in hiding, praying the Wardens would pass us by. That really was over, wasn't it—the running, the fear of being caught? After so many days on constant high alert, I found it hard to accept that I'd finally made it through.

"You say that, and yet you wanted them to be a part of this," she said. She stopped abruptly. "Did I sound that horrible, Kaelyn, when we talked over the radio? You can see why I would have hesitated to share anything with them that might help them, can't you? If there was someone specific you were worried wouldn't get the vaccine, you could have just told me. I don't understand why all this was necessary."

"It's not about just one person," I said. Now that she'd brought up the subject, a floodgate seemed to open inside me, and everything I'd been thinking over the last day poured out. "I know so many people who've done things that you might think makes them too dangerous to get the vaccine. Even me and my friends. I mean, we've all been terrified, and desperate, and I don't see how we can assume that even the people who've done the worst things would have done them if they'd seen a better way. The people who are really messed up"—Nathan's sneer floated through my thoughts—"we should have other ways of dealing with them, don't you think? Won't they just get crazier, even more dangerous, if they're the only ones left who still have to be afraid of the virus?"

"Maybe," Dr. Guzman allowed.

"I get it," I said. "I was so angry at everyone who's gotten in our way. . . . Everyone who's hurt us. But somebody's got to stop being angry sometime, if we're going to get out of this, right? I saw a direction that looked better than the one we seemed to be headed in. So I took it."

My throat was closing up. I swallowed hard. Dr. Guzman touched my elbow. "Well, I hope you're right."

"If Michael breaks his word, if he tries to take over the production of the vaccine, I can make sure you get all the information you need to produce it here on your own," I said. "And I'll do the same thing for Michael, if the CDC stops working with him. No matter what happens, someone will be making the vaccine."

"That's one thing I do agree with," Dr. Guzman said. She started to walk again, and I followed. "Having a vaccine at all is more important than who's making it."

As we approached a bend in the hall, I noticed a cluster of photographs and notes tacked to the wall over a small pile of random objects: a teacup, a pair of loafers, a lacy scarf. Beside the photos, a list of words formed a line down the wall. When we reached the corner, I realized they were names. Dozens of them.

"A memorial?" I asked.

"Yes," Dr. Guzman said. "All of those people worked here. Most of them died here."

Another reminder of how many lives we'd lost to the virus. How many people had died trying to save the rest of us from it. My throat tightened again.

"Could I . . . Could I add to the list?"

Dr. Guzman looked startled. Then her expression softened. "I think that would be all right."

She disappeared down the hall, and returned with a permanent marker. I bent down over the pile of mementos and wrote four names at the bottom of the second column.

Gordon Weber. Gavriel Reilly. Tobias Rawls. Anika.

I didn't even know Anika's last name. By the time we'd met her, last names had hardly seemed important. But I knew her well enough now to see she deserved to be included here, in this list of heroes.

"We wouldn't have the vaccine at all, if it wasn't for them," I said.

Dr. Guzman lowered her head. "I'm sorry."

We wandered back the way we'd come in silence, and I guessed the whole purpose of the walk had been for Dr. Guzman to hear my explanation. "I have work to do," she said as we arrived at the staircase that led down to the dormitory area. "Please know that the three of you can stay as long as you want. Help yourself to food from the kitchen. And let me know if you need anything else, and I'll see what I can do."

"Thank you," I said.

Downstairs, our dormitory room was dark. I lay down on my cot, but I was nowhere near drifting off when Leo and Justin came back in. I got up, grasping Leo's hand when he joined me.

"Everything's okay?"

"From what they could tell so far, yes," he said. "Some of the tests take a while."

"And you?" I asked Justin.

"One hundred percent healthy, except for this stupid leg," he said, sinking onto his cot. "And even the leg, the guy yesterday said it should heal completely in a few weeks."

"Good," I said. So I'd done all right by him, at least.

"So what are you two going to do now?" Justin said. "Are you staying here?"

Right. Because we could think about the future beyond delivering the vaccine now. The answer came to me as soon as I reached for one. "I have to go back to the colony to get Meredith," I said. "She's probably worried to death now that we've been gone so long. And then, I guess, back to the island."

Leo nodded. "Sounds good to me. I'd like to be home again. Or at least somewhere we can make 'home.' Here's definitely not it."

"We could all head north together," I said to Justin. "You could see your mom. Dr. Guzman might be able to find us a vehicle we can use, and we should be able to drive away from here now without the Wardens swarming us."

But then, if we all left, no one would be around to recover Dad's notebooks from their hiding place if one group defected.

Before I could even express that worry, Justin solved the problem for me. He straightened up, gripping one of his crutches, and said, "I was thinking. . . . I don't know if I'm ready to go back yet. Maybe I could stick around here, help keep an eye on the Wardens. It seems like this place could use someone who knows what they're all about. And after everything Michael did—I'd like to make sure he stays in line."

"You'd be okay here?" I said. "Dr. Guzman and that one doctor seem all right, but no one else has been very welcoming."

He shrugged. "I don't need them to be friendly. I just want to keep helping. That's enough to keep me going."

I couldn't argue with that. "Okay," I said. "Is there something you'd want me to tell your mom?"

"Tell her the stuff I've done so far," he said. "All of it. Well, all the awesome stuff anyway."

He cracked a grin, and for the first time in what felt like ages, all three of us started laughing.

Leo and I waited five days, while the first batches of the vaccine were made. Both sides in my forced compromise remained cautious—first they exchanged ten batches, then twenty—but there was no bloodshed or backstabbing. On the fourth day, when the young doctor I'd talked to in the kitchen was getting ready to go out to offer vaccinations to the local survivors, I asked if I could join him.

"I won't get in the way of anything," I said. I just wanted to see.

Michael had promised that the Wardens wouldn't interfere with the CDC's efforts as long as they didn't try to hinder his operations. No one stood in our way when we drove out in a military-painted Range Rover, one soldier in the front passenger seat and the other beside me in the back. And I saw plenty. I saw an elderly woman weep when we caught up with her outside one of the vacant stores. I saw a middle-aged man question Ed from behind his porch railing until he was convinced he could trust him, and call his little son outside to be vaccinated too. I saw a young woman peer cautiously from an upstairs window and then slip out the door, her face glowing at the news.

"This is really it?" she asked, over and over, as Ed prepared the needle. "It'll work?"

"It will," he replied with a smile.

A few figures lurked in the shadows, marking our movements but never coming within range of the soldiers' rifles. The Wardens weren't the only gang around, just the biggest. But apparently Dr. Guzman had taken my words the other day to heart, and passed the sentiment on to her colleagues. "Whenever you're ready!" Ed called out. "The vaccine's for everyone."

Only one of the skulkers emerged: a teenaged boy with tangled hair and a scabbed-over cut along his jaw. His thin shirt barely disguised the bulge of a weapon wedged in the waist of his jeans, and his hand twitched toward it when Ed got out of the car. But he stood still and held out his arm, and when the needle came out his expression was so relieved I thought he might cry.

"Thanks," he muttered, and bolted back into the alley he'd come from.

"What'll you do when you run into people who are already sick?" I asked Ed after we'd given out the last dose and were driving back.

"We'll bring them in, do the best we can for them," Ed replied. "We may be able to make use of the antibodies produced by people who've taken the vaccine. At very least, we can keep them as comfortable as possible."

So we didn't have a perfect solution. But it was so much more than I'd dared to imagine a few months ago, while I'd watched the virus tear apart the island.

We pulled back onto the CDC grounds unscathed. I stepped out of the car and looked around, and the knowledge hit me all at once. I'd done it. Maybe only temporarily, maybe not quickly enough to help everyone I'd wanted to, but I'd seen my mission through to the end.

Which meant it was time to move on.

Dr. Guzman provided us with a car—a creaky sedan that had belonged to one of the doctors now listed on the wall—as well as a week's supply of food and a tube and bucket for siphoning gas. We were going to have to scavenge fuel along the way, but I imagined it'd be a lot easier without murderous pursuers on our tail. We said our good-byes to Justin with hugs and a repeated promise to pass word of his exploits on to his mother. He accepted a note from me explaining where I was going, to pass on to Drew if he got the chance.

I stopped by the memorial corner before I headed out, and touched the four names I'd added. My eyes welled up. But when I got into the car beside Leo, and the soldiers pulled open the gate, all I could think of was Meredith, calling out my name as she raced to welcome me back.

Leo leaned over to kiss me before he started the engine. There was going to be a little weirdness, too, returning to the colony. Tessa had broken up with Leo when she'd decided to stay there, but I didn't know how she'd feel seeing the two of us together. I couldn't even be sure, until we reached it, that the colony had stayed safe the last few weeks. But I had enough hope to live with that uncertainty for now. The world outside already felt like a far brighter place than the one I'd left when I first stepped inside these walls.

"I'm happy," Leo said. "It seems almost wrong, with all the awful things that've happened."

"I don't think it is," I said as we eased past the gate and turned north, toward home. "I think that's how we stay alive."

ACKNOWLEDGMENTS

I am exceedingly grateful to the following people:

Amanda Coppedge, Saundra Mitchell, Mahtab Narsimhan, and Robin Prehn, for being my first readers for this trilogy and helping steer the early drafts on course.

Jacqueline Houtman, without whose scientific expertise my explanations of viruses and vaccines would make much less sense.

My editor, Catherine Onder, for pushing each book to be as good as I could make it and championing the trilogy from beginning to end.

My agent, Josh Adams, for being the books' first champion and expertly guiding my career before and after.

The readers here and around the world who've let me know the series has found a place in people's hearts.

My friends and family, for being there when I needed them and not being there when I needed to hole up and write.

And my husband, Chris, for patience, belief, and love I hope I match.

Franklin Pierce University
00202358